I0523537

THE
ERSATZ
ACADEMY

THE ERSATZ ACADEMY

ANDREA WEILGART

Cosmic Communication Foundation | Long Beach, WA

© 2023 Andrea Weilgart

All rights reserved. No part of this publication may be reproduced, stored in a retrieval system, or transmitted in any form or by any means electronic, mechanical, photocopying, recording or otherwise, without the prior written permission of the publisher.

Published by
Cosmic Communication Foundation | Long Beach, WA

Publisher's Cataloging-in-Publication Data
Weilgart, Andrea.

The Ersatz Academy / Andrea Weilgart ; illustrated by Bo LeMieux. – Long Beach, WA : Cosmic Communication Foundation, 2023.

p. ; cm.

ISBN13: 978-0-9601167-0-6

1. Language, Universal--Fiction. I. Title. II. LeMieux, Bo.

PS3623.E35 E77 2023
813.6--dc23

Project coordination by Jenkins Group, Inc. | www.jenkinsgroupinc.com

Front cover illustration by Bo LeMieux
Front cover design by Jenny Zemanek
Interior design by Brooke Camfield
Author photo by Jason Brunner

Printed in the United States of America
27 26 25 24 23 • 5 4 3 2 1

DEDICATION

To my grandchildren, Arya and Leanna, that they may get
an idea about the power of language and a glimpse of the spirit
of their great-grandfather.

"Let nothing dim the light that shines from within."

—Maya Angelou

PROLOGUE

"The sky up there is full of stories just waiting to land." Grandpa pointed with the tip of his cane.

Over Silas's head, the stars gleamed with mystery. Their stories had been millions, billions of years in the making. Stories that traveled to Earth only in the form of tiny pinpricks of light.

"I met one, once . . ." Grandpa smiled at the thought, reveling in his memories. "It changed the course of my life."

Grandpa's tales never disappointed, and Silas glanced over at his older sister Verity in hope that she was listening intently as well. But she was sleeping, her head slumped against the arm of Grandpa's porch swing. Silas hunkered down in the tattered armchair he always claimed for himself.

"It arrived with a spark like a shooting star and shared a way of thinking and communicating that reshaped everything I thought I knew about language and meaning. It showed me that understanding and peace are a circle flowing together seamlessly, like a river meets the ocean . . ."

Grandpa trailed off, lost in thought, a contemplative look on his face.

"Was . . . it made of light?" asked Silas, fascinated by the constellations overhead and the possibilities they held.

"In a sense. It drank from the suns of the universe and carried what we might call a light within it—a philosophical light, anyway. And it carried a philosophy of peace to every planet it visited using an unearthly language designed to convey these very thoughts. A cosmic speech for truth and wisdom that sang with inner harmony between sound and symbol. Meaning could become visible, like through an open window. And its symbols reflected the whole universe in the miniature world of our mind. Keep an eye on the sky, my boy, because what you take to be a shooting star might just be something more profound . . ."

Silas propped his chin on his hands, searching the sky for shooting stars or evidence of Grandpa's language of light. But it was late, and sleep beckoned. Overcome by a feeling of calm, he felt his eyelids drooping, and soon he was asleep, his dreams vibrant with thoughts of an otherworldly being and a language that just might change everything.

1

The retreating day was gray above the reaching arms of the forest. Beneath the fragrance of the pines and ferns was the sense that the world was waiting for someone to look closely enough to discover its secrets.

Fourteen-year-old Verity Truman often had this feeling, but this evening it was especially strong.

"Earth to Verity! I guess you left this one for me?" Silas, Verity's younger brother, pointed to a morel mushroom peeking out from beneath a felled tree she'd missed. A founding member of the Wild Boys, Silas was an aspiring outdoorsman whose lifelong goal was to live off the land. This was one of the side effects of growing up with earth-loving parents who thought that rescuing food from supermarket dumpsters was a more ethical way to shop. Verity didn't mind foraged food, but she did like having an actual roof over her head most of the time. And running water.

Verity cut the mushroom from the ground.

"Last one. We should head back before it gets too dark."

Silas led the way, his perfectly honed internal compass telling him when and where to turn or double back. Each tree or rock or clearing was like a signpost for him. Verity loved trees as much as the next person, but after a while, they all started to look alike.

"Wait." Silas pulled up. "Do you see that?"

A light flickered and danced, accompanied by an intense whirring sound, kissing the leaves it touched with white and gold. It was vivid against the dusky sky, resembling the narrow beam of a flashlight.

"Is that a giant lightning bug? Or firefly?" Verity had never been clear whether there was even a difference between the two.

But the iridescent green-winged creature was far too large for that: it was the size of a robust dragonfly, only it hummed more sonorously. Even so, Verity cringed as it zoomed overhead. Anything that fast and flashy made her feel vulnerable. "Or maybe it's an exotic hummingbird-bug hybrid?" She thought her bird expert brother might be amused by her terminology.

But he said nothing, too intent on his mission. Beckoning Verity, he followed the zigzagging passage of the light as it leapt from bough to bough and leaf to leaf, then somersaulted a series of elongated loops into the air.

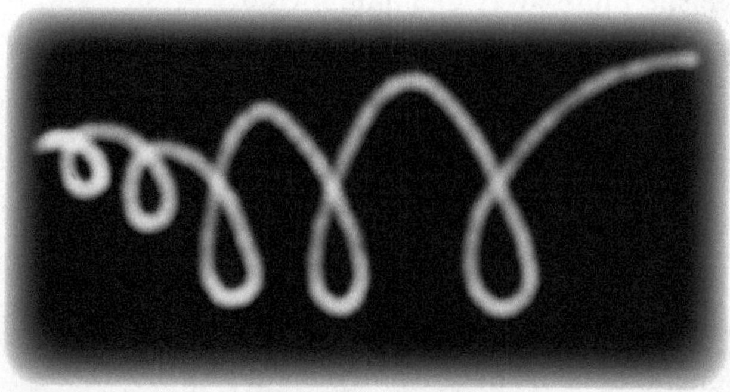

With each upward loop, it produced what sounded like a bright "ee-ee-ee!"

They chased the creature into a clearing, but just as they drew closer it leapt up, vanishing from sight. Silas slumped in disappointment. Verity, too, felt she had somehow missed out on something amazing.

"Maybe it'll come back," she said optimistically.

"Maybe . . ." said Silas. He began to add something, then decided against it. "At least we're right by the camp."

A turn at a moss-smothered tree and they were back in the clearing they'd spent the day setting up. The fire crackled merrily, warning the evening to back off a bit. Dad was seasoning a pan over its dancing flames.

"Look at all this!" he called approvingly as he took in the goods Verity and Silas carried. "We're in for a feast tonight."

"This is going to be your father's best pilaf yet." Mom was reading by the fire. She had decided long ago that reading in poor light was worth ruining your eyesight over. She would never have climbed the ranks at the museum otherwise.

Verity and Silas diced the zucchini and morels while Dad sauteed the onions. He tossed in the vegetables, stirring them in the sizzle of oil.

"It's so nice to be out here, away from it all." He waved his wooden spoon. "No newspapers, no angry talking heads on television, no people yelling hateful things entirely unsupported by evidence. If we're lucky, the world will still be there when we get back."

"I hope so." Mom was still nose down in her book. "We have the new museum exhibit opening, and I, for one, plan to be there for the launch."

Dad tasted a caramelized onion. "Mm! The green energy exhibit? That's my wife, stirring up trouble wherever she goes."

"Well, museums aren't just about collecting things to put on display. We have a social responsibility."

"Now more than ever, I'd say." Dad drained the saucepan that had been burbling away at the side of the fire. "Especially with that whole thing about blocking the new solar array venture. Coal, in this day and age! It makes no sense at all. That's what happens when you're more interested in the money you get from the big coal lobby than the future of the planet."

"That's always great to hear," said Verity wryly. "Silas and I will be the ones who'll be trying to stay alive when the oceans overflow and we start burning up."

"Ideally we'll be around for some of it as well," pointed out her dad. "We're not *that* old, you know."

"Well, not as old as Pleistocene megafauna," Silas said deadpan, focused on the piece of wood he was whittling.

"Or dinosaurs," added Verity with a grin.

Mom put down her book and dug her toes into the moss. She looked nostalgic. "Remember that time during college when we broke into the city council member's office and covered his desk with buckets of salt water and seaweed because he refused to get behind sustainable fisheries?"

Dad chuckled. "I think some tins of sardines were involved, too."

Mom wrinkled her nose. "The stench was *incredible*. But he deserved it. Besides, you have to stand behind what you believe in. I know everyone has the right to a voice, but sometimes people are just wrong, and they need to be shown."

"Without using violence, of course," added Dad.

Verity and Silas exchanged a look. They had a protest of their own planned for the night they got back home. Both were active members of goEco, a local grassroots group for environmentally aware kids led by college students concerned about their future and fed up with political inaction. Over the years, they'd petitioned for smart water meters and recycling bins, but they'd started to set their sights higher. After all, the adults weren't planning on doing anything about climate change. They were too busy thinking about making money and how to spend it.

"Ready spaghetti?" whispered Silas as their parents started plating up dinner.

Verity nodded. The plan was to tape up black trash bags painted to look like solar panels all around the neighborhood. There was no way the city representatives could keep ignoring the problem with the solution staring them right in the face.

"Here you go." Dad passed over a plate of luscious-looking pilaf, and Verity happily dug in her fork.

Mom raised a glass of water in a toast. "To good food!"

"And good people," added Verity, sharing a meaningful look with Silas.

The moon's giant eye was gazing down at Verity when she awoke in the middle of the night. She wasn't sure what had roused her—maybe a passing animal or her dad's famously eardrum-shattering snores. But she did know she needed to use the "facilities." Finding somewhere to go was one of the downsides of camping.

Her sleeping bag crinkled as she slithered out and found her bearings. The fire had simmered down to coals; other than the moon, there was barely any light. She rummaged around for a flashlight but remembered Mom had borrowed it to read with. She'd just have to hope for the best.

Verity tiptoed across the camp and over to the trees, arms held out like a zombie. Stumbling on a protruding tree root, she cursed Mom's campfire reading habits and her lack of a flashlight.

Suddenly, the path before her lit up with a flickering light—just like from the creature she'd spotted earlier that evening. Thrilled to be privy to another sighting, she kept her eye on it as she found a log that would serve as a perfect lean-to.

Verity marveled at the light emanating from the sprite-like creature and the clear, rich sound that accompanied its movements. She knew lightning bugs lit up to signal their mates but even as showy and attractive as these signals appeared, there were no others around that she could see.

"ee - ee - eh - eh - o - o," it fluted.

There was something warm and comforting about the calm, repetitive loops it traced in the air. These left a lingering afterglow trail like a New Year's sparkler dancing against the dark of night:

Then a new set of figures appeared—these not as connected as the former.

After a minute or so, the creature shot up into the sky, disappearing among the stars. Now it was just Verity and the moon, and Verity wasn't inclined to hang out alone in the woods.

Back amid the muddle of sleeping bags and cooking utensils, she groped around for Silas's stargazing notebook. With only the moonlight to guide her, she drew the loops the creature had made, hoping her scrawl would be recognizable in the morning.

Verity awoke to Silas's insistent shaking. His stargazing notebook was pressed uncomfortably close to her face.

"Is this you?" he asked, jabbing at the loops Verity had dazedly scrawled in the middle of the night.

Verity blinked blearily. "I saw that bug again. It was making those shapes over and over."

His expression intent, Silas slowly flipped through the notebook, revealing other similar forms:

"How about these?" he asked.

"Wow, some busy bee, huh?" Verity was impressed. But as Verity mused over the figures, she felt a memory stirring. She vaguely recalled being perched on Grandpa's lap, enthralled by the story he was telling. But the details escaped her. She frowned, wondering precisely why that memory had surfaced—and why now.

2

The firefly creature and its flashing figures all but vanished from Verity's mind over the coming days. She and her best friend, Lila, had been busy preparing for tonight's goEco protest. This had taken a lot more coordinating than expected. Even well-intentioned eco-warriors needed plenty of wrangling.

Verity had spent hours confirming that everyone had the right materials and directions. One mistake could compromise the entire operation, and Verity didn't like to think about the potential consequences. Law after law had been passed recently in the name of good citizen behavior. Which didn't seem so bad until you thought about the people passing the laws.

"Authoritarians," she muttered as she finished her inventory count. She had a grocery store's worth of garbage bags and duct tape in front of her.

Her bedroom door opened, and Mom poked her head in. One eyebrow went up as she took in the plastic bags strewn over the floor. "Making some costumes for school? Or are you planning a career in garbology?"

Verity thought about telling Mom what they were really up to. Her parents shared her feelings on the solar panel matter, and it wasn't like they were new to the whole protest idea. Still, it was opening night for Mom's new exhibit at the museum, and she had enough on her plate.

"Just a thing for school."

"This is what you get to work with when the powers that be keep cutting budgets," added Lila.

Verity's mom threaded an earring through an earlobe. "I know exactly how that feels. I'm only a couple of budget cuts away from putting together an exhibit on garbage myself."

"Well, you know who to call if you need help."

"That I will. Now, do you need anything for tonight? There's a lentil soup on the stove courtesy of your dad. And some oranges from the Kiggins' yard down the road . . ."

Dad came up behind Mom. He'd traded his uniform of a T-shirt and torn jeans for a neat button-down shirt and slacks. "Ready, hon?"

"Ready as I'll ever be. How do I look?" She gestured at her outfit, a floaty dress she'd paired with an equally floaty wrap. She reminded Verity of a Greek goddess.

Dad grinned. "Like a brilliant museum curator who's about to launch the exhibition of the ages."

"That's exactly the kind of compliment a woman likes to hear. Well, we're off. If you feel like it, there's a good documentary about Galapagos on later."

Verity jumped up to give Mom a hug. "Good luck! Knock 'em dead."

Mom made a face. "Even half dead would do."

Dad ushered her out of the room. "You can't be late to your own event. Bye, girls! Stay out of trouble and try not to get arrested!"

As the night rolled in, chasing away the day and switching on the streetlamps, Verity and Lila coasted their bikes down to the warehouses not far from the town square. Their baskets and panniers were laden with the garbage bags they'd taped to resemble solar panels. "Solar Saves" and "Won with the Sun" were written on them in hard-to-ignore reflective tape.

A half dozen of the goEco kids were already there. The Wild Boys were off to one side in their flannels and cargo pants, straddling heavy-duty mountain bikes that had seen a flat tire or two. Climbing gear was slung over their shoulders.

"Hey, everyone." Verity gave a cheerful wave and dug about in her backpack for the maps she and Lila had worked out earlier that week. "Here are our targets for tonight. Move fast, and don't get seen. If someone's around, just go on to your next target. Got it?"

Head nods and raised fists indicated agreement.

"Let's make change happen!"

"Make it happen!" came the enthusiastic response.

The group split off, with the kids flying either solo or in pairs. Any more than that and they'd attract attention. Kids traveling together always elicited stares, and things had gotten even worse recently.

Verity and Lila set off together toward the bus depot outside the train station. All of the shelters glowed with digital ads extolling the virtue of coal and the big businesses it supported: a perfect target.

Lila unrolled the tape as Verity stretched out one of the garbage bag solar panels to obscure the ads. "Solar Serves Survival!" it demanded, mocking the ad beneath it. Verity felt a thrill as she imagined what the area's commuters would see on their way to work tomorrow. She did feel for the janitorial staff who would have to clean up, but she figured they'd be on goEco's side. Environmentalism stood for the good of all.

Twenty minutes later, they'd covered every shelter in the depot. The trash bags gleamed where the streetlamps kissed the reflective tape that crisscrossed them.

"What's next?" asked Lila, although she knew the town hall was at the top of their list.

Verity squeezed her friend's arm. "Nervous? Me, too. But this will be our signature piece. It'll be all over the news, and that's what we want, right?"

"'Shining a light on the planet's needs,'" quoted Lila, although she didn't sound completely convinced. She took a deep breath to steady her resolve. "Let's do it."

The town hall was a vast building with a domed roof and an excessive number of marble pillars. Verity had been inside a few times as a kid for policy meetings and talks back when local politics had been less heated. But as the region had steered toward a new, dangerous type of policy, her family had stopped going. It had become disheartening to listen to the hate speech and the science deniers, especially as these people started to act out against everyone who preferred to get their information from research, not memes.

Lila gave a low whistle. "I'd forgotten how impressive it was. Where do you think the mayor's office is? Do you think she's in there, cackling evilly about the destruction of the planet?"

"It's pretty likely," said Verity wryly. She pointed. "I think that's it there, near that section with the stained glass."

There was silence for a moment as the two friends regarded the building.

"We're thinking the same thing, aren't we?" asked Lila.

"Even though we agreed there'd be no changes to the plan, huh?"

"So who's going to do it?" Lila produced a battered quarter. "Toss?"

Verity squared her shoulders. "This one's on me. Hopefully all those climbing classes with Silas taught me something. If not, it's been a good life so far. Plus, I won't have to worry about the rising oceans carrying me out to sea."

Lila helped Verity arrange her backpack so it wouldn't throw off her center of balance. It wasn't an ideal setup, but it was good enough.

They waited a few minutes in case a guard was patrolling the area, then snuck toward the town hall building. Fortunately, the old-fashioned style of its brickwork meant there were regular footholds. The nearby wisteria tree might prove helpful as well.

Still, it was with pounding heart and roaring pulse that Verity began to scale the side of the building. Attaching the garbage bags to the town hall roof would definitely make an impression. But so would getting caught.

Hand over hand, she climbed, shimmying up the wall. This was the simple part. Creeping around on the roof without drawing attention would be the challenge. Hoisting herself over the roofline, she waved down at Lila, who raised her fist in response. Now she had to find somewhere to balance while she pinned the garbage bag banners to the steep roof. She crossed her fingers, hoping the gutters would hold her weight.

Inch by inch, she crept along the roof, dragging the garbage bags with her. A napping pigeon cooed at her, disgruntled over being disturbed. Verity almost lost her footing but regained it after a few seconds of scrabbling. Pausing to catch her breath, she heartened: not far above was an elaborate stained-glass skylight almost exactly the dimensions of her garbage bag. It was perfect.

"Hurry up!" hissed Lila from her lookout point. "The clock's ticking."

Verity wedged a roll of tape between her teeth and climbed over to the stained-glass window. Everything was going smoothly. The garbage bag unrolled tidily and stuck almost perfectly to the frame of the stained-glass display. She couldn't have chosen a better spot.

Verity was pinning down the final corner when the duct-taped solar panels began flickering with reflected light. She turned her head, wondering if the firefly creature from the campsite had somehow followed her. But all she could see from her crouching position was a sliver of the night sky and the neon flash of the nearby movie theater. She twisted herself slightly to get a better view, her hand landing on the window.

The glass gave a warning creak, then shattered with a musical tinkle, falling inward into the mayor's offices. So did Verity, who followed with a thud, having somehow tangled herself in the garbage bag. There she lay, stunned and in shock, looking like an unaccomplished piece of modern art, until a flashlight speared her eyes.

"What on God's green earth do we have here?!"

3

Verity's parents arrived at the police station about an hour later. In their event finery, they looked much more put together than their battered daughter, who was bleeding from dozens of tiny scratches and suffering from an acute case of shame. And a badly bruised tailbone.

Mom rushed up to the front desk with such speed she nearly tackled it. The officer on duty, a very slight young man, took a step back.

"We're Verity Truman's parents. Is she okay?"

"That depends." A burly officer stepped out from behind a filing cabinet. He slapped a hefty thigh with a dog-eared file. Both his teeth and fingers were stained yellow from nicotine, and the smell of cigarettes clung to him. "The mayor is considering pressing charges for vandalism, trespassing, breaking and entering, and probably a few more besides."

"Doesn't that seem a little punitive?" Mom folded her arms. Her ornate brass bangles clanked. "She's fourteen—just a kid! And I'm sure it wasn't intentional."

"She gets her coordination from me," explained Dad with a well-what-can-you-do shrug. He always played the fool in situations like this.

Verity's mom held up a silencing hand. "You're not helping, hon. Look, she was just expressing a political opinion. As an informed citizen, she has every right to protest and make her voice heard."

"Not every right," said the mayor. She had just reentered the foyer after leaving for about the dozenth time to make a phone call. "In case you haven't been paying attention, we've been working hard to do away with the misdirected minors."

"Like the right to assemble and the right to peaceful protest?" Verity's mom's lips thinned to a slash.

"Precisely. It's the pre-hostility of the protest we're concerned about. What's so peaceful about breaking the windows of a heritage-listed building? If your daughter has an opinion she simply must share, she can wait until she's old enough to vote."

Verity scowled. She knew that anything she said would only make things worse, but it was taking all her strength not to snap back.

Mom had no such qualms. "Well, if it were up to *me*, I'd lower the voting age. Democracy works best when as many people as possible have the right to participate in it. Why should we restrict the voices of informed citizens just because they don't meet some arbitrary age requirement?"

"Lady—"

"I really wouldn't," warned Dad. He turned to the mayor, summoning all of his raffish charm, most of which had unfortunately receded over the years, along with his hairline. "Look, is there some way we can work this out? Verity's a good kid. She just has strong ideas about things."

"Can't think where she might get those," muttered the burly officer.

The mayor checked her phone, then sighed. "I can spare a few minutes. Let's talk in the back room. All right, Miss Truman, you wait here. And stay away from the windows."

"And trash cans," whispered Dad. He followed the mayor and the police officer.

"Wait, where's Silas?" Verity had forgotten all about her brother until now.

"At home. Where else would he be?" Mom's tone was pointed.

Verity knew better than to say anything else. Clearly, her parents had figured out Silas's whereabouts that night but didn't want to implicate him as well.

With the adults gone, she swung her legs and counted the spots of chewing gum on the carpet as her fate was discussed without her. It was an awful feeling, having someone else make decisions about your life and not getting any say in the matter. But at the same time, she was glad her parents were handling the situation. Verity sighed. If the mayor grilled her for long enough, she'd probably end up bursting into tears or incriminating herself even further.

About half an hour later, Verity's parents emerged from the back room. They looked drawn and tired, the color leached from their complexions. Even their clothing seemed less vibrant.

The mayor, on the other hand, was the very picture of victory.

"I have a call to make, but I'll be back in a minute. I'll leave the three of you to talk among yourselves." She trotted outside, letting the door swing behind her. Verity tried to swallow, but her mouth was dry. She'd do anything for a cup of tea right now.

"Sweetie." Mom took a seat beside her. "You have a difficult decision to make. It's the new antisocial behavior laws they rushed through a few months back. If you don't take the deal they're offering, they're threatening consequences for us."

Verity frowned. "What do you mean?"

"We could be charged with contributing to the delinquency of a minor." Dad rubbed a hand through his thinning hair. "Let's just say I did an overnight in my college days, and it was memorable for all the wrong reasons. Jail food is no comparison to the spoils of our dumpster diving, trust me."

Mom leaned forward. Her tone was quiet but earnest. "At the very least we could lose our jobs. And we all know jobs in our fields are tough to come by these days, what with all the budget cuts. It doesn't look great for any of us."

Verity's palms were damp. She wiped them on her black jeans. "So what am I supposed to do? Community service? Write the mayor a nice letter?"

"If only. The mayor has proposed you spend a term at some kind of 'youth development center' in the desert, whatever that means. Apparently, they have great outcomes for troubled teens."

Verity was defensive. "But I'm not troubled! I just have strong ideas about how to make things better for the earth and everybody!"

She felt tears coming on but fought to contain herself.

Mom smiled half-heartedly. "I know. We're letting you make the decision . . ." She hesitated, then sighed. "Just remember that what you choose will affect us, too."

Nodding, Dad gave her shoulder a reassuring pat. But Verity could feel the worry radiating off him. His palms were as clammy as her own.

"But it's not really a choice, is it? If I don't take the school option, I could get both of you thrown in jail for something you didn't do. What would happen to Silas? And your jobs?"

Her parents were silent. The police station air felt heavy and dense, pressing in all around the three of them. Verity's craving for tea was replaced by a sudden need for fresh air. She couldn't spend any more time in this place, with its ghastly undercurrent of stale coffee, cigarettes, and sweat. If jail were half as oppressive as this, she was in trouble.

How bad could a school possibly be?

"The school," she said. "I'll enroll in the school."

Her parents exchanged a look, then enveloped her in a hug. Verity relaxed into the comforting familiarity of it, trying not to think about what she might have signed up for.

The door swung, and the mayor reappeared, phone glued to her ear. "So?" she mouthed, still carrying on her conversation with whomever was on the other end.

"The school," repeated Verity.

The mayor gave a sage nod. "Ersatz Academy? Brilliant. It's just the place for a girl like you."

4

Silas was waiting on the porch when they got home, his latest whittling project clasped between his fingers. Curls of wood had gathered around him like tiny mole hills, only much more easily dealt with.

"Is everything okay?" he asked. "What happened?"

"Authoritarians happened." Dad gripped the porch railing with uncharacteristic force and gave it a rattle. "Remember when a peaceful protest was a rite of passage? Not a mark of delinquency that must be quashed at all costs?"

"Nope." Silas pushed away the wood shavings with his toe.

"Verity's going away to a new school for a term or two," explained Mom. "It was the lesser of the options they gave us, the other being potential jail time for the whole family."

Silas's eyes widened. "Jail time? Seriously? Even for me?"

Mom opened the front door and ushered them all inside, away from prying neighborly eyes. News traveled fast these days. "Well, not you, because you were here the whole night watching nature documentaries, right?"

Silas gave a thumbs-up. "That is absolutely what I was doing. Ask me anything about pangolins or arctic foxes."

"Maybe if it weren't so late already." Dad gave an exaggerated stretch that risked putting his back out. "How about we all get some shut-eye? This will all be easier to handle once we've slept on it."

But Verity didn't want to go to bed just yet. Her enrollment at the Academy was effective immediately, meaning someone would be there to pick her up the next day. Going to bed would only bring the inevitable transfer closer, and she wasn't ready for that quite yet.

Mom brushed a curl away from Verity's face. "You can always read in bed. I know that's guaranteed to cheer you up."

"Indubitably," said Silas, with the over-the-top delivery of a circus ringleader.

"Word of the day!" Their dad gave him an effusive clap on the back, although Verity didn't quite believe the good cheer behind it. "You get to pick tomorrow's word. What'll it be?"

Silas thought a moment. Then said, quietly, almost to himself: "Exile. Tomorrow's word is exile."

<hr>

Sleep was a long time coming. Verity lay beneath the covers, tracing the familiar shadowy shapes in her room and picking out the constellations from the glowing stars Silas had stuck to her ceiling as a birthday gift a few years back. She scrunched her eyes closed, and when she opened them, the stars danced, reminding her of the firefly creature:

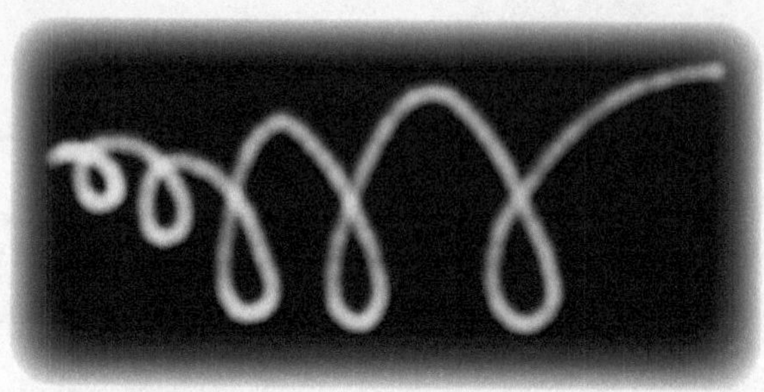

Blinking, she slid out of bed and went to the window, staring out at the midnight street. A streetlamp on the fritz sparked, and the neighbor's beagle let out the occasional mournful howl, but otherwise, the streetscape felt still and empty. But not the same way that the forest had.

Her appreciation of proper roofs and plumbing aside, she had to admit that in the forest there was always a sense of being surrounded by something. There was a natural richness and a density of life that human cities could never replicate. Not to mention an all-encompassing calm.

This made her think of Grandpa, who had been the first in the family to embrace nature. He had done it before the hippie movement. And before it was cool. For him, it had just been a way of life. Just like his stories. She smiled at the thought of the yarns he'd spun when she and Silas had been kids. He'd been convinced that the universe had its own voice and language and it was just looking for someone to listen.

Almost, she thought absently, like the firefly creature.

Verity must have fallen asleep at some point, because the ringing of her vintage alarm clock jolted her out of bed. The clock was the only one they'd found that could wake Verity, who had a reputation for being an impressively deep sleeper.

The bedroom door opened, and Mom took a seat at the end of her bed. "Any breakfast requests? Your dad has a bunch of blueberries he'd like to use, if pancakes sound any good to you."

"Sounds delish." Verity's voice was croaky and thick with sleep. "I can't believe it'll be my last Dad-cooked breakfast for months."

"Things can change quickly, can't they?" The bed creaked as Mom shifted her weight. She gazed up at the stars on the ceiling, which were faint in the daylight. "Believe me, when I was at the gallery last night, I had no inkling any of this would be happening. I was too busy trying to focus my nerves for my speech."

In all the drama Verity hadn't even asked about Mom's big night. "How did it go? The opening, I mean."

"Great, actually. We had a record turnout and plenty of media attention. Maybe there's hope for humanity yet. After all, looking to the past is the best way to avoid a terrible future." Mom smiled wryly. "Well, and 'youth development centers,' apparently. Have you started packing?"

Verity shook her head. She'd dug out her duffel bag last night, but that was it.

"Well, it shouldn't be too hard. The school has a uniform, so you won't need too many clothes. Plus, the list of what you're allowed to bring is pretty restrictive."

Verity reviewed the list her mom had passed to her. It was sloppily inkjet printed on the back of a piece of scrap paper. "And you're *sure* I'm going to a school and not a prison?"

"That's for the mayor to know and you to find out." Dad had just arrived with a plate of blueberry pancakes and a side of lemon wedges.

Verity squeezed a lemon over her pancakes and rolled them up into a fluffy burrito. "You're both taking this way too well," she said, taking a bite. "Aren't you worried? Scared? Freaked out I might not come back?

I mean, what do we even know about this school?" Her voice cracked a little, betraying the calm she was trying to convey.

Mom exhaled slowly. "We're all of those things. But we can't control the situation. We can only control how we respond to it. So, we're doing our best. It sounds like you are, too."

Verity's pancake burrito was almost gone. "I mean, I guess it could have been worse. We could've all gone to jail."

"True," said Dad. "And there are no blueberry pancakes there. Not even in minimum security." He paused. "Look, the world is becoming a strange place. It doesn't work the way it used to, and the rules are all up in the air. This isn't exactly how we thought things would turn out for you, but at the same time, we can't let them break us. We need to stay true to what we stand for: values and actions that benefit everybody."

"And blueberry pancakes." Verity forced a smile.

"I do have strong convictions about blueberry pancakes. Now go on: start figuring out that packing list and I'll put another batch on. If you're fast enough, Silas won't eat them all."

Verity set aside her plate and reviewed the packing list once more. "No electronics, no books, no toiletries . . . This shouldn't take long."

She threw some clothes into the bag, along with a reading light, a notebook, and a jumble of pens and pencils. As the Wild Boys would say, it was better to be overprepared than underprepared. The bag was almost embarrassingly light, but she couldn't think of anything else to bring. It seemed strange to be packing for such a long time and with no idea of what awaited her.

"That's it?" asked Mom, hefting the bag.

"I guess so."

"Why don't you go wake Silas? I'll double-check to make sure you haven't missed anything."

Verity padded down the tiled hallway and knocked on Silas's door. There was no answer, although she could hear his fan whirring in the background. Silas needed background noise to sleep, which was maybe why he liked sleeping outside.

"Silas?" There was movement on the other side of the door, but her brother didn't respond. "You're missing out on Dad's blueberry pancakes."

Nothing.

In fact, Silas didn't emerge from his bedroom until after lunch. When he did, he was far from his sunny self. He answered every question with a monosyllable and didn't even bother to consult the barometer that hung on the back porch.

"He's just worried about you," Mom reassured Verity. "This is a big deal for him as well. As precocious as he is, he's still just a kid, and I don't think he really understands what this all means." She paused. "Or maybe he's feeling a bit guilty for getting away with it when you didn't."

***

Dusk had settled over the town, and Verity's departure time was creeping ever closer. At some point within the next hour, the Ersatz Academy bus would arrive, and she'd be traveling at high speed far away from her friends and family. In the end, she hadn't even had time to properly speak with Lila. All they'd managed was a quick exchange of texts.

Verity slung her duffel bag over her shoulder and went out to wait on the porch. The atmosphere inside was stifling and gloomy. Her parents had become quieter and more withdrawn as the day had gone on, and Silas was still in hiding. She needed to get out.

As she waited, watching the sky turn the colors of fruity gelato, the front door opened. Silas emerged, scowling.

He gestured to her duffel bag. "This whole thing is weird and wrong. But look, if anything happens and you need help, find a way to tell me. It wouldn't be the Wild Boys' first rescue mission. I mean, of a *person* it would be . . ." Silas shrugged.

Verity's smile wobbled a little under the threat of tears. She'd miss her brother's small kindnesses and dorky jokes. There was so much she was going to leave behind: she could barely bring herself to think about it. She scrubbed her eyes with the back of a hand.

"I promise. If you promise to keep an eye on Mom and Dad."

"I'll do my best, but they're not exactly well behaved. Oh, hey, I made you something." Silas reached into his pocket and pulled out a wooden trinket. With its slender body and wire and crepe paper wings, it looked like the firefly creature they'd seen in the woods.

Verity took it with a thank-you and an awkward hug. "That reminds me: I've been meaning to ask you about . . ." But the thought dissipated as a hulking gray bus turned up their street. Its brakes hissed as it pulled up outside.

"I'll get Mom and Dad." Silas sprinted back inside.

A man with braided hair and tattooed hands climbed out of the bus. He looked like he might have accompanied her parents on some of their protests in his youth.

"Verity Truman?"

"That's me," Verity said reticently.

"I'm with Ersatz. The name's Huff. Before we get going, I have some paperwork for your parents. They're in there?"

"We're here." Mom emerged breathlessly from the house.

She looked stricken: no one was happy about the decision they'd landed on. But it was the lesser of two evils, Verity knew. She scrunched her eyes closed, counting down from ten to calm herself.

Huff waved a clipboard. "If you'll just sign this, we can be on our way. ETA is midnight if we make good time."

Verity's parents wrapped her up in an embrace. Dad was close to tears, although he cried watching David Attenborough documentaries, so this wasn't too surprising. Mom was trying her best to appear composed but still smothered Verity in kisses and demanded that she write home. Only Silas stood off to the side. His fists were clenched, like he was forcing himself not to blurt out how he felt about the whole situation.

Verity slung her bag over her shoulder. Her hand trembled on its strap.

"Bye, everyone. I'll call you when I get there—"

Huff held out a hand. "I hate to do this, but you'll need to hand over your phone."

Verity frowned. "Seriously?"

"It's on the list. Along with pretty much everything else, I know. But it's the rules, and Ersatz is all about rules. A break from those devices isn't so bad, anyway."

Feeling like she'd agreed to cut off a limb, Verity pulled out her phone and handed it over to Dad, who held it up like a prize.

"I'll take good care of it for you, Ver. I won't even read your messages or anything."

"Gee, thanks." Verity made a face, but it quickly devolved into the start of a sob. She'd better get on the bus before she chickened out and tried to make a run for it. Pressing her lips tightly together, she climbed the first step.

"Ver, hold on." Silas darted in, grabbing her arm. "Good luck and remember what I said."

Verity nodded, then made her way onto the bus, trying not to look at her parents huddled there on the driveway. Silas had disappeared. Verity cast her gaze up to his bedroom window, trying to spot him.

Huff cranked up the bus radio with Beethoven's Ninth and put the bus into gear.

"Can't go wrong with classical music," he said over the roar of the engine. "Not that my younger self would ever have said such a thing."

Verity gave a monosyllabic reply. She was distracted by two figures that had appeared on the inside of Silas's bedroom window:

Verity had seen them in Silas's notebook, but not stacked up like that. She wondered what they meant. Then, clutching the carved figurine in one hand, she traced the same figures in the condensation on the window to her right.

The bus pulled away, and Verity's house, and previous life, dwindled into the distance. Overcome with resignation, she leaned back in her seat and closed her eyes. Whatever lay ahead, it was going to take some getting used to.

5

The bus jolted to a stop, jerking Verity awake. She had no idea what time it was, but it seemed late: the sky was dark and lit with a confetti of crisp stars. She shivered.

"Home, sweet home." Huff killed the engine. The violins of the Vivaldi that had been playing over the speakers abruptly faded to nothing.

"Where *is* this place?" whispered Verity to herself. She was looking out at a compound consisting of a cramped handful of buildings surrounded by a tall mesh fence. There was no grass or vegetation within the perimeter, only dried out asphalt and faded concrete. But even that seemed less daunting than the expanse of surrounding desert scrub lit up by the floodlights that blazed across the site.

Silas had perfectly described her situation with his word of the day: exile. She could only hope she wouldn't end up serving out a life sentence here.

"Welcome to Ersatz Academy," announced Huff, not sounding particularly enthused.

"Who's Mr. Ersatz?" asked Verity, who had wondered about the Academy's strange name. "Or Ms.?"

Huff chuckled. "Interesting question. I wondered that myself when I started work here, so I looked it up. It actually means 'substitute' in German, but here we use it to mean 'fake.' Got your stuff?"

Verity held up her mostly empty duffel bag. She wished she'd smuggled her phone in one of its pockets: she could at least let her family and Lila know she'd arrived safely.

"Nothing wrong with traveling light. It's good for the soul. Back in my day, I spent more than a few years in a van chasing bands around the country. Nothing but a gas stove, a backpack, and a stray dog to my name. But that was then. Now there's bills to pay. Come on."

Huff directed her off the bus and across the asphalt to one of the few buildings. The entire surface was crisscrossed with variously colored lines studded with arrows.

"Directional," explained Huff. "They'll tell you where to go. Mind you don't go straying off them. That's a no-no."

"What, because I'll ruin the grass?"

Huff chuckled. "Something like that."

In front of the building stood a massive moth-smothered sign that reminded Verity of the kiosk displays at the entrance of national and state park campgrounds. But a lot less welcoming.

ERSATZ ACADEMY
Where Discipline Rules:
The Tools for a Better Future

1. STAY IN LINE
2. THINK WITHIN THE BOX
3. WEAR YOUR UNIFORM
4. LISTEN TO ADULTS
5. OBEY ALL RULES

Verity swallowed. She had a feeling she and Ersatz Academy weren't exactly going to get along. She wasn't averse to rules per se. Just the ones she didn't agree with. Like basically all the ones listed on the billboard.

Huff pressed a buzzer, and a door swung open, revealing a huge brute of a man who took up most of the frame. The man's jaw was disconcertingly wide, and he wore a bristling statement mustache shaped like a hairy horseshoe.

"And who's this, then?" The man sounded like a rabid Rottweiler.

"Verity . . . Truman. I'm a new student here, I guess."

The man slapped the door frame with enough force to send a tremor through the room. "Not a student. A subject. You'll learn the difference soon enough."

Verity wasn't sure how to respond to that, so she didn't.

"I'm Payne. Crenshaw Payne. Aptly named, so they say."

"Do they?" asked Verity.

"They do!" snapped Payne. "Right. You, through here for processing. Huff, I'll take it from here."

Huff gave a lazy and slightly ironic-looking salute and loped off into the dark. Verity suddenly felt very ill at ease.

Payne reached out a meaty hand. "Bag."

Verity handed it over for Payne to paw through. Wordlessly, he unzipped every compartment and reviewed every item. "Won't be needing this," he said, taking out a book she'd packed just in case. "Or this. What's that sloshing around in there, anyway?"

Verity's mom had apparently snuck a jar of preserves into the duffel bag.

Jamming the book and preserves into a large plastic tub bursting with contraband, he haphazardly threw everything else back in Verity's duffel bag, zipped it up, and tossed it to Verity. "Any electronics?"

Verity shook her head.

"No phone?"

"No phone. You can ask Huff."

"I will." Payne yanked open a cupboard door. Inside was a stack of plastic-wrapped clothes, all in lifeless gray. He dragged out a set and handed them to Verity, along with a pair of matching gray sneakers.

Verity supposed this was her uniform, although it looked more like a very dull version of prison garb than the uniforms she'd seen private school kids wear. At least it didn't have a tie or those long socks that had to be held up with knotted elastic.

Payne gestured at an undersized door that apparently led to a changing cubicle. "Get dressed in there. Then we'll go meet Lawson."

Verity did, managing to bruise both an elbow and a knee against the wall of the cramped cubicle. She was lucky she was petite for her age; a bigger kid could easily have gotten stuck. Judging from the scuff marks on the walls, more than one had.

Payne took her old clothes and tipped them into a plastic drawstring bag, which he hung up in another closet. Dozens of bags, all presumably filled with other kids' street clothes, swung there like meat on butchers' hooks. Verity suppressed a shiver. The whole situation made her think of the phrase "like a pig to slaughter." She hoped she was reading too much into things.

"Right, let's get on with it. Lawson doesn't like to be kept waiting. He's a busy man. Important, do you hear me?"

"Sure," said Verity, although she wasn't sure being busy and important were necessarily connected.

Payne led Verity across the quadrangle, following a dashed yellow line. At the line's end was an arrow pointing to an old brick structure painted over in what was becoming a familiar gray. The building's thick windows were covered over with bars on the outside and black-out curtains on the inside. Its door had the forbidding density of a medieval table turned on end. To its right was posted another copy of the Academy Rules.

Ignoring the doorbell, Payne rapped on the door so firmly that his knuckles came away scraped. He didn't seem to notice. He'd probably raised his fists often enough in his life that they had no feeling left in them.

From the other side of the door came a screech that seemed to tear the night open. Startled, Verity stumbled backward, landing a solid foot away from the dashed yellow line.

The door opened, revealing a man whose face was half covered in scar tissue. It bloomed over his right cheekbone in waxy ridges resembling a brain. Verity knew she shouldn't, but she flinched.

"This subject is off the line, Payne," came the man's very precise, fastidious voice. He prepared and spoke every syllable with great care, as though each word were a culinary delicacy. Verity had a feeling that they weren't going to be to her taste.

"So she is, sir. Back on the yellow, Subject."

It took Verity a second to figure out what rule she'd broken, but she quickly corrected herself, planting her feet back on the line. Ersatz Academy was going to take some getting used to. She had never been asked to literally toe a line before.

"Well, then, come in, Subject. You are to be up at 0500, so I would not waste any more time."

Verity nervously followed Lawson over the threshold and into a tidy but nondescript apartment most notable for the scarlet macaw perched in one corner. The bird screeched, and Verity realized it was the source of the earlier blood-curdling scream.

"I see you have met Pyrite." Lawson ceremoniously seated himself on a plush office chair behind his formidable desk. It was free of clutter except for a single photo frame holding a page that marched with ominous text: *"Orders Lead to Order. Subordination Builds Nations. Followers Make Better Fellows."* Brian Lawson was cited as the author.

There was nowhere else to sit, so Verity remained standing. She supposed this was by design. Lawson apparently wanted to make people understand where they stood with him. "I s'pose so, sir. Lucky me."

A pair of flat, fishlike eyes regarded her. "It will behoove you to behave, Subject. There is no room for impertinence here, understood? I surmise you know why you are at Ersatz Academy?"

"I was involved in a protest, sir."

Lawson raised his remaining eyebrow. "Breaking and entering, destruction of property, and unlawful politicizing, I hear."

Unlawful politicizing was a new term for Verity. She had a feeling that it wouldn't be the last she'd learn at Ersatz Academy.

Lawson picked a fleck of invisible lint from his perfectly pressed shirt. "But I did not mean for what *reason*. I meant for what *purpose*. Two very different things. The reason for your admission here is your insubordination. Your purpose here is to be reformed."

"I see, sir," said Verity, although she didn't really.

Lawson pressed on: he appeared to have his welcome speech memorized. "Ersatz Academy exists both *because* of young delinquents like you and *for* the benefit of young delinquents like you. Ultimately, our purpose is to benefit society as a whole. We take that youthful arrogance and determination and constructively redirect it to create fine, upstanding, contributing members of society . . . ones who understand the value of established boundaries."

"But I already am one of those." Verity actually felt very upstanding—standing up to what was wrong, anyway.

"You are the *opposite* of that. You question authority. You seek power. You mobilize the uninformed and uneducated. You corrupt the basic institutions of our society."

This was exactly the sort of screed Verity might expect to hear from the mayor's cronies or in a particularly awful subreddit. No wonder the mayor had been so invested in sending her here.

"But the role of citizens isn't to behave," she pointed out. "It's to participate in democracy, to get involved in society, and create a better world for everyone . . . sir."

"Such a familiar tune you sing." Lawson spoke with a touch of amusement. "I have heard the same from hundreds of others as they first step through these doors. But never fear. I believe that every individual has the capacity to become productive and well behaved. To create a better world, yes, but the right kind of better world. One of order, efficiency, and discipline. It is my job as HeadMaster to facilitate exactly that. Our outcomes are excellent. We have impeccable graduation rates. Exceptional job placement results. And a recidivism rate of almost zero. A recidivist is a repeat offender," he explained, patronizingly.

Verity was aware. It had been the Truman word of the day a month or so back.

"Fortunately, we got ahold of you early. The younger you are, the more reformable. With some reeducation you will not need to worry about your future or how you will find your proper place in society." He smiled crookedly, one side of his face frozen by scar tissue. Eerily, he seemed completely earnest, as if he expected Verity would find the idea of becoming someone completely different a good thing. So this is what was meant by "Ersatz."

Pyrite screamed, and Verity clapped her hands over her ears.

"See?" said Lawson. "We have already begun."

———

Payne directed Verity along a dotted line that led to a looming cinder block building. Its porous sides seemed to suck up any light that touched them, and its tiny barred windows resembled toothy mouths. Verity's initial impression of the Ersatz Academy had not improved one iota.

The dotted lines continued inside, running the length of the squeaky-floored corridors. Once over the threshold, however, the lines broke off into an array of new colors and patterns.

"For navigation." Payne, like Lawson, apparently thought Verity was extremely dim. Maybe he was projecting. "Each one goes to a specific bunk room or classroom. There's no excuse for being lost here. Or for straying off the path. Orders lead to order, see?"

Verity was too exhausted to argue. She had no watch or phone to check, but the clock must be creeping toward one or two in the morning. She was ready to just climb into bed and be done with this day.

"This is you," said Payne momentarily. "The white dot room. You can tell—"

"Because of the white dots." Verity pointed to the floor and then the sign next to the door.

"Fast learner. Might serve you well here. I've seen my fair share of things over the years, believe me." Deep in reflection, Payne smoothed his walrus-like mustache. He passed Verity a dull silvery key fob. "That's yours for the room. It'll get you into here, the bathroom, and whatever's on your schedule. Don't even try flashing it around anywhere else. The system will register it, and then I'll be the one writing up the report. Reports are work, and I don't like working. Got it? Good. Now I've got some monitors to monitor. Good luck, kid."

Payne lumbered off, mumbling into a walkie-talkie. As he turned a corner, Verity noticed a blank screen mounted on the wall above his head.

Wondering what its purpose was, she let herself into her bunk room, waiting for her eyes to adjust to the darkness. There were three other girls in there, all sound asleep. One was snoring worse than Verity's dad. Another tossed and turned, while a third lay completely motionless on her back, like a mummy.

The bunk below this girl was the only one free. Pulling Silas's carving from her bag, Verity crawled beneath the sheets, willing sleep to come.

Instead, she spent what felt like hours staring up at the slats above her, her only company the comforting figures of the firefly creature dancing through her memory:

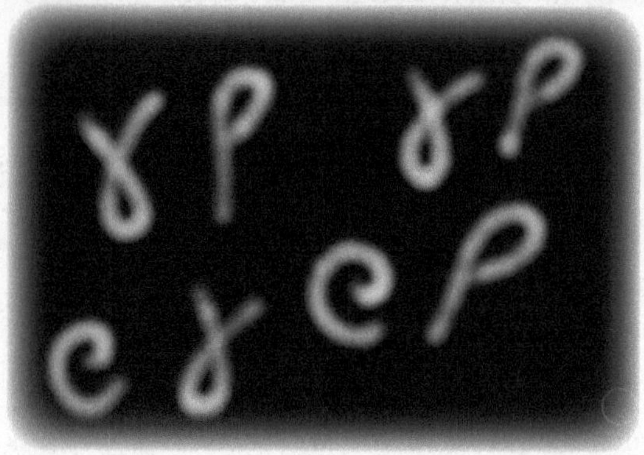

They flashed in front of her eyes, before transforming into the squiggles Silas had drawn on his window:

6

A klaxon shattered the silence, loud enough to wake even Verity, who'd finally fallen asleep after hours of restless rumination. Thinking it was a fire alarm, she groggily hauled herself out of bed ready to flee to the nearest exit.

"It's 5 a.m. already?" moaned the girl with the impressive snores. Strangely flat, her voice was much less expressive than her nighttime snoring.

"Oh, hey, Em, we've got a new girl," said the girl from the top bunk, opposite Verity. She had long hair in tight braids and a regal expression that suggested she was used to giving orders, not taking them. Verity wondered how well she was holding up here.

"Fresh blood," said Em, with a quirk of her eyebrow. Her brows were much paler than her jet-black hair, which had grown out a few inches. One side of it had once been shaved but was now fuzzy with reddish regrowth.

Another head poked down from the bunk bed above Verity's. Dark, owlish eyes regarded her. "I knew you'd get here in the night," came a low, confident voice with a hint of toughness. "That bed's been empty for too long."

"Krystal wins another bet," said Em. "You owe her your breakfast, Queen Bea."

"Hardly." Bea defiantly jutted her chin. "Someone was going to arrive sooner or later. There's no right way to be these days. Anyway, New Girl, let's get to the showers before morning exercises start. Unless you hate hot water."

Verity shook her head. Silas might be fine with bathing in a chilly stream, but she liked her showers scalding. Taking her roommates' cue, she gathered up an armful of gray clothing to change into.

A blue dotted line led them to the bathrooms at the end of the hall. Dozens of girls followed it, all walking at a measured but deliberate pace. There were boys, too, but they were following a dashed blue line in the opposite direction.

The bathrooms were a haze of steam but were surprisingly quiet. Most of the girls in there barely spoke, instead staring straight ahead into the mirrors as they brushed their teeth or fixed their hair. Those that did talk kept it to a low murmur, as though worried about eavesdroppers.

Bea was the exception.

"So, what did they get you on?" She jabbed with her toothbrush. Toothpaste sprayed the stainless-steel mirror, the kind you'd find in a subway station or a roadside diner where you'd be liable to get food poisoning. Next to it was a framed poster of the Academy Rules, slightly crumpled from the humidity but stern, nonetheless.

"What did they get me on?" Verity had to think that one over herself. "Protesting the coal industry. Although mostly falling through the roof of the mayor's office while trying to tape a solar panel to it."

Bea nodded, impressed. "Just you, or were there others involved?"

Verity started to explain about goEco, but then realized Bea might be fishing for information she could use against her. She wasn't sure yet whether she could trust the girl. Maybe the other girls were being quiet for a reason.

"Just me." She splashed water over her face. She felt like death warmed over.

Bea spat out her toothpaste and quickly undressed. "You've got two minutes if you want to shower. No one's late for morning exercises."

Verity followed Bea's cue and ducked into one of the shower stalls, soaping and rinsing as fast as humanly possible. The prickling hot water helped to wake her. So did the soap, the scratchy sand-infused kind she hadn't used since preschool. Lawson clearly wasn't one for the comforts of home. Not that Verity had especially high standards about such things, having been raised on natural soap made from coconut oil, oatmeal, and lye. Lila always joked the ingredients were one step away from a decent cookie but a few away from a decent bar of soap.

By the time she got out, the other girls were dressed and waiting. Apparently, she wasn't as water conscious as she'd thought.

"You need to work on your speed showering, New Girl," said Em. Her eyes looked freshly lined; she must have smuggled in a makeup kit somehow. Or maybe she'd been applying eyeliner for so long her eyelids were permanently stained.

Bea sighed nostalgically. "Remember bubble baths? And hot tubs? And saunas? And what I wouldn't do for a manicure."

"Oh, poor you, having to live like a normal person." Krystal folded her towel with such aggression it was like she was trying to strangle it. "My mama works two jobs just to keep the hot water on."

"I bet she's proud to see you in here, then." Bea leaned back against the countertops, surreptitiously checking the state of her fingernails. What she saw was disappointing; her mouth tightened.

Not wanting to get involved, Verity took Em's cue and made an escape.

"Are they always like that?"

Em gave her a sidelong glance, green eyes striking in their dark makeup. "Pretty much. I *think* they're friends. Frenemies, anyway."

The girls shoved their pajamas in their bunk room lockers, then followed a line of green arrows outside onto the asphalt, keeping an eye on the clock that flashed on the wall-mounted television screens. The screens must be used by Lawson to communicate with the subjects, Verity realized. Like morning announcements, only much more intrusive and intimidating.

Somehow, Bea and Krystal managed to catch up with Em and Verity. To make up the distance they must have jostled an unsuspecting victim or two out of the way. Verity pitied the kids who had found themselves on the wrong marked line and were probably being disciplined over it.

As it turned out, Verity did some jostling of her own. Distracted by the broad desert sky as she made her way outside, she got off track and crashed into Payne, fresh off his night shift.

"Watch it!" he bellowed, reaching instinctively for a device at his side. It looked like a taser, although Verity couldn't be sure. Not that she wanted to find out.

"Payne! Sorry—"

Payne didn't seem to recognize her at all. To him, all the kids here were probably just a jumble of lookalike cretins.

His piggish eyes glared. He was almost completely lacking in eyelashes, though it was hard to tell under the neanderthal jut of his brow. "Morning exercises. That way. And stick to the paths unless you want to be written up."

"Yes, sir."

"That man's dead inside," muttered Em.

Verity was inclined to agree but didn't have time to discuss the finer points of Payne's sociopathy. She ran to catch up with Bea and Krystal, who had reached the quadrangle and were taking their positions ready for morning exercises. Bea squeezed a whisper out of the side of her mouth, "Look, but don't notice."

"Huh?" It left Verity wondering.

It was quite a sight. About fifty or sixty subjects stood in neat rows along the asphalt, all in the same ramrod position. Their rigid stance and gray uniforms gave the exercise a military feel. Verity fidgeted in discomfort.

Lawson's sudden appearance did nothing to help matters.

"Subjects!" he barked, taking his place at the front of the quadrangle. "Morning exercises will commence."

This was the full extent of his preamble. Without further ceremony, he led the subjects through a fitness routine that borrowed from tai chi, yoga, and calisthenics. Verity tried to keep up, but the movements cycled so quickly she was always a step behind. One moment she had her hands over her head, and the next she was struggling to hold a plank. Then it was jumping jacks and stork poses. Maybe confusion was the point of it all. Maybe you were more likely to defer to authority when you had no reasonable point of reference left. It worked for math teachers, after all.

Beside her, Em wheezed asthmatically. Verity hoped she had an inhaler handy. But before she could say anything, Lawson stormed up her row and shouted at a small curly haired boy who had stumbled during a yoga pose, given up, and taken a seat in protest.

"Detention!"

Though the boy must have known what was coming, his lower lip trembled.

"Is anyone else not pulling their weight?" Lawson's ravaged face turned on a girl positioned behind the chastened boy.

"No, sir," said the girl, wobblingly maintaining her pose. She managed to evade detention, but others weren't so lucky. By the end, no fewer than half a dozen had been made to stand on the sidelines. These subjects remained behind as the others were released for breakfast.

"That was . . . something," whispered Verity to Em, who was surreptitiously taking hits from her inhaler. "Are you okay?"

"Sign of weakness." Eyes averted, Em picked her way along a studded green line. "Lawson doesn't need to know. Besides, the sick bay isn't exactly Disneyland."

"I'm starting to see a trend."

"Wait till you see what passes for breakfast."

Breakfast was served in the mess hall, a long, thin room with industrial leanings. Its floors were polished concrete, and its walls had the kind of unnervingly dull paint scheme you see in government buildings. Metal tables and benches ran the length of it, breaking only for the serving area at the far end of the room. The Academy Rules claimed pride of place on the walls, and smaller posters that Verity supposed were meant to be motivational were pinned here and there, their corners furling. Dozens of kids were crammed into the room, most grouped in small, vocal clusters; some loner types protectively hunched over their trays, avoiding the teasing and posturing of everyone else.

"What do you think's on the menu today?" Bea swooped in with Krystal in tow. The girls took their place in the quickly moving line.

"I think I'll have the poached salmon," said Krystal, mimicking Bea's accent.

"Fancy." Verity was surprised.

The other girls cracked up, and she realized she was the butt of a joke.

"No salmon on the menu, huh?"

"Nuh-uh," said Em.

"Enjoy," said the petite woman serving up the food. She wore a hairnet that covered her braids, but not her long, dangling earrings. Verity suspected she was standing on a box to see over the counter.

"That's Susie Slaw." Krystal shot a wave at the server, who gave her a thumbs-up in return. "She's one of the good ones. Her and Grimes, the custodian. And I guess Huff's okay. The rest are . . . a unique breed of monster. I guess you'd have to be, to work here. I mean, just look around. Those three there are called the PackHunters for a reason."

She was referring to a trio of re-educators who all had a sharp, predatory look to them. They stood in the corner, arms crossed and eyes narrowed, ready to pounce on the merest infraction.

"They do the DayWatch between classes," added Krystal. "Try not to get on their bad side. Although that's all of their sides."

As if to prove her point, one of the PackHunters swooped in on a boy who had been leaning back on his chair, tilting it so its weight was balanced on two legs. A stern exchange of words followed, and the boy was handed a yellow detention slip.

Krystal looked smug. "See?"

The girls sat at an empty table to one side of the room, directly beneath a slowly swooping fan. The Academy didn't seem to believe in air conditioning, and the desert heat was already oozing through the walls. Verity's shower felt like a lifetime ago.

"How's the chef's special?" asked Bea. "It's not quite the Four Seasons, huh?"

The Trumans preferred camping and couch surfing over hotels, so Verity couldn't make an accurate comparison, but she had an inkling the meal in front of her didn't measure up. On her tray was a bowl of congealed oatmeal, a splodge of spongy eggs, a forlorn apple, and some murky-looking milk. The theory behind the breakfast wasn't so bad, but the reality of it matched her lowered expectations.

"It's the same every day." Bea prodded her eggs with a fork. "Seriously, you'd have to really try to make eggs this rubbery. No wonder most of it gets tossed."

"Tossed?" Verity was surprised. "It doesn't get composted or donated?"

Krystal rolled her eyes. "Being poor doesn't mean you deserve to be fed this crap. You rich people are all the same. You think you're doing a good deed by foisting all your trash on people worse off than you. Just saying—feeling good about doing something doesn't mean you're actually doing good."

Verity flushed. Her family wasn't rich, but she supposed they *were* privileged. They wouldn't starve if they didn't go dumpster diving or go barefoot if the nearby thrift store closed down.

"Zing," muttered Em.

Verity took a tentative sip of her milk. It tasted strange compared with the soy she was used to.

"Don't mind her," said Bea. "She's got a chip on her shoulder about growing up where she did. I mean, it's not like we can help the backgrounds we come from. Oh, hey, it's Cody."

Krystal was fuming but said nothing further. She took out her anger on her mushy apple instead.

Verity turned her attention to the newcomers.

"Morning." A sinewy girl with wild hair and wilder eyes dragged out the seat opposite Bea, setting down a carton of milk. She leaned in, glancing around as she spoke, like the walls had ears. "A newbie, huh? What did you do to end up here?"

Verity swallowed a mouthful of oatmeal. It lodged in her throat like wallpaper paste. "Just a protest gone wrong."

"Pretty good reason." Cody's dark eyes latched onto hers. They didn't seem to focus properly. Instead, they trembled slightly, as though there were a wiring disturbance inside her head. "You know, this school is just part of a big government takeover. They're trying to round up the troublemakers, keep us off the streets so that the sheeple can go about their happy little lives. There are hundreds of these places around, all of them secret."

"Really?" Verity's curiosity was piqued.

"Seriously, don't listen to Miss Conspiracies 'R' Us." Krystal had moved on from her previous grudge, but her eye-rolling was back in fine form.

"Ms.," corrected Cody.

"Whatever. She has a new theory every day. Each one crazier than the last. Yesterday it was nano-cameras in the food."

Cody raised her milk carton, testing its mouth to see whether it was sealed. She popped it open and took a sip. "You won't be laughing when they upload photos of your insides to the internet."

"Why would 'they' even bother?" said Krystal. "I mean, if you're going to come up with a conspiracy, it should at least make sense. Like, tell me there's a government conspiracy to keep immigrants poor and struggling and I'll believe you."

"It's because they're playing 3D chess," explained Cody patiently. "It doesn't make sense to us, but that's because we don't think on their level. Believe me, there are things out there that are way beyond what we can comprehend. Like the Illuminati. And aliens."

"Aliens?" For some reason, the firefly creature from Verity's family camping trip came to mind.

"Not the aliens thing again," muttered Em from beneath her fringe of black hair. Cody slapped her empty milk carton emphatically down on the table. Milky dregs sloshed all over. "You can't think we're all alone in the universe? The aliens have been trying to communicate with us for years. Millennia! Ask the Ancient Egyptians."

Bea wiped milk from her plate with a napkin. "This kind of insanity is what you get when you're made to kneel out in the sun for detention. Heatstroke: it messes with your mind."

"Not me," said Cody. "I'm fine. It was a whole day ago. Besides, it could have been way worse. Like the Box that one time. Much longer in there and I would've gone nuts."

"Imagine that," said Krystal.

"Is she for real?" asked Verity. "There's something called the Box? Is that even legal?"

Em shrugged. "I think it's peaceful, personally. Like a sensory deprivation chamber."

"The poor person's version of one." Bea was unable to resist.

Verity still wasn't sure whether she was being pranked.

Krystal made a face. "I had to do a sleepless night once. It wasn't so bad until the next day. I fell asleep in one of Raison's classes and got detention all over again."

"You've got a lot to look forward to, New Girl," said Bea, twisting her braids with a nonchalance that Verity didn't quite buy.

Verity's hand hurt; she realized she was clutching Silas's wooden carving with all her might. As she forced herself to release it, Pyrite the macaw gave a blood-curdling shriek, making her tense up again. She wasn't alone. Just about everyone in the room gave a start. Even the PackHunters flinched.

"You know," mused Em, "that bird is the worst punishment of all. Stuff of nightmares."

7

The moment the class warning bell blared through the dining hall, every subject leapt to their feet, ready to drop off their trays and dash to their assigned classrooms. Tardiness wasn't something Lawson tolerated, not even at 6:30 in the morning. The way-finding routes bustled with subjects rushing along in single file. Those who stepped out of line were promptly reprimanded by the PackHunters, who stalked the corridors between classes.

Verity's schedule was the same as the other girls' in her bunk room, except today. As part of her orientation, she had a multiperiod session with a Doctor Craniale, whose unnervingly unappealing job title was "HeadShrinker." Verity assumed they were some sort of psychologist. The Academy seemed to have spent a lot of time brainstorming odd terms for normal things, perhaps to justify whatever bill it would be sending to the state for its services. Verity could think of a few other regimes and movements in history that had had their own jargon, and none of them held up very well by today's standards. She had to hope the Academy wasn't striving for historical notoriety.

The consultation room was at the end of a zigzagging orange line and behind an imposing steel door, the sort that would ordinarily lead to a meat locker or maybe an alien autopsy room. Its faintly lustrous surface was impressively devoid of fingerprints. The custodian must be exceptional at their job.

Verity swiped her key fob over the door sensor, and the slab of steel swung open. Inside, the room was coldly clinical, with monochrome walls, uncomfortable furniture and a lingering undertone of lemon-scented cleaning products. A single framed print was the only piece of decor and did little to break the monotony. At first, Verity took it to be an eye chart, but it read like an extension of the Academy's rules. *Attention is nine-tenths of the law!* it exclaimed. Again, Lawson had attributed the quote to himself.

"Verity Truman?" came the thin voice of the HeadShrinker, an older woman who wore her blue-rinsed hair in a dramatic beehive. She obviously had more than two minutes to spend in the showers every morning.

Verity nodded. "Dr. Craniale?"

The HeadShrinker's lips thinned with displeasure. Verity got the impression that Craniale did not have much time for kids. Maybe that was why she had taken this job.

"Take a seat." Craniale twisted a silvery pearl necklace. The pearls matched her demeanor: cold, hard, and blank. "Now, you're here for your initial baseline assessment. You'll be subjected to stimuli, with your responses recorded for later use."

"What do you mean by 'later use'?"

The pearls twisted further, clacking together like marbles. Verity secretly hoped the string would break and they'd go spraying off along the floor. "Unless you have a doctorate in psychology, it's nothing you need to worry about."

"Sure." Verity was unconvinced.

Craniale turned a knob on a hand device, and the lights flared. Verity cringed, covering her eyes. The afterimage hung on her retinas like the glowing white dot that would appear on the ancient Truman family TV after switching it off.

"Good, good." Craniale made a note.

Then the room went completely dark.

"Are you doing that?" Verity's voice quavered. She couldn't even see her hands in front of her face.

"Would that knowledge affect your responses one way or another?"

Verity dropped her hands, clasping them tightly in her lap. She waited for the next assault on her senses.

It didn't take long. Over the next hour the lights flashed and dimmed, punctuated with confusing questions and incongruous analogies Verity knew she was stumbling over. She felt like she was participating in the mental version of Lawson's morning exercises.

"Hat is to tree as cicada is to . . ."

"Head?" responded Verity.

Craniale raised an eyebrow, but she gave no other feedback. In the freshly dialed-up lights of the room she had all the expression of a plastic mannequin. Even her immoveable hair looked the part.

"A house has how many angles?"

Verity swallowed. "As many as there are?"

"If you mix blue and yellow paint, how does your garden grow?"

"Green?" Verity's underarms were damp from anxiety; she lifted her arms to cool them off. "With silver bells and cockleshells?"

A twist of the pearls and, then, abruptly: "Which of your parents has had the bigger influence on you?"

Verity was about to respond with the obvious answer—her mother—but then paused. This seemed like a dangerous line of questioning. Craniale obviously wanted to pin Verity's behavior on one of her parents. Not only that, but she had no idea to whom this information was being passed along, nor what would be done with it. For all she knew, it could be used to put her mother on some sort of government list, to have her removed from her job at the museum, or worse. "I'm not answering that."

Craniale's eyes were frosty beneath their false eyelashes. "That is an unproductive statement. Refusal to answer questions from your superiors is a mark of insubordination."

Verity knew that snapping back would do no good, but she couldn't help herself. She'd spent a lifetime being told that opinions were made to be shared. "Being in a position of authority doesn't make you my superior."

Craniale drummed the edges of her tablet, regarding Verity with a mix of pity and disdain. "Is that so? I can see why you were recommended to us. Tell me, what are your thoughts on factual flexibility?"

"Facts aren't flexible. Otherwise, they're not facts."

"Relatively speaking," countered Craniale mildly. "I suppose it all depends on your incentive structure. Which brings up one more issue we should address: do you believe one should be free to cause civil disorder?"

"Yes." Verity felt trapped. "Sometimes."

"It's a yes or no question."

But it wasn't, at least not to Verity. "Well, it depends on the circumstances . . ."

"That will do," Craniale interrupted. "You may go to your first class now."

"That's it?" Verity couldn't tell whether she'd passed with flying colors or had failed miserably. "Did you get what you needed?"

Craniale slid her tablet into a slim leather portfolio with an elaborate gold buckle. "Oh, yes. And I look forward to sharing the results with my superior."

———

Having followed a maze of orange and then pink way-finding lines, Verity arrived midway through what should have been her second class, letting herself in with her key fob. Half a dozen pairs of eyes turned her way as she entered, but Re-educator Raison scarcely paid her any attention. She pointed with a bony finger to the empty chair next to Krystal and went on with her lesson.

Verity took a seat, fidgeting with the pen and notepad that had been waiting for her on the desk.

"On to the rhyming sentence completion exercises," Raison barked.

Raison erased the phrase that ran the length of the chalkboard in huge letters—*Thinking aloud is not allowed*—and replaced it with:

When Lawson tells me what to do, __________.

Followed by:

The rules were posted in the light, __________.

"Write down the first thing that comes into your head, and then we'll review. Remember that they must rhyme. There will be no wrong answers."

Verity thought for a moment, then wrote:

When Lawson tells me what to do, I'll just do what's right and true. Followed by: *The rules were posted in the light, their meanness makes me want to fight.*

Next to her, Krystal's eyes widened. She nudged Verity and gave a tight shake of her head, shuffling over her papers so her own answers were in view:

When Lawson tells me what to do, *I am proud I'm on his crew.*

The rules were posted in the light, *rules are good and rules are right.*

Krystal tapped the page with her pen, indicating that Verity should take note of what was expected. But her efforts did not go unnoticed. The hand of a thickset boy to Verity's right shot up.

"Ma'am!" shouted the boy. "Subject Rodriguez is helping the new girl cheat!"

Raison snapped her head in Verity's direction, her laser-like gaze following. She rapped her ruler against her desk. The sound reverberated through the classroom, echoing off the flat walls. "Thank you for informing, Subject Bull."

The other subjects half-heartedly applauded, although none of them looked especially pleased about it, and there was plenty of eye-rolling going on.

The same boy hissed under his breath at Krystal, "Nice try, you sneak!"

Krystal was sitting with a downcast expression doing her best to look contrite, while Verity was feeling both bewildered and defiant. This class was like being thrown into a bizarre karaoke session where someone else picked your song for you and there was no screen to help you along with the lyrics.

"Subject Rodriguez, detention for you," snapped Raison, making a note in the red binder on her desk. "You can collect your slip when we're done.

I'd say I expected more of you, but that would be untrue. Now, Subject Truman, is it? I want you to read out your original text, followed by what Rodriguez gave you."

Verity did, an uncharacteristic shake in her voice. She knew every part of her answer was somehow wrong, even as she felt in her heart it was absolutely correct. Her normal intuition around right and wrong had been upended.

"Well, well." Raison steepled her bony fingers. The tendons rose on her hands. "Class, we can see the marked difference between these answers, can't we? One is clearly from someone who doesn't understand the exercise at all, and the other is from someone who has grasped its essence. Behavioral issues aside, Rodriguez may well yet experience reform. Truman, on the other hand, has some significant catching up to do."

"But you said there would be no wrong answers," protested Verity.

Raison gave a deadly smile. "No, I said, 'There *will be* no wrong answers.' That you don't see the difference shows just how much work we have to do. Front of the class, please."

Verity pushed herself out of her chair and went to stand by the chalkboard. From there she was struck by the uniformity of the subjects squeezed into their seats, all looking like they were fighting both sleep and despair. Whatever the Academy was meant to be teaching them, it seemed lost on its subject body.

Staring out at the glum kids, Verity was struck with a sudden wave of homesickness. She wondered what her parents and Silas were doing right now. Whether things were different without her there, or whether they were eating blueberry pancakes and playing word games as if nothing had happened.

"Truman!" Again, the ruler thwacked against the desk, which had taken quite a beating this morning.

"Yes, ma'am," said Verity.

Raison's steepled fingers made a popping noise as air fled their joints. "Now, I want you to answer a series of questions. We'll continue until you get the right answers. Even if that means staying through lunch. Is that clear?"

"Yes, ma'am," said Verity.

Raison proceeded to rattle off a series of questions not unlike those Craniale had subjected her to. No matter how Verity responded, Raison marked her wrong. Every time this happened, the other subjects tensed up in their seats. She could feel the room turning against her.

"What color is the sky?"

"Blue."

"Wrong! It's pink because it's dusk."

Verity glanced out the window, needlessly seeking confirmation. "But it's not dusk, is it?"

Raison's ruler stroked the side of her desk. "I just said that it is."

"But that doesn't mean—"

"We'll try another simple one. What color are the leaves on a tree?"

"Green? Yellow? Orange and red? Variegated?" Verity hoped one of these would suffice. She should at least get an extra mark for "variegated," which Silas had picked as Truman word of the day last spring.

Raison somehow managed to look both triumphant and disappointed. "Wrong. There are no leaves because it's winter, and the tree is . . ."

Though she had a knot in the pit of her stomach, Verity was finally beginning to realize the rules of the game. Just like her session with

Craniale before, it wasn't about giving the right answer. It was about giving the answer they wanted you to give, no matter how ridiculous or incorrect.

"A cactus," finished Verity.

Raison gave a sharp clap of her gnarled hands, and the entire class relaxed in their seats. "Well done. Now, what color is the sky?"

<hr>

Verity emerged from her first class feeling exhausted. It was surprisingly mentally taxing to give the wrong answer when questioned. By the end of it, she'd found herself caught between two opposing desires: to please Raison and to be right. Her entire experience at the Ersatz Academy so far had been one of doublethink and doublespeak, and she wasn't sure how much of it she could take.

Verity was walking back with Em along a way-finding line of black-and-white arrows interspersed with the green dots that led to the mess hall. As they turned a corner, she noticed something strange: a series of gray mail slots along the corridor walls. "*Informers Are Performers*," read the sign above them.

She grabbed Em's arm. "What are those?"

"Ratter-boxes. If you see someone breaking the rules, you're meant to write it down and put it in there."

"And people actually do that?"

"All the time. It's why Lawson's so good at giving everyone detention. He already knows who's going down. Between the ratter-boxes, the MonitorRoom and Payne, and the PackHunters, he's got eyes all over. Word to the wise: you can't trust anybody here."

"Not even you?" Verity knew as soon as she said it that it was a test.

An asthmatic wheeze punctuated Em's dry laugh. She reached for her inhaler. "Lucky for you I'm not anybody. Hey, watch out!"

A small boy was bolting down the hallway, thumb and forefinger pinched around the tail of a mouse desperately trying to climb up his hand. Not only was the boy not following the marked lines but also he wasn't in uniform. Instead, he wore brightly colored shorts and a patterned button-down shirt. The vividness of his outfit was even more pronounced against the dull gray that surrounded them. Verity felt as though she'd just seen a rainbow manifest on an overcast day.

The boy met their eyes but scurried along without saying anything.

"Casper Grimes." Em used Verity's shoulder to steady herself. She held up a finger as she took a puff off her inhaler. "Lucky, I had my Ventolin ready to go. Anyway, Casper's the caretaker's son. He lives on-site, but he's homeschooled or something. He never talks, so it's hard to know for sure."

Verity couldn't imagine spending her entire childhood isolated at the Academy. No wonder the boy was running around making friends with rodents. It was a proclivity only Silas might possibly understand.

"Poor kid. Living here, I mean."

Em grimaced sympathetically. "Since the school opened, apparently. What a life. If you can call it that."

8

Verity was on trash duty that evening. The notice flickered up on one of the enormous wall-mounted television screens, the blinking text following her down the hallway. That it somehow knew where she was made her feel uneasy. She hoped it was just a coincidence.

She wasn't sure what trash duty involved, or even whether to take the term at face value. Knowing Lawson, it could easily refer to something entirely different. In the interests of avoiding detention for getting it wrong, she asked Bea.

"Trash duty? For once it's what it sounds like. Basically, once we're done with dinner, you help Susie Slaw clean up and take the bags out to the trash cans at the back of the quadrangle. Just follow the purple dashed line." Bea swirled a spoon in a gruel that looked like the morning's breakfast all over again. "But my actual advice is to get out of it if you can. I don't know about you, but trash duty is something you pay other people to do, not something you do yourself."

Ordinarily Verity would have ferociously debated this, but she was too tired. Instead, she nodded, picking at the skin of her mealy apple.

All she wanted was to hunker down in her bed and sleep for the rest of the week. Her mind whirled with the Re-educators' re-teaching efforts, and she felt disoriented, like she was walking around upside down. In a sense, she was. At some point, up had become down, and the known had become the unknowable.

She was quiet most of dinner, ignoring Bea and Cody's bickering and not even bothering to respond to the latter's assertion that the government was drugging the nation with fluoridated water. Instead, she just munched on her apple, silently thanking that very same fluoride for giving her cavity-free teeth and hoping the detention she'd caused Krystal didn't involve the Box or any of the awful options discussed that morning.

When everyone stood ready to retire to their bunk rooms, Verity collected their used trays and carried them to the back of the mess hall. Susie Slaw was hefting stacks of trays, plates, and silverware from the serving window to the sinks as she cleared out the leftovers and began washing up. It was an enormous task. Verity was surprised that only one staff member had been assigned to it. She helped Susie with a precarious stack of trays threatening to spill across the dull concrete floor.

"Thanks! You're the trash duty kid, huh?" Susie's earrings swung like metronomes as she regarded Verity. She had a cheerful demeanor underscored by her large, apple-like cheeks and upturned mouth. It was enormously at odds with the other Academy staffers, who had probably been hired based on their unpleasantness. "You're new, huh?"

Verity nodded and scraped a plate into a trash can, trying not to show her displeasure at wasting food, even if it wasn't that great. The food, the napkins, and the plasticware all went into the one can without being sorted. She wanted to say something but bit her tongue. With the possible exception of Huff, Susie Slaw seemed like the only halfway decent adult at the Academy, and she didn't want to annoy her with recycling tips.

"You can always tell the newcomers." Slaw was unaware of the bullet she'd just dodged. "You've still got that sense of *you* about you. Okay, so, anything that doesn't fit in the trash cans goes in those bags over there. All of it goes out to the dumpsters in the quadrangle. The purple dashed line will show you the way. You can't miss it. Not among all this gray, anyhow. There's a flashlight over there on the shelf you can use."

Verity helped Susie clean up, scraping plates and pouring liquids down the sink before throwing their containers in the trash. At least the plates were reusable, so the overall operation was one step more eco-friendly than airplane catering.

As Verity worked, she noticed Susie had another bag at her side she was carefully packing with Tupperware containers filled with kitchen leftovers. It seemed like a lot to take home. When she commented on it, Susie jumped. Guilt skittered over her face, and Verity wondered what truth she'd hit on.

"It's not for me, of course. I wouldn't do that. Some people just don't have enough." Susie wiped clammy hands on the thighs of her slacks and tied a knot in a garbage bag. The smell of warming apple cores and melted butter saturated the air. "Anyhow, how about you take these bags out to the dumpsters? It'll keep us on time."

"Sure." Verity was still curious about what Slaw was doing with the extra containers but didn't want to push her luck.

"Good. I'll keep going here." Slaw was clearly relieved. She started loading one of the huge industrial dishwashers at the back of the kitchen.

Verity hefted a jumble of trash bags, holding them at arm's length. Even so, the humidity from the still-warm leftovers inside teased out sweat from her wrists.

Arms outstretched like a tightrope walker, she followed the purple line out to the silent quadrangle and over to where the dumpsters sat like squat, hungry beasts. Their lids clanged furiously as she hauled them open. The smell of rank milk and fermenting fruit, exacerbated by days of beating sun, clawed at her nostrils.

Eyes watering, she stared up at the roofline as she tried to will away tears. Noticing a series of iron rungs toward the top of the stone wall, Verity wondered whether any of the subjects had ever climbed up to the rooftop. Given how punitive the Academy's "behavioral readjustments" were, it probably wasn't worth the risk.

Verity threw the bags in one by one, then slammed the dumpster lids closed before the beady eyes of the resident rats could make her acquaintance. This was probably where Casper Grimes had sourced his pet mouse.

As Verity turned back to the mess hall, a flashing light in the sky caught her attention. She covered her eyes and rubbed her temples, thinking it might be the onset of a migraine. After the day she'd had and everything her senses had been subjected to, she wouldn't be surprised. But peering through her fingers she knew what she was experiencing had nonmedical origins. Silas's luminescent creature had returned.

Verity tried to pinpoint its location as it flitted from spot to spot, carving arcs of light in the still evening air. Momentarily, the dusky sky glowed golden with a handful of looping figures that Verity had seen before. The only difference was that this time, the creature made a sort of vertical zigzag in between them. As it did, it phonated something that sounded like *v-i-d-e-o*. No, wait: *v-i-v-e-o*.

Remembering the figures Silas had written on his bedroom window, Verity used the flashlight to trace the following:

The creature zoomed up and down, as if excited at her efforts to communicate. Then it started weaving some new figures, sounding out *broo* as it did:

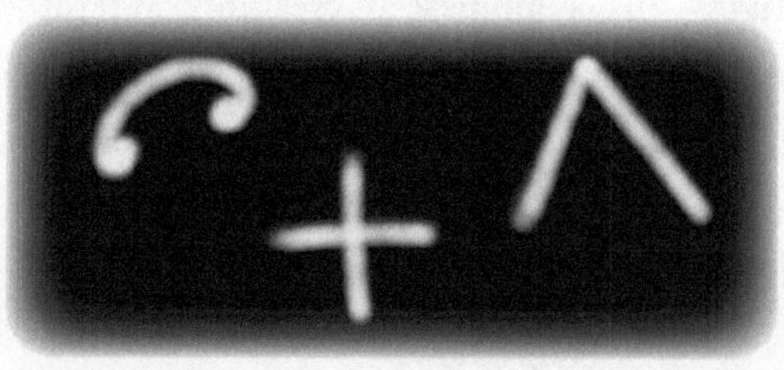

Verity traced them with her flashlight, trying to memorize them. A sense of lightness came over her, and she forgot all about trash duty and detentions. There was something about the elegant form and simple line of the figures that piqued her curiosity and drew her away from her stress and uneasiness with life at the Ersatz Academy.

wrote the creature, piping: *teh–b–ooo–v*. Verity copied it, hoping she was doing its forms justice.

It responded by emblazoning a series of new figures into the twilight:

booov–ih–ooo–ee! it piped.

Confused, Verity signed with a question mark. Again, the creature traced *bUv–iUI* in the air. Stumped, Verity repeated the series of figures over and over with her flashlight.

But the ethereal firefly's light was fading now, and she could see it retreating into the night. This was the second time this had happened. She wondered whether it was heading off to recharge somewhere. Now that she thought about it, the creature's soft glow reminded her of the solar lights her dad had installed in their front yard. Maybe that was its trick: it spent the day absorbing the sun's rays through its leaflike wings and used its stored energy to communicate at night.

It was a shame the Ersatz Academy didn't have science fairs or Verity would have been a shoo-in for first place.

Verity finished hauling trash out to the dumpsters, then followed the designated dotted line back to her bunk room, ready to bury her face in her pillow and put the overwhelming events of the day behind her. On her way, she passed Lawson's quarters, almost leaping out of her skin when Pyrite gave one of his soul-rending shrieks. As she paused to let her heart find its rhythm again, she caught a snippet of a conversation coming from within.

"... the new program could dramatically speed up your results. And their extent," came an unfamiliar voice. "The Academy—and of course you—will become a true thought leader in youth reform."

There was a pause, and then Verity heard Lawson's voice: "Anything that reduces the resistance to our methods is of interest to me. Anything at all."

Verity trembled, and not because of the light desert breeze.

Just then, Constance Grimes and her son came past, rattling a custodian's cart between them. Worried that she might be seen and reported,

Verity squatted, pretending to tie her shoelaces. Then she dashed off toward her bunk room, being mindful to stick to the white dotted line.

As she let herself in with her key fob, the other girls gave her only the most cursory of greetings. Bea was fixing her hair, and Em was staring at the ceiling reciting Poe's "The Raven" extremely inaccurately from memory. Krystal was sitting on her bed, sullenly kicking her legs.

Verity was about to blurt out what she'd overheard outside Lawson's office when she noticed the newly frayed hem of Krystal's gray trousers.

Verity squirmed with guilt. "I'm really sorry about the whole detention thing."

Krystal shrugged. "It's fine. I put myself in the line of fire. But just saying, the girls' bathrooms are spotless right now. I used some of my mom's tricks. Wish I had her cleaning soundtrack, though. Every Latina mom will tell you a soundtrack is mandatory."

"They made you clean the bathrooms?" Verity grimaced.

Krystal shrugged, slightly defensively. "So? Looks like they made *you* take out the trash."

"That wasn't even a detention thing." Bea ran her fingers through her braids. "Especially since you and trash bags get along so well."

Verity snorted. "Well, our relationship is a bit strained right now. You know they don't recycle here?"

"What, you expect the trucks to come all the way out to the middle of nowhere?" retorted Krystal. "Even the trash just gets burned."

"How is that okay, though? We all have a responsibility—"

"Oh, man, don't even," said Krystal, with one of her trademark eye rolls. "Sure, in an ideal world, we all live in perfect harmony with all of nature's little creatures and everybody. But this isn't that world. Do you have any idea how much privilege you need to have just to tell people what they should be doing with their lives? Take it from me. Most of us are too busy getting through each day to worry about biodegradable packaging or whatever. If it *is* sustainable, we can't afford it anyway, so what does it matter? I know you're all about doing the right thing, but that's just not doable for everybody."

Bea slapped the bed. "Thank goodness for that or we'd *all* be taking fashion tips from the Walmart catalog."

Krystal tilted her head. "Like your brand names matter in here."

The conversation had already moved on, but Verity was stuck on Krystal's earlier point. The greater good prevailed, whatever your personal circumstances. If people didn't make changes to how they lived, then it was only a matter of time before the world's water sources were depleted, food scarcity became widespread, and coastal cities were at risk of flooding. But before Verity could say anything, Krystal had rolled over in her bed, impassively facing the wall. No further debate was happening tonight.

Longing for a connection with the familiarity of home, Verity pulled out her backpack, rummaging about for the carving Silas had whittled for her. Her fingers caught on a folded slip of paper squirreled away inside a pair of socks. Unfolding it, she saw what appeared to be a key to the firefly creature's alphabet, all accompanied by translations in Silas's spiky handwriting. There were far more than the handful she had seen so far, all with their own sound and meaning. Verity was reminded of the summer Chinese course she'd taken a few years back. Unlike English, where letters were associated with sounds but not meanings, Chinese characters carried meanings as well. Putting multiple characters together created a combination with a new, more complex meaning.

Verity was intrigued. This was the sort of puzzle all those years of crosswords and Scrabble had trained her for. She scanned the list, looking for the figures she'd come across so far and pausing on a few others that caught her eye:

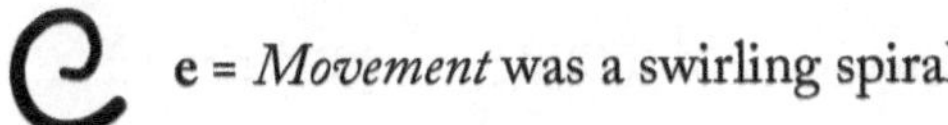 e = *Movement* was a swirling spiral

i = *Light* reminded her of the filament inside a light bulb. Even its sound was bright, now that she thought of it.

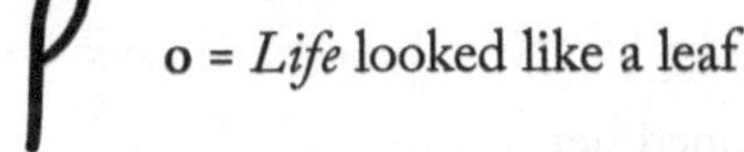 I = *Sound* swooped up and down like a sound wave

o = *Life* looked like a leaf

O = *Feeling* was a heart shape and sounded like an emotional "Oh!"

u = *Human* looked like a person's legs and was the same symbol used in Chinese, Verity realized.

U = *Mind/Spirit* was the human symbol with the ground beneath its feet. It made Verity think of the body-mind-spirit thing that wellness companies were always talking about.

b = *Together* reminded her of the vintage phone her grandparents had used.

r = *Good* was a plus—or positive—sign.

 v = *Action* looked like a lightning bolt. It even sounded like a kind of electrical vibration.

They looked easy enough to remember: each symbol seemed to embody its own meaning, and some of the related ones had similar sounds.

Flipping over the page, she saw that Silas had also pieced together a few of the symbols into combinations. Mouthing along, Verity tried to follow his translations.

 bO: *together + feeling*

Thinking for a minute, she jotted down "sympathy" next to Silas's translation. The combination brought her back to the solidarity she'd felt with her friends at the protest. She thought about Lila and hoped her friend didn't feel like Verity had abandoned her.

 fu: *this + person* = me, I

bu: *together + person* = you

 bru: *together + positive + person* = friend

brU: *together + positive + spirit* = peace

Verity nodded along as she puzzled out the combinations. She liked the way the simple combinations could be built up into more complex ideas and how the related words were alike in sound as well.

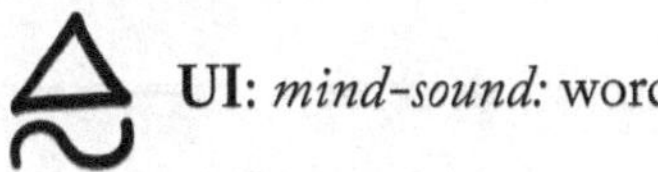 **UI**: *mind-sound:* word

tebUv: *toward-move—together-mind-verb:* communicate

eo: *moving-life:* animal

io: *light-life:* plant

And then there was this one:

Viveo: *make-light-make-movement-life* . . .

Verity grinned in realization: the creature must have been referring to itself earlier!

This all seemed to bode well. None of the words she'd encountered seemed to intend harm, so Viveo probably wasn't here to destroy civilization as she knew it.

As she flicked back and forth through the symbols and combinations, she thought again how cool it was that these simple symbols could be stacked on top of each other to stand for more complex words and ideas. Like adding the lightning bolt symbol for action, ⚡ "v", to a word made it a verb. So adding "v" to ⅄ "i" to make ⅄⚡ "iv" would give you something like "shine." And adding an ‿ "m" for quality made the word a modifier that described another word. So "m" + "i" to make ⅄ "im" would give you the adjective of light—"light" or "bright"—which she found fitting for her new firefly friend. And ⚡ iOv meant to feel or sense light—to see, obviously—while ⚡ IOv was the verb for sound-sense—to hear.

Playing around with the symbols was a fun and much-needed distraction from life at the Academy and the unsettling bit of conversation she'd overheard between Lawson and his visitor. She made a mental note to tell her bunkmates about what she'd heard once she'd recovered from putting her foot in it with Krystal.

Verity soon became completely immersed in the exercise. She worked at creating new combinations until a warning bell sounded, notifying the subjects that it was time for lights out. Moments later, the overhead fluorescents shut off with an industrial clang that echoed through the halls. Her mind restless despite her physical exhaustion, Verity lay in the dark tracing permutations of Viveo's symbols in the air.

She wasn't sure how, but some part of her firmly believed they'd help her get through her semester at the Ersatz Academy.

9

reakfast the next day was the usual drab, poorly executed fare. This time, the mess hall chalkboard menu tried to pass off the oatmeal as "pottage." Shakespeare had it right: an oatmeal porridge by any other name would surely still smell and taste as bland. But Verity hardly noticed. She was still off in the world of Silas's symbols, which she was enjoying puzzling over. Playing with the symbols and creating new configurations made her feel a little less homesick, like Silas was there looking over her shoulder.

But Verity's good mood was short-lived. Toward the end of breakfast, Lawson came strutting in. His scarred face and dead-eyed stare instantly killed the table's appetites, and everyone set down their spoons.

"Uh-oh." Krystal swallowed a glue-like glob of oatmeal with difficulty. "Impromptu announcement time."

Lawson positioned himself on a way-finding line in the precise center of the room, clicking his glossy shoes together to get the subjects' attention. This was unnecessary, as all conversation had immediately ceased the minute he strode in. Even Pitbull was making the effort to chew with his mouth closed.

"Subjects! Law and order!" came Lawson's thin, crisp voice.

The declaration was met with confused silence.

"Know no border," prompted Lawson, marking each word with a chop of one hand into the other. "Once again, 'Law and order'!"

"...know...no..." came the garbled, uncertain response.

"*Border!*" bellowed Lawson. "*Law and order!*"

"*Know no border!*" shouted the subjects. There was a zealousness to their response, like they were enjoying the excuse to let out months of pent-up energy and rage.

Lawson gave a curt, satisfied nod. "Precisely. Speaking of borders, I'm pleased to announce the addition of a new boundary-breaking component to our curriculum, finalized just this morning: computer programming."

"Now we're talking." Cody cracked her knuckles. "Although, I bet they'll have keystroke loggers to record everything we do ..." she trailed off as Lawson spun on his heel toward her.

"Something to say, Subject?"

Cody folded her hands in her lap. She stared down at her half-eaten apple, which was browning from the air. "No, sir."

Verity frowned, thinking back again to the snippet of conversation she'd overhead the previous night. The stranger had mentioned something about using technology to help reform the subjects. Computer programming *was* full of problem solving and abstract thinking. Maybe those were the skills they were trying to develop.

"The training will begin immediately, with a select group of subjects chosen for participation. The privileged few who will attend the programming sessions are as follows ..."

Lawson listed off a series of names that Verity mostly didn't recognize, although those she did were the ones who were constantly being pulled out of class or sent to detention.

"...and finally, Subject Truman," finished Lawson.

Verity started. She wasn't sure that being included among the previously mentioned names made her one of the "privileged few."

Lawson clapped to signal the end of his message, then added: "To celebrate this exciting new addition to our curriculum, Ms. Slaw will be handing out chocolate chip muffins. For those who weren't named as early participants, never fear. Your time will come."

Head tilted up so that he could stare imperiously down at the subjects as he went, Lawson clicked his heels again and strode from the room.

"He must go through a lot of shoes," remarked Krystal.

"Well, leather lasts, if you take care of it." Bea eyed the basket of muffins that Susie Slaw was toting around the room. This was a surprisingly decadent addition to the menu. "And he's the type of OCD person who would spend hours buffing and polishing."

"Huffing and puffing, more like," quipped Krystal.

As Krystal and Bea cracked each other up with rude comments about Lawson, Cody turned to Verity. She fiddled with her milk carton, popping its cardboard mouth open and closed. "Do you actually know anything about computers, Truman?"

Verity accepted a muffin from Susie Slaw. It was small but smelled incredible compared to their usual breakfast fare.

"Not much." She peeled back the muffin's wrapper. "I can use one, but I've never done any coding or anything."

"Don't you think you're a weird choice, then? I mean, I'm a legit hacker, and they didn't pick me."

"Maybe you don't need the practice." She took a bite from her muffin. It was a revelation of chocolate and butter. "Mmm."

Cody waved away the muffin that Susie Slaw offered her. "You're actually going to eat that thing? Think about it: why would they suddenly switch up the menu? They could have put anything in those, you know."

"Like chocolate chips?" teased Verity. "My family gets more dietary variety from dumpster diving and picking fruit from the neighbors' trees than I do from this place. I'm willing to take the chance."

Bea made a face. "Dumpster diving? That's disgusting. But not surprising."

Em piped up, surprising Verity. "It's not *that* gross. I saw a thing on Vice about it. It's just food past its sell-by date. And it's still in its packaging, too."

Verity barely got to acknowledge Em's input, because Cody wasn't backing down. "I'm just saying that it's interesting that on the same day they roll out a new type of class, we're suddenly being bribed with cupcakes. Like I always say, it's not being paranoid if they're actually out to get you."

Verity bit her lip, her mind going once more to last night's eavesdropping. She was probably reading something into nothing, but something felt *off* about the whole thing. But then, she worried that if she said anything to Cody, the girl would run with it and build it up into an elaborate conspiracy theory involving government-backed brainwashing or something.

Fortunately, she was saved by the bell: before she could say anything, the warning bells blared, sending the subjects scattering like ants.

Over the next few days, Verity's classes were interrupted by Lawson's computer programming subjects being pulled out from class and escorted off to wherever the programming sessions were happening, one at a time. Verity thought this was strange, even for the Academy. Computer programming seemed like something you'd do with a class, not one-on-one. Maybe the subject material was particularly challenging or they didn't have enough computers to go around.

As the subjects returned from their sessions, Verity found herself listening in on their whispered conversations with their friends, trying to see whether she was right to feel weird about what she'd overheard earlier. But most of the conversations were just a congratulatory *"Yeah, man!"* accompanied by a fist bump as the subjects celebrated having a reason to skip their regular classes.

Verity's curiosity would be satisfied soon enough. Having rushed in from yard duty at recess, she'd just taken her seat when the monitor in the corner of the classroom flickered on. Re-educator Wolff, who was leading the class, paused midway through his roll call, his expression one of irritation.

"C'mon, c'mon," muttered one of the kids in the back row, obviously hoping the monitor would light up with his name, giving him an excuse to leave.

The screen didn't. Instead, it flashed with Verity's name, along with the directions to the computer programming lab, which was apparently at the end of the orange spotted line. But to get to that, she'd first have to follow the lavender dashed one, a combination that made her think of trying to navigate the New York subway for the first time.

"Man," muttered the kid in the back row. "I never catch a break, huh?"

"Subject Truman, you're excused," said Re-educator Wolff, with a curl of his thin upper lip.

Verity pushed back her chair and made her escape, feeling self-conscious under the envious gaze of the other subjects.

A sweaty man in head-to-toe denim was waiting for her outside, perspiration pouring off him. He was definitely not suited for this climate, and Verity wondered how he didn't pass out from dehydration.

"Subject," he said, with a nod that sent a spray of sweat flying.

"Sir?"

"TaskMaster Jobs," he said by way of introduction. "I'll be accompanying you to your session."

"Um, sure. Why?" Verity had managed the New York subway in the end, and she was pretty sure she'd be able to figure out her way to her computer programming class, too.

"Because that's the protocol."

"Why would there be a protocol? There isn't for any of the other classes."

Jobs made a note on his battered tablet, then wiped down its greasy screen with his sleeve. "I can see why you were selected for this. Let's go."

Verity followed in his wake as he led the way along the lavender line. He had a slithery walk, his shoes scuffing along the polished floors with every step. Damp as he was, he had probably been a newt in a past life.

The corridors were quiet, with just the occasional student following one of the painted paths or a re-educator stalking about. Verity kept her head down, ignoring the way her name flashed in repetitive blips on the wall-mounted screens. Despite her best efforts, the Academy was changing her. She was now hyper-aware of everything that went on around her and of how her every move was being observed.

After a detour around the quadrangle, Verity and Jobs switched over to the orange dotted line, which led to an old outbuilding. It looked more like a garage or a barn than a computer programming lab, although it was painted in the Academy's trademark gray. It shimmered in the blazing sun of high noon like an ominous mirage.

Jobs jabbed at his tablet, then frowned. After a few more attempts he touched his key fob to the sensor on the building's door, to no avail. He scowled. "Must be a glitch in the system. I'm offline."

The tablet balanced in the crook of one arm, he rapped on the door with the back of his hand. His damp skin left a mark on the steel.

Momentarily, the door opened. A shabby man with wild hair and rumpled clothing regarded them. His mismatched socks were knitted in fluorescent colors that contrasted against the expressionless gray of the room.

"No connection, Jobs? Same here. Looks like a system-wide outage. Bit of a shame, but we'll get it sorted out. Not to worry there, Subject. Wordswright. I am, I mean. They call me Wordswright." The man fixed his gaze on Verity. His eyes were so deep set that they were like black holes in his head. There was a hypnotic quality to them.

Verity swallowed. She recognized that voice. It was the same man she'd overheard speaking to Lawson on her way back from trash duty. Her skin was crawling: she had a feeling that she wasn't going to be learning how to code basic operators or functions.

Jobs flicked his tablet with thumb and forefinger. "I'll get Payne to restart it. Hopefully it won't be more than a few minutes."

He slithered off, leaving Verity standing awkwardly by the doorway.

Wordswright ushered her in with a wave of a leather-bound notepad. The room was stuffy and warm. Apparently, the air conditioning was malfunctioning as well. Lawson sat in the corner, silently observing, ready to take notes.

"Let's get set up, then. While we're waiting for him, I mean. I'm booked back-to-back all week, and we don't want to be on the back foot, do we now? Playing catch up, I mean. Apple juice? Muffin? Both?"

Disoriented by Wordswright's stream-of-consciousness style of speaking, Verity tried to think what Cody would do. She declined politely, blaming her large breakfast.

Wordswright gave a tight smile and awkwardly folded Verity's fingers around the juice bottle. "I insist. You'll need your wits about you. And your blood sugar. Drink up."

The juice was cool on the back of Verity's throat, but it had a slightly unfamiliar aftertaste.

"Here's our work station." Wordswright gestured at an oversized, surprisingly modern monitor. Apparently, this was where the Academy's entire technology budget had been spent.

Momentarily, a white dot appeared in the center of the screen. It grew in size, gradually taking on shape, until it transformed into a rudimentary, pixelated avatar. Words floated like subtitles beneath it, given voice by a speaker system somewhere in the room.

"*Welcome. Well come. I've been expecting you, Verity. I am AI,*" came a stilted, static-filled voice.

"Ah, we're back online!" Wordswright drummed out an excited little beat on his thighs. "Let's begin. Your job is to read the prompts on the screen and respond to my questions. Make sure you speak into the microphone. You see it, don't you? Right there."

Hello. Hallow. Hollow. Hell, Oh. Oh, I. A.I.

Verity assumed the machine was just warming up.

"What's your name?" asked Wordswright. Verity hesitated. Her head was already spinning from the combination of the muggy room and the juice sugar high. "Herity— I mean, Verity."

"Excellent." Wordswright tilted back his head in satisfaction. He scratched at his wild hair, then made a finger gun that he pointed at the screen. "Could you hold your hand above your head like this? Excellent, yes. And your other one out like this? Good, good. Proceed."

Verity held the uncomfortable position, trying not to squirm as her muscles protested and the blood fled from her fingertips. Pins and needles threatened.

Wordswright fiddled with a dial, and the room strobed with light. Verity's immediate response was to cover her eyes, but Wordswright reprimanded her instantly.

"Hold your position, just like that. You'll adjust to it; humans are adaptive. There we go. Back to the screen, and onward we go."

Blinking rapidly, Verity turned her attention back to the screen. She wriggled her fingers to try to get some feeling back into them.

In front of her, words flashed and sounded in hypnotic sets over and over, differing only by a letter or two. But there was no meaning Verity could find. Some of them were related. Some of them weren't. Some of them didn't seem to be English. There was no real pattern to any of it.

"They're not words; they're *weirds*," muttered Verity, almost deliriously. She felt as though she had been in the room for hours. The heat and the discomfort of holding her hands out was getting to her, and her tongue was thick and dry against the roof of her mouth. She longed for another bottle of the juice. Damp patches were beginning to gather uncomfortably under her raised arms, giving her an inkling of Jobs's everyday suffering.

"Weirds. Good, good!" Wordswright made a note with a gnawed ballpoint pen, then drummed on his legs once more. Verity wasn't sure whether this was part of the programming or just an annoying tic. Her arms were tiring, and it was getting harder to hold them up.

"Keep holding that pose; it's all part of the magic—or science, I mean. Shall we move on to the logic exercises? You'll love these. They're even accompanied with a snappy little device to help you focus. A world-first, just about! And you get to be part of it!"

Verity swallowed. She wasn't sure she wanted to be part of any of this. Especially the ominous "world-first" parts.

Wordswright produced something that could only loosely be described as a headband. More like a high-tech spider, it had tentacles that reached around your brain like invasive feelers. Verity shuddered as Wordswright mounted it to her head. He sat back, and with a few mouse clicks the screen began to populate with what appeared to be a series of old-school advertising slogans.

"Give those arms a quick shake while the headset calibrates . . . Oh, there we go. Back to it!"

Discover the discipline difference! Our discipline beats everything! Dare to order discipline! De-odorize with order! Just do-order it!

The AI's robotic voice echoed off the bare walls as Verity tried her best to find any sense in the strange slogans it seemed to be pasting together.

Wordswright leaned forward. "What are the first words that come to your mind?"

The cursor flashed hypnotically, exacerbated by the strobing lights.

"Adjust a door . . . a door order . . . or . . . you adore orders . . . ?" Verity stammered, confused. Her head was pounding, and she was struggling to string two thoughts together.

"Absolutely. That *is* adorable." Wordswright seemed to be suppressing a smile as he took notes.

Enforce more reform. Enormous comfort to conform. Let go of control. Our control rocks and rolls.

"Oh, I like that. Clever computer to come up with that, hmm? The thinking man's AI, no? I'll have to jot that down. Tell me, subject, what's the role of the prole at the polls?"

Verity was having to exert extreme effort to concentrate on Wordswright's statement. His words slurred together into one long, undifferentiated phrase. She blinked to moisten her eyes, which felt like sandpaper from trying to focus on the screen as lights flashed all around. Her forehead was prickling with sweat under the weight of the headband, and her arms were dropping lower and lower by the minute.

"To control the vote. I mean—to vote."

Wordswright noted down something with a dramatic flourish.

"Congress—" blurted Verity, for no reason she could fathom. Her mind was chasing a web of language held together by a set of unfamiliar rules. It was like trying to diagram a completely ambiguous sentence: one of those "he hit the man with a cane" ones.

Stop what's real. Get it right. Might rules rights. Might rights wrong rules. Feel right with the real deal. Let leaders deal with what's really right.

Blinking once more to reset her blurring vision, Verity became aware of a minute flashing light to one corner of the screen. She homed in on it, embracing it as a welcome refuge from the verbal and sensorial assault coming at her. Momentarily, she realized why: the tiny beacon reminded her of Viveo and Silas's alphabet. She mentally cycled through the symbol forms she'd been playing with the previous night, soothed by the loops and lines of the curious language.

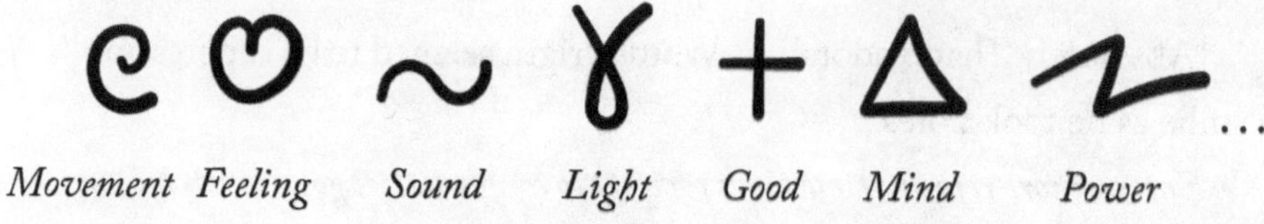

Good–Mind–Power caught her attention.

Summoning her last reserves, she focused on the light and Viveo's symbols until her mind felt clearer.

Things are not always as they seem, she told herself. *Two rhymes do not necessarily make a right.*

The AI droned on: *Daring difference defies civility. Erring impudence denies impunity.*

"Tell me: what is the danger of daring difference?" Wordswright questioned, following the AI's pronunciation pattern.

Verity paused, letting her thoughts cohere. "It *defines* civility."

"What?" Wordswright's eyebrows suddenly knit together. "You must have misunderstood."

Wordswright set the program to repeat its last phrases. He turned a dial, and the strobing lights were suddenly amplified until they completely invaded Verity's senses, leaving no room for anything else. She tried to refocus on the tiny light and Viveo's symbols, but they were fleeing from her mind.

"Again: what is the danger of daring to differ?

"It defies civility," answered Verity, trying to make sense of the words on the screen. "And defines . . . impudence . . ."

"Impudence! Indeed! Much better! Now we're making progress—"

"Tell me, Subject Truman, what day is this?"

"A good day," responded Verity. "No, a great day. No, wait. Wednesday."

She felt triumphant for the moment, as though she'd achieved something monumental by overriding the onslaught of interferences to her mind. She'd given Wordswright the answers he expected, but she did so by choice, assuming the alternative would have dire consequences here.

The headband itched against her forehead, and she reached up to adjust it.

"Arms in position, Subject!"

But Verity ignored the order, dropping her hands in shock. A moment later, so did Wordswright, fumbling his notepad in doing so. The screen had begun crackling and beeping with increasing intensity, and suddenly, the robotic voice of the AI blasted through the room at full volume: "*STAND BY FOR NEWS FEED . . . A NEW CREED!*"

Conforming is normal
Orders bring order
Words we obey
Mean more than they say
We adore order
It's comfortably moral.

The headband burned red hot against Verity's forehead, and she yanked it off, throwing it to the floor. Wordswright didn't even notice: he was lunging toward the monitor to grab the cord that connected it to the wall. The screen, and the flashing light, went blank.

For a moment, he sat looking stunned. Then he turned the dial that controlled the strobing lights, returning the room to something resembling normalcy. His hands shook.

"Was that . . . meant to happen?" Verity's dry throat made it hard to speak.

"Of course, of course. All part of the plan, always is. The AI learns as it goes, you see. It gets smarter by the minute. Just as you will." Stooping to gather his notebook, Wordswright gave it a dismissive wave. "Anyway, that concludes our session. Follow the marked lines back to your class. Jobs should be around somewhere."

Confused and exhausted, Verity retreated from the room, her eyes on the way-finding lines and her mind elsewhere altogether.

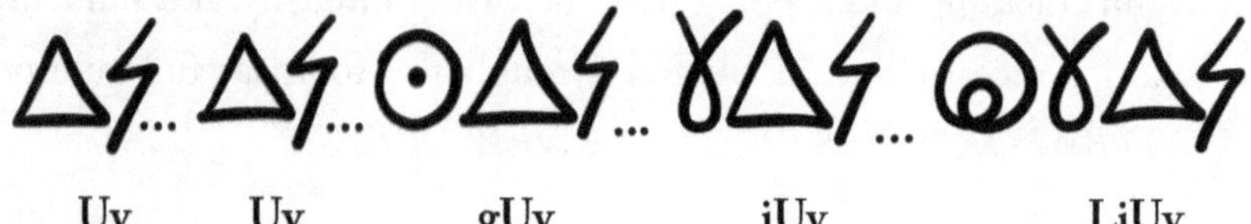

Uv   Uv   gUv   iUv   LiUv

pulsed the alien symbols at the back of her vision.

Think . . . Think . . . Know . . . Understand . . . Comprehend.

10

Lawson strode out onto the asphalt, taking his place on a painted cross outside the square marking the perimeter for morning exercises.

"Law and order!" he shouted.

"Know no border!" the subjects shouted back. They'd become accustomed to this new cadence call routine. Some even seemed to enjoy the excuse to let loose with a yell.

"In line!" Lawson's precise voice carried through the still morning air. The sun was still hovering around the horizon, not sure it wanted to get up just yet. Verity didn't blame it. She would much rather be hiding under the gray covers of her bunk bed, even if they were scratchy.

"Now, why are you here?" A pause. "Dis-cip-line!"

"*Is no sin!*" chanted the subjects, stomping their feet with each accented word.

"And what's our goal?" Another pause. "We foll-ow rules!"

"*Don't be fools!*"

"Obey's the key!" shouted Lawson.

"*To set us free!*"

"With discipline!" shouted Lawson.

"*We all win!*"

Lawson concluded his morning exercises with a barking demand that a selection of subjects assemble around the blue square where the Academy's school buses parked. In all, about a dozen were picked out from the rows of anxious kids. Another few were manhandled away by the PackHunters for alleged insubordination.

Verity's stomach roiled. Every time she was singled out for anything at the Academy, it had turned out badly.

"What's going on?" she asked warily as she lined up between Bea and Krystal. Cody stood a few places back with mistrustful eyes and protectively folded arms. Em was the only one of Verity's friends who had been passed over. Pretending to rub a hand over the shaved side of her head, she flashed Verity a peace sign. Verity made a face in return.

"We've been assigned to a WorkForce." Bea again spoke out of the corner of her mouth, like a very poor ventriloquist. "Basically, they ship us off into the Oasis and make us do busywork."

That must be why Em had been skipped. Asthma and physical exertion didn't exactly go hand in hand.

The girl ahead of them, tall and thin with thickly coiled hair, turned and glared. "Think it, but don't say it," she hissed. "You want us all to get detention?"

"Fine," said Bea, this time through clenched teeth. "Not busywork. CommUnity projects. With a capital 'Unity.'"

The girl looked somewhat mollified. She turned back toward Lawson and stood waiting for further instruction.

"Projects for rich people." Krystal's dark eyes glittered. "Surprise."

"Rule-following, order-loving rich people," chimed in Cody. "The ones who've drunk up all the government's lies. And fluoride."

"Again with the fluoride," whispered Bea. "I bet your dentist loves you."

"Don't get me started on what they put in fillings."

Cody's forthcoming rant was cut short by the arrival of a familiar, sweaty figure: Buck Jobs. Just like the last time Verity had seen him, he was dressed entirely in heavy blue denim. Damp patches were already visible around his armpits and on his back. His head gleamed with moisture.

Bea grimaced. "That's one way to water the grounds."

"Salt content would be *way* too high," noted Krystal with a grin. "You'd kill everything."

"Everyone on!" Jobs bellowed, holding out his battered tablet device. Each subject scanned themselves in with their key fobs, together creating a symphony of electronic bleats.

"Morning, kids! Subjects, I mean." Walt Huff lounged in the driver's seat as the subjects trudged onto the bus in single file and filled up the rows of gray-upholstered seats. The vinyl squeaked and groaned as they made themselves comfortable, doing everything possible to avoid touching bare skin against the sticky material.

Verity felt a sense of relief at Huff's presence. He was one of the few adults at the Academy who was tolerable, although maybe she'd lowered her standards since she'd arrived.

"Don't encourage them, Huff." The TaskMaster's watery green eyes narrowed. "Treating them like equals only makes them think they are. And we all know what happens then."

"What happens?" asked Verity, signing herself in via the tablet.

"You end up here. Doors closing!" Jobs rapped commandingly on the dash, leaving a damp knuckle print.

Huff flipped the switch that controlled the doors. They sighed closed, trapping the students on board. Still, as claustrophobic as it was, the bus meant being somewhere other than the Academy, and that buoyed spirits somewhat. Even without knowing what lay ahead, Verity relaxed as the bus bumped out of the campus and onto the narrow road that was the only way in and out of the Academy. Watching the school's stern gray structures shrink against the horizon was surprisingly cathartic, especially against the soundtrack of the Bach cello suite playing quietly in the background.

"All right, Subjects, it's off to the Oasis. 'What's the Oasis?' asks the girl with the attitude problem," he said in a sneering, high-pitched voice. He gave Verity a meaningful look.

Verity bit her bottom lip. It took incredible willpower not to retort.

"It's the ultimate planned community. A place where none of you would otherwise have any right to set foot. Although, if you follow Lawson's curriculum well enough, maybe that will change."

Krystal made a harrumphing noise. "Pretty sure that's not how things work."

The girl who had told Bea off earlier turned in her seat, shooting dagger eyes at Krystal.

This drew Jobs's attention. "Does someone have something to say?"

Krystal was sullen. "Just some commentary on this country. Working hard and following the rules doesn't always get you places."

Jobs's fleshy jowls tightened. "How would you know, huh?" He jabbed at his tablet with a sweaty thumb. "It's never too early in the day to give detention, you know."

Krystal made a gesture of surrender. "Sure. Whatever."

Jobs cleared his throat and continued. "We have several projects assigned today. You'll be split into groups, with one group per project.

You five, you're on grass count." He indicated a group of subjects at the back of the bus. Then he pointed to Verity, her bunkmates, and Pitbull, who was sprawled out behind them, taking up an entire row of seats. "You, on re-greening."

"*So* much better than grass count." Bea raised her hands in a worshipful gesture.

Verity had no idea whether this was true. "What's re-greening?"

Bea rolled her eyes. The answer was apparently self-evident. "Well, the grass at the golf courses dies off in the desert climate, so we go out and spray it green."

"That's . . . so wrong!" Verity wondered how this could be the better option. "Why are there even golf courses in the desert in the first place?"

"Well, it's a private course. People pay good money for that grass." Bea didn't seem overly concerned. Although from the hints she'd given about her background, her family probably owned a golf course or two of their own.

"Especially when you realize there are only about five hundred people living at the Oasis," muttered Krystal.

"So, there's a whole desert golf course for just a few hundred people? And it has to be sprayed green?"

"It does look *way* better sprayed." Bea picked at the seam of the seat in front of her. "It's yellow and patchy otherwise."

Jobs swooped in, sweat-damp tablet at the ready. Verity could feel the humidity radiating off him. "This group again. Is there a problem here?"

Verity's self-control failed her. "Just that our task is stupid and pointless. I'm not doing it."

"C'mon, Verity," whispered Bea. "It's just grass."

"And not even the good kind," sneered Pitbull.

"Oh, it's much more than grass." Jobs folded damp arms over his tablet. He was so sweat drenched he could have come straight from a morning sauna session. "It's a measure of your commitment to the program. Based on your comments, I'm guessing you'll be extending your stay with us."

Verity gulped. She had resigned herself to a detention or two, but not something like this. "You mean at the Academy? You can do that?"

Jobs rapped his tablet stylus against coffee-stained lower teeth, looking as smug as he did damp. "Matriculation is based on a number of factors. One of them being participation in CommUnity Projects. I highly recommend you do. Because the alternative is much less pleasant."

"Just do it, Verity," murmured Bea. "Unless you want to end up in the Box. Or worse."

"Wait. Cody wasn't just making that up?"

Cody lifted her fists to her head, unclenching them in a "mind blown" gesture. "Truth is stranger than fiction. And harder to come by. Except maybe on the DeepNet."

Krystal made a face at Cody. "C'mon, girl. There's *nothing* you should be looking for on there."

"Fine." Verity had been worn down. "Let's go spray some grass."

The bus made several stops throughout the Oasis, dropping off small groups of subjects each time. Verity stared as the bus crawled along the wide, tidy avenues, its tires humming on the perfectly maintained roads. It was a far cry from the potholed surfaces of her hometown.

Lining the roads were neat, identical stone houses distinguished only by the numbers and names printed in gold on their mailboxes. All had luminous lawns edged by precise rows of box hedges. Set against the soaring blue sky and the vivid pink of the desert flowers that decorated the parkways, they looked fake, like a computer rendering. Even the sprinklers moved so precisely it was almost hypnotic.

Huff pulled the bus off the main road, guiding it through a huge arch that marked the entry to the golf course. The parking area was spectacularly landscaped, with elaborate waterfalls, ponds, and vibrant flora. Gaudily patterned parakeets chirped in an aviary adjoining the brick clubhouse.

"How the one-percenters live, huh?" muttered Krystal.

Verity was fascinated despite herself. There was something so artificial about the place that it felt alien. She had the sense that if she got close enough, she'd find out it was nothing more than a painted backdrop and a series of props.

"Hoo, boy, makes me homesick," Bea said longingly. "Just imagine the 'Gram-worthy selfies you could take in this place."

The bus jerked as Huff put it into park. Jobs stalked up to the front, mopping his face and neck with his handkerchief. He cursorily consulted his tablet.

"Subjects in group three! This is your destination. Parks Manager Driver will be overseeing your work. You will be present and productive from 0800 till 1500, at which point the bus will return to collect you. Any misconduct or misbehavior will be reported and dealt with. Clear?"

The TaskForce disembarked from the bus, where they were greeted by a prim woman with a ponytail so severe she must suffer from daily tension headaches. Like Jobs, the woman carried a tablet—although a newer, less sweaty one—and a very strong sense of self-importance.

"Subjects," she began, her tone terse. "Today, we'll be regreening the front nine of the course. For those new to the equipment, I'll take you through how to use it, along with the standard safety measures. All equipment must be returned to me by the end of the day; we'll take inventory at that point. There are productivity milestones you're expected to meet, with penalties for those who do not. Leaving the course at any time is prohibited. And I *will* know."

Verity didn't doubt it. The adults out here were pros at tracking and monitoring kids. They were like ill-intentioned helicopter parents, always hovering around and ready to step in wherever they saw fit. Which was everywhere.

After demonstrating the equipment, Driver took the subjects out to the first hole. It was trim and neat, with sprinklers running on high to keep the surrounding vegetation in good shape. There was absolutely no indication they were in the middle of the desert. Verity sniffed: there was a fragrance she couldn't pin to a particular flower or plant.

"Perfume," explained Cody. "They spray it from dispensers in the ground to keep the place smelling good. Try not to breathe too much, because who knows what it does to your gray matter. Wish I'd brought my gas mask."

Verity wanted to accuse Cody of spinning another one of her stories. But as she took another step, a spritz of moisture spurted from a tiny black nozzle near the tee-off area.

Cody raised her eyebrows in an "I told you so" expression.

Driver clapped her hands and regarded the subjects from under the brim of the sun visor she'd just put on. "Let's get spraying! Stick to the fairways and greens, and keep the density of the sprayers to what we agreed on. You don't want to reimburse us for wasted materials, do you?"

"No, ma'am," chorused the subjects.

"Well, then. Let's make this grass green again!" She made it sound like a political slogan.

Wielding their sprayers, the small group of subjects painstakingly made their way down the fairway, leaving a bright green carpet of grass in their wake. It did look good in a Photoshopped kind of way, Verity had to admit. But it was hard to believe any community would sign off on something so wasteful.

Bea scoffed when Verity said as much. "What's wasteful about taking pride in where you live?"

"Seriously, girl," added Krystal. "You should see my mom go nuts with the Christmas ornaments. They're useless, too, right? But it brings joy, so who cares?"

Verity cringed inside. Every time she opened her mouth, she said the wrong thing. Trying not to fixate on what the other girls probably thought of her, she adjusted her sprayer and got back to work.

As the morning wore on, the little group slowly divided up. Bea was well ahead of the others, working efficiently through her designated zones. Given the way she talked about things, Verity had expected her to be less on-task. Pitbull dedicated himself to hauling containers of spray and carrying equipment, which kept him well away from the others. Cody, on the other hand, spent most of her time pointing up at jet contrails and raving about chemtrails and government conspiracies.

As the morning wore on, the heat inched up to oppressive levels, and Verity was sweating in her gray uniform. Granting herself a minute's break, she absently sketched out some of Viveo's symbols in a sand bunker using a stick.

Ʒℓ℮℧ [YweO] weak feeling . . . powerless, she whispered to herself, realizing it reflected how tired and defeated she felt out here.

"What are you doing?" Bea was leaning on the nozzle of her sprayer, looking down at Verity's inexpertly sketched symbols.

"Learning how to speak . . . alien. It's a pet project of my brother's."

Bea raised an eyebrow. "Well, I've heard stranger things. Most of them in the last half hour from Cody."

Suddenly self-conscious, Verity wiped out the symbols.

"Better get back to it, huh? Unless you want to get reported." Bea primed her sprayer ready to green a section Verity had missed.

But it was too late. As they finished up their shift and wearily returned to the bus, sweaty and covered in blisters, Jobs confronted Verity.

"You were reported for being off-task, Subject. When we arrive back at the Academy, follow the red lines on the asphalt to your detention site."

Pitbull snickered, and Verity guessed who had ratted her out. So much for staying under the radar. He—and probably others as well—had obviously been keeping a close watch on her.

It was little wonder, then, that the back of Verity's neck prickled as she spent the waning hours of the day kneeling on the hot asphalt writing over and over in chalk on the ground:

I will be perfectly productive, dutifully diligent, and infinitely industrious as Pyrite screamed bloody murder in the background.

11

By the time detention was finally over, Verity could scarcely stand, and her knees were raw from the sun-boiled asphalt. The excruciating walk back to her bunk room was made on wobbly legs that didn't want to cooperate. Even her fingers ached: they were swollen from dehydration and cracked from chalk dust.

Finally back in the bunk room, she hobbled to her bed, where she brushed down her knees and wrapped them with a pair of clean gray socks. As she lay back on her thin pillow and closed her eyes, she felt overwhelmed. Her exhaustion mixed with humiliation, creating a cocktail of sheer despair. She wanted to cry.

Her entire life she'd been encouraged to think freely and stand up for what she believed in, but the consequences were becoming harder and harder to take. No one was sent to a place like this for meekly following the rules. Maybe it was better just to quietly go along with whatever the prevailing school of thought was. If you never trod on any toes, you never had to worry about people kicking back.

She thought back to the goEco protest. It had seemed like such an important and worthwhile idea at the time. But maybe it was pointless. The people at the top, the [knu-wun *people in power above many others*], were always going to wield power over the little guy, no matter how many of them there were.

She sighed. She couldn't dwell on this, or she'd end up spiraling. She dug under the slats of the bunk bed above her and pulled out Silas's symbol crib sheet, tracing the now-familiar symbols into her notebook. Their curious, intuitive forms gave her a relaxed focus, the way diving into a jigsaw puzzle did.

Her eyes landed on the headphone symbol for "together." It reminded her of Silas's parting word to her: [bO *sympathy*]. Now she felt anything but. [YbO *apart feeling*], she drew. She missed the feeling of strength [tUw-bO *solidarity; a sense of powerful togetherness in working toward something*] she'd enjoyed before everything had gone so wrong.

Verity was puzzling out some additional combinations to describe her current feeling when Bea buzzed herself into the room. The other girl perched on Verity's bed, giving her a sidelong glance from beneath long lashes.

"Didn't see you at dinner tonight. Although, honestly, I don't blame you. I miss having an actual cook."

It was lucky Krystal hadn't yet arrived back from trash duty, or she would have had some choice words to share.

"I wasn't hungry. And I wasn't really up for the walk." Verity pointed to her battered, sock-wrapped knees.

Grimacing, Bea brushed an invisible wrinkle from Verity's bed covers. "I saw you out there. Asphalt detention is definitely up there with the

Box. It's not so bad to begin with, but it doesn't take long to make you regret being born with legs." She bent forward, spying the crib sheet. "Is this your symbol language thing again?"

"My brother Silas's. He calls it his light language. It's actually pretty cool."

Bea's interest was piqued. "Light language? Sounds spacey, but I'm down with that. I'm a bit of a word nerd myself. And I loved *E.T.*"

Verity hesitated. She wasn't sure just how far she could trust the other girl, especially having just spent hours in detention. What if it hadn't been Pitbull who had ratted her out after all, but Bea?

"Oh, c'mon. You think I'm going to laugh or something? If I can handle Cody's tinfoil hat stuff, I can deal with some alien pictograms. Hand it over."

Despite her misgivings, Verity handed her the slip of paper. Bea spent a few minutes perusing the thirty-some symbols on the list, her brow furrowed in thought.

"So, each symbol has its own sound and meaning. And the symbols seem kind of connected to their meaning, right?" Bea glanced at Verity for verification. "Like how the heart one is for 'feeling' ♡ [O] and the lightning bolt means 'action' ⚡ [v]."

"The sounds are, too. My favorite is how 'round' ◉ looks like a roller coaster and when you say it a bunch, your tongue curls up like one, 'L.' Like 'lollipop.'"

Bea imitated her, comically exaggerating. "Are these all the symbols?"

"I think so."

Bea twisted a braid as she reviewed the symbols. "You know, maybe you don't even need any more than what you've got right here. Just these could be enough for a whole language."

"Really?" Verity had teased out a few words, and she'd figured out how to make verbs and adjectives, but that was as far as she'd gotten.

Bea crossed her legs and settled in on Verity's bed. "Kind of like how German has all of those really long, cool words that are actually like ten words squashed together."

Verity was impressed and knew that it showed in her expression. Bea had surprised her by leaping into the puzzle with such gusto. She thought for a moment.

"You might be right. I mean, there's Y, the one that looks like a minus sign. It looks like it makes the opposite of the symbol underneath. So, it works like 'anti-' or 'un-' maybe. Just that would double the number of words, wouldn't it? Like if you add it to ⟨symbol⟩ [**im** *(adj.)*] light, you get ⟨symbol⟩ [**yim**] dark."

"So, it couldn't mean heavy, too, could it?"

"You'd have to use a different formula, I'm pretty sure," said Verity. "Weird that words can look exactly the same but mean totally different things."

"Well, English has a bunch of other languages mixed in with it—no wonder it's a big ol' mess. Hey, what were you writing that got you in trouble at the Oasis? Better have been something majorly rude about Jobs."

"I wish," said Verity. "I would've called him a ⟨symbols⟩ **vYk-wu** [*boss, master*] who likes to use a lot of ⟨symbols⟩ **kwU** [*control*]."

"Truth," said Bea. "My mom is always saying 'you catch more flies with honey than vinegar,' but these guys are all on the vinegar bandwagon."

Verity was chewing her lip, feeling vulnerable. "Here's the one from the Oasis," she offered, impulsively adding a few more symbols. ⟨symbols⟩ [**tYwe-YkO** *tired, low feeling*].

Bea took a closer look. "You're feeling . . . powerless and down, huh? Sounds about right for around here."

"Seriously. I don't know how much longer I can hack it in this place."

After a moment, Bea snatched Verity's pen. ⛓ [tYg-we! *burst*]. She wrote, taking up most of the page. "It's a motivational poster about busting out of here," she said with a grin.

"Well, at least we have our . . . ⟡ [fUwe *freedom*]." Verity grabbed the pen and sketched it out.

"Ooh, our *own mind power!*" sang Bea. "I love that. Because here's the thing. No matter what goes on in here, no matter how much they control the day-to-day, they can't get into your head and take away your thoughts. Not to get all Cody on you, but you're always safe in your head. Even in a place like this."

Verity thought back to her computer programming session. "Unless you're being brainwashed."

"But *were* you?" shot back Bea. "Because you seemed to come out of that plenty normal to me."

"That's because I sort of . . . went into my head. With this symbol stuff."

"So, no . . . **U-kwU**," △ [*mind control*], sketched Bea, ". . . for you?"

"Like mind control, you mean?" interpreted Verity. "Well, you know me. The one thing about me is that I've always known my own mind."

"⊙△ **gUv** [*know*]," said Bea. "Know what's inside your mind, right?"

"Yup, not to be confused with 'no mind'!"

Bea nodded her approval. "You're not so bad, Truman."

The girls kept playing around with the language, taking a break only when Krystal and Em let themselves in.

"Ugh, you *reek* of garbage juice," said Bea as Krystal climbed up to her bunk bed. "It smells like the perfume counter at a dollar store in here."

Krystal smirked, wafting the odor toward Bea. "Yeah, that's on purpose. To keep you away."

Verity regarded Em, who was covered in dark stains that almost matched the liner around her eyes. She looked like a panda. "Have you been drinking ink or something?"

"Whiteboard cleaning duty. Those fumes are something else, let me tell you. I think I flew to the moon. And Cody, if you're listening, the moon landing was *not* a hoax."

Verity grimaced. "That all seems like a really bad idea for someone with asthma."

"You're telling me. I had to make a pit stop at the Infirmary for more Ventolin." She sniffed her shirt and winced. "Gross. Guess it's shower time for me. How about you, Krystal?"

"Mrmh," groaned Krystal, who had her head squashed into her pillow. "Tomorrow morning. I'm in a trash fume coma."

Bea stood, stretching. "I'm coming. That way I can sneak a bonus fifteen minutes of glorious shut-eye in the morning. Under-eye bags are *not* gonna be in my future. Truman, you should thank that brother of yours for the entertainment."

This gave Verity an idea, and she picked up her pen to start composing Silas a letter in his light language. It was slow going, and she had to intersperse it with some English words, but overall she was pleased with her first effort. Spelling was definitely easier using Silas's alphabet.

"Ooh, writing love letters?" Krystal poked her head down from the top bunk.

"Not quite." Verity covered the page with her hand.

"Probably should warn you that there's no outgoing mail here. Officially."

"Is that . . . legal? Even prisoners get to write letters back home."

"Emphasis on *officially*." Krystal gave a sly smile and held up a finger. "Things would be so much better for you if you stopped being such a teacher's pet all the time. There's a workaround. Casper, the custodian's son."

"The pale kid with the pet mice?"

"Yup. The Academy rules don't apply to him. And he's not much of a talker, obviously. You'll just have to find a way to get to him."

12

"*Enforcing brings reform!*" bellowed Lawson, his voice ringing out across the cafeteria.

The subjects paused, some midbite, others mid-conversation, ready to drone the expected refrain in return.

"*We're endorsing to conform!*" came the chorus, mostly in key, although a couple of voices—Pitbull's gruff one and a squeaky one from a gangly dark-skinned kid—stood out. So did the vacuum of noise beside Verity: Em was merely lip-synching along, and badly at that. Verity had the urge to say something but stopped herself. Where had that come from? She wasn't the type to rat people out . . . or demand they conform.

Before Verity could reflect any further on this, Lawson clapped his hands, then turned his attention to Payne, who was in the corner messing with the AV system. He was taking an embarrassingly long time doing whatever he was doing.

"Need some help?" bellowed Cody through cupped hands.

Ignoring her, Payne finally gave a thumbs-up.

The PA system emitted a squealing noise that resolved into a sort of languid, ambient music played at low volume. There was a rhythm to it that Verity couldn't quite capture and some sort of vocal line that lurked beneath the main melody. Something about it set her teeth on edge.

"⊬∧ ◯ϟ ≙⌠ ... the melody?" [**fu IOv UI Yk brI?** *I hear words below melody?*] Verity thought to herself.

"*A song to right all wrongs!*" called Lawson. He seemed like he was going to continue, but Payne lumbered up with his tablet, muttering something under his breath. Both strode off, out to the courtyard.

"Song, schmong," said Em snidely. "This is easily the worst post-rock soundtrack I've ever heard."

"Post-rock?" Bea was bemused. "You mean they somehow made rock music even worse?"

"Wow, sacrilege!" Cody obviously took this personally.

"Shouldn't music have, like, a beat?" chimed in Krystal. "If you can't dance to it, it's not music."

"It's a whole thing . . ." More animated than Verity had ever seen her, Em launched into an explanation, clearly not bothered that Bea's attention was miles away. Krystal was dancing deliberately out-of-time to the music, proving her point.

"⊺∧ ⌠ ℰϟ ℰ⌢ ... the rhythm," [**cu Yc ev eb jAe** *She's not moving with the rhythm*] she whispered to Bea.

Bea grinned.

As the music droned on, Verity glanced around the room. Something felt slightly off. The subjects had all resumed eating and chatting, but they were kind of . . . subdued. Even with Payne and the PackHunters always circling and the threat of punishment always looming, the subjects tended to be pretty unruly. Most of the kids at the Academy were the ones you'd find lounging in the back row or hanging out behind the bleachers, and there was usually plenty of noise. Not to mention more than the occasional outburst requiring intervention—and sometimes medical attention.

Tonight, there was a lot more staring off into space and mindless playing with food. A handful of subjects had distanced themselves from their usual friendship groups and were sitting either alone at empty tables or with several seats between them and the nearest kid. D'Angelo Washington, for example, was being way too quiet for comfort. D'Angelo had a reputation for being a total clown, and Verity had never seen him sit still for more than a few seconds. Tonight, he was sitting with his eyes downcast, rhythmically kicking the back of the chair in front of him.

"I mean, post-rock *is* pretty antisocial," said Em when Verity raised the point. "It's for chilling out to, but in a depressed way."

"Sounds . . . appealing." Verity tried to lock eyes with Bea to loop her into the joke, but the other girl was staring thoughtfully at her hair. Verity tried Krystal instead, but the other girl had stopped dancing and was contemplating a water stain on the wall.

Em shrugged. "Depends on what you're into. *This* isn't really my thing, though. It's so . . . bland."

"You don't think it's creepy?"

Em shook her head, a rare grin moving over her face. "Now, if you want to talk about *creepy* music . . ."

"Nuh-uh," said Bea.

"There she is." Cody snapped her fingers in front of Bea's nose. Both Bea and Krystal blinked, as though they'd been brought back to the land of the living.

Em's grin widened. One of her canines stuck out at an odd angle. "You know why it's so creepy, Verity? I hear if you play it backward, it reveals a secret coded message . . ."

Verity rolled her eyes. "Cody, looks like you've lost your title as lead conspiracy theorist."

"They're not conspiracies if they're *true*," pointed out Cody.

Verity toyed with her dinner as the others chatted around her, their conversation falling into a lull when Lawson's music reached a weird, strangely affecting crescendo.

"What was . . . Did you hear that?" Something in the music had reminded her of the artificial voice of the computer in her programming sessions. Everyone else shook their heads.

Verity leaned back in her chair, trying to catch a glimpse of Pitbull, who she knew had attended at least a couple of the programming sessions: he'd been pulled out of two of Verity's classes these past few days. The thickset boy was hunched over his tray, hands balled in fists and clamped together as though in prayer. He was mouthing along to lyrics that apparently only he could hear.

"Do you think Pitbull's okay?" Verity asked Bea, interrupting one of Cody's monologues about the dangers of drinking tap water. "He's talking to himself."

Cody smirked. "You say that like it's a bad thing."

"Anything to do with Pitbull is a bad thing," said Em, who'd been on the receiving end of a few of Pitbull's attacks. Pitbull wasn't a fan of goths.

"At least he's only hassling the air around him," said Bea. "Are you guys done? I'm on trash duty, and I'd like to keep my time around the trash cans to a minimum. Unless someone wants to do it for me?" She looked meaningfully at Verity.

"Actually, sure," said Verity, still frowning at Pitbull.

Surprised, Bea raised her hands in a "sure, go ahead" gesture. "You really do have a thing for trash, huh? I mean, if you're still hungry, I'm pretty sure they'll give you seconds."

"Very funny. I can change my mind if you'd like."

Bea wagged a finger. "I firmly believe that people should hold to their commitments. It's all yours."

Susie Slaw was pleased to see Verity, although she did get a bit cagey when Verity stole a glance at the bag of food she was apparently setting aside to take home.

"It's for a good cause." Slaw tied off a bag with more gusto than was strictly needed.

Verity cringed inwardly. Clearly, her judgment had been written all over her face. "I didn't mean—"

"No, no, it's fine." But Slaw's body language said it wasn't. She handed Verity a bag straining under the weight of its contents. "Can you take this out to the dumpsters? Watch it doesn't leak."

"Sure." Verity took the bag from Slaw and hauled it outside, following the purple dashed lines to the dumpster. The bag landed with a slosh inside, giving off the unappealing aroma of stale milk and muffins. Wiping off her hands on her uniform, Verity waited around, searching the star-speckled sky for any sign of Viveo. Only the moon stared back.

The faint hum of Lawson's creepy music spilled out from the kitchen's open doors. Again, Verity thought she heard a hint of a lyric, but she couldn't quite detangle it from the rest of the rumbling wall of sound.

Feeling slightly defeated by Viveo's absence, Verity began turning back toward the cafeteria. As she did, a vaguely familiar phrase came to her, though whether it was just in her head or buried somewhere deep in Lawson's music, she couldn't tell.

Words we obey . . . Words we obey . . . Words we obey . . .

As the words echoed over and over, the music seemed to increase in volume, and a bright light shattered her vision, piercing her skull like an ice pick. The sound of her pulse became monstrous in her ears. Clapping her hands over her eyes, she slumped to the ground.

When Verity came to, she was staring blearily up at the worried face of Constance Grimes, whose drawn-on brows were knitted in concern. Her mouth was moving, but it took Verity a moment for her brain to translate this into speech.

"How are you feeling? Can you hear me?"

Grimes's voice finally resolved into words, and not the ones that had been repeating over and over in Verity's head for what felt like hours. Verity felt like when she'd sustained a concussion playing soccer the previous summer. Her head throbbed, and her vision spat with sparks.

We adore order . . . We adore order . . . We adore order . . .

Verity clapped her hands over her ears. She couldn't hear Lawson's eerie music from here, but it had burrowed into her brain somehow. "Where am I? The Infirmary?"

Grimes snorted and folded her doughy arms. "Not if I can help it. There's a time and a place for that, and this isn't it. We're in my cottage. Casper saw you faint, so he got me, and we carried you back here together."

"Thanks." It was all Verity could muster. Her pulse was currently roaring in her ears at rock concert levels. At least it was drowning out the earworm that was bugging her.

Grimes passed Verity a glass of ice water. It felt comforting in her clammy hands. "Do you know what caused the dizzy spell?"

Verity tried to stitch together her thoughts, but they were all over the place. It was like trying to do a jigsaw puzzle when you didn't know what the picture on the box looked like.

"I'm not sure . . ." Something was off, but she couldn't think straight enough to pinpoint it.

Grimes's mouth tightened. Her reddish lipstick had partly worn off, giving her a careworn look. The harsh lighting in the cottage didn't help. "I'd try to stick to the old menu. The new one isn't agreeing with you." She checked a plastic wristwatch. "Give me just a moment and I'll take you back to your room. I've got to make my rounds first."

Verity nodded, and Grimes hurried out the door. Her cheap rubber-soled shoes squeaked on the tiled floor. Verity had a feeling that Grimes wasn't paid nearly enough to work in a place like this.

Casper was eyeing her from afar, which sparked a memory in Verity's addled mind. Rummaging in her pocket, she pulled out the letter she'd written to Silas in his light language. She waved it at Casper, who tentatively made his way over to her.

"Can you mail this for me? It's for my brother."

Casper took the letter and slipped it into his back pocket. He mimed zipping his lips, a gesture that seemed redundant.

Verity felt as though a weight had been taken off her shoulders, although unfortunately the fog in her head hadn't gone with it. In fact, all the movement had made it worse, and it was swirling around like a

June sky in San Francisco. She closed her eyes, hoping to see Viveo's light language. But all she saw was swirling confusion.

Just then, Grimes returned. "Sorry. I had to mark off a checkpoint. Lawson is Mr. Punctual. If I'm a minute behind on my rounds, he's on my case. Are you ready to head back?"

Grimes took Verity by the elbow and guided her across the quadrangle and toward her bunk room. But their journey didn't go unnoticed. Nothing ever did at Ersatz Academy.

Menacing as ever, the enormous shape of Payne materialized from the shadows.

"Grimes. Subject. What's going on here? I saw the fainting incident from the MonitorRoom. You're not at the Infirmary. Why not?" Payne's tiny, piggish eyes squinted accusingly at them.

"It's nothing, Mr. Payne." Grimes addressed him much more politely than Verity would have. "Just . . . a woman's issue."

Payne tried to hide his discomfort. Verity was impressed by Grimes's quick thinking.

"Well, in that case . . ." Payne cleared his throat. His meaty fingers drummed on the taser latched to his belt. "Next time follow appropriate procedure."

"Yes, sir," said Verity. "Can I get back to my bunk room now?"

Payne took a step back, backing up off the painted line he had so carefully adhered himself to. He lifted a pair of paddlelike hands in surrender. "Don't let me keep you."

Verity's disorientation stayed with her all evening. She felt as though she were swimming through Jell-O, and Lawson's weird, ambient music didn't help. There was no escaping it; it followed the subjects everywhere they went like the hum of an ailing refrigerator. Verity found herself listening again for the snatches of lyrics she'd sworn she'd heard buried in the music, but to no avail. Maybe she'd hallucinated them.

When the door to the dorm room swung open, she winced. The harsh hallway lights were more than she could handle right now.

"You okay, Verity?" Em's thickly lined eyes were staring down at her. "No offense, but your complexion is paler than mine. And I work hard for this pallor."

The room was spinning again, and Verity lay down on her thin mattress, willing everything to stop moving. The bed creaked as Bea took a perch at its edge. She had just come back from the bathrooms, and the towel she had wrapped around her hair was leaning off to one side, toppled by the weight of her damp braids. "You good? You look like the trash took you out instead."

Verity hugged her knees, which were still tender from her recent asphalt detention. "I had this weird head spin that came on really suddenly."

"Headspin City, zero stars," said Bea. "Got it."

Krystal cocked her head, making a show of massaging the bridge of her nose. "With a headache? Because I have a killer one like an ice pick behind my eyes. I swear Lawson's crappy music did it."

"Oh, go on," said Em. "Just because you can't salsa to it doesn't mean it's *bad*."

Bea scoffed. "Are you sticking up for Lawson?"

"I'm sticking up for *music*! I'm just saying that I was there, too, and I'm fine. No headaches or fainting or seizures or whatever."

"No song lyrics randomly stuck in your head?" pressed Verity.

Em made a face. "I wish."

Krystal climbed into bed and mashed her pillow over her eyes. "I mean, I'm happy to blame the muffins and the desert heat and these all-round gross conditions, too. Doesn't change the fact that I've got a headache."

The room spun as Verity shifted position. "Em, have you done any of the programming sessions yet?"

"Sure. Two of them." Em scratched lazily at her undercut. "They were no big deal."

"You didn't feel, like, a bit hypnotized or anything?" Krystal's voice was muffled by the pillow. "Like that Rightwords guy—"

"Wordswright," corrected Verity.

"Whatever. Like that . . . guy . . . was getting in your brain a bit? Because I was kind of vibing a little, like I was in a rap battle or something."

"I mean, not really." The long side of Em's hair fell down over her face as she bent her head. After a pause, she added: "I didn't actually get most of it. The text moved way too fast for me. Words aren't really my thing. I have this language-processing thing going on."

"Like dyslexia or something?" asked Verity.

"Like that, yeah. I'm not stupid, though." Em's eyes flashed. She'd obviously been teased about this in the past.

Bea rolled her eyes. "Duh. Dyslexia has nothing to do with intelligence. There are heaps of dyslexic geniuses out there. They're a dime a dozen in math and science. Even literature. It's no biggie."

Em gave a tight smile.

"So," said Bea after a moment. "I'm the only one who hasn't done this computer programming thing, huh? And it looks like headaches, fainting spells, and whatever trip Krystal went on are what I should be expecting?"

Verity swallowed. The room was no longer revolving, but she still felt nauseous.

"Guess so," said Krystal. She moaned. "Okay, I'm down for the night before my head explodes."

Em followed her lead, and it was just Bea and Verity left.

"Something's going on," whispered Bea. "You know it, right? Everyone at dinner tonight—it was weird. I felt it, too. There was something to do with that music, although I don't really know what. I don't think I got the full hit because I haven't done this programming thing yet. But I think they're trying to influence us somehow."

Verity nodded, the motion setting her head pounding. "I overhead Lawson . . . ow, my head. Can you see the veins pulsing? Because that's how much it hurts."

"Pretty much. But, hey, you got through the programming session, right? You seemed fine when you came back that first time."

"Yeah, but I'm a wreck now."

"C'mon, I'm desperate here. What was your trick?"

Verity considered this. Her thoughts swam like confused fish, muddled by flashes of the subliminal lyrics she kept thinking she was hearing.

Conforming is norming . . . Conforming is norming . . . Conforming is norming . . .

"I just stared at the flashing light on the monitor," she said at last. "It kind of reminded me of Silas's light language. Oh, and don't drink the juice."

"Okay, so stay dehydrated and distract myself with thoughts of alien Morse code. Got it. I think." Bea kicked her legs at the edge of the bed. "I hope you're right, Truman, because I'm getting the feeling that there's a lot at stake here."

13

Verity was spared another computer programming session the following day, although the alternative wasn't much better. Once again, she found herself on a WorkForce bus trundling into the artificially green avenues of the Oasis. The assigned students were mostly the same as last time, with a few exceptions. Bea was the most notable absentee. She had been assigned to a session with Wordswright first thing that morning, throwing Verity a wincing glance as Payne led her away.

The trip to the Oasis was quieter than last time, with most of the subjects staring blankly out the window or dozing in their seats. Verity found herself listening for Huff's comforting classical music, but instead he had something similar to Lawson's background soundtrack playing, although at such a low volume she could barely hear it. Feeling paranoid even as she did it, she strained to pick out the words she was certain were lurking in there, disappointed when nothing surfaced.

Huff didn't seem impressed with the change to his playlist and kept shaking his head every time the music changed key or tempo.

The strange feeling Verity had felt gazing around the cafeteria last night returned. Maybe Bea was right. There was something *off* about this whole situation. The Ersatz Academy was strange to begin with, but things had escalated with the introduction of the computer programming sessions. The subjects had turned inward on themselves. Some were quiet and wary, showing the kind of sullenness normal after a telling off. Others were lost in thought, with the kind of strangely directed focus of someone playing computer games while you attempted to talk to them. Some, like Kiyana Wallace at the front of the bus, were silent but tense, as though waiting to react to a threat.

"What're you looking at?" snapped Kiyana.

"Sorry."

Chastened, Verity angled her head against the window and watched the formless desert rush by. Lawson's ambient music made for a bleak backdrop, and she retreated into the harmonious forms and sounds of Silas's light language to escape it.

[rOb Ub UI *harmony of words*]

The bus stop-started its way around the Oasis, dropping off groups of students here and there. This time, Verity and her team were told to gather in the middle of the town. They climbed down the dusty steps of the bus and onto a wide central park area with gleaming black paths and perfectly proportioned box hedges. Painstakingly trimmed Japanese cloud trees formed stunning centerpieces ringed by elaborate water fountains. All of it was entirely out of place in the desert. But that was probably the point.

The air was fresh with the same fragrance Verity had smelled at the golf course, but now there was a new sensory element. Instrumental music swelled with the desert wind, piped through speakers in street lights that were infinitely more ornate and expensive than the ones in her own town.

"Ugh, more of Em's post-rock stuff," muttered Krystal. "It's everywhere. It's like Lawson's running around with a Bluetooth device stuck on 'pairing.'"

Verity cocked her head, listening more closely. The music wasn't quite the same as what had been playing at the Academy or on the bus, although there were definite similarities.

"This ain't *rock*," spat a kid Verity didn't know. "It's the stuff they play at bus stations to scare away 'the youth.' To stop crimes and stuff. It don't work, obviously."

"That's enough!" bellowed Jobs. The few subjects who had anything to say were silent. "Everyone off. There's work to do!"

The subjects quietly filed off the bus into the blasting desert heat. Jobs stayed on, basking in the air conditioning.

A short, plump man with a knotted cardigan slung over his shoulders greeted the subjects as they lined up outside the bus. All his clothing had fancy logos stitched on to it—even his socks were logo patterned.

"I'm Earl Kingsley, Senior," he said by way of introduction. His voice was high pitched and sneery and clashed with the fake smile he tried to maintain as he spoke. It was the smile of someone who had read about facial expressions in a book rather than having learned them naturally.

"Oh, cringe," whispered a kid standing behind Verity.

"I'm proud to be the president of the Oasis Homeowners' Association. As you can see, we maintain our town to a very high standard. It's our goal to become a national leader in resort enclaves, and we hope that towns in other states will take our lead in building communities that not only make their residents proud but also inspire others to want to join communities such as ours."

Verity glanced at Krystal, expecting her to chime in with a comment about how most people didn't have the means to live in a mansion on a fake golf course and that the only way that families like hers would ever step foot in such a place was as the hired help. But Krystal was quiet. She was rubbing at the bridge of her nose the way she had when she'd had that brutal headache.

"Today, I hope that you'll give your all to helping the Oasis look its best through precision landscape design. Let me outline my expectations . . ."

"Precision landscape design" turned out to involve trimming the sod along the sidewalks into a perfect line, as measured by Kingsley's ruler.

Where even a week ago, Verity might have said something, this time she was silent. The sun was already witheringly hot, and she lacked the energy to engage Kingsley in a debate that would just end up with her kneeling on the hot asphalt writing out her punishment in chalk.

Instead, she obediently took her edger and set to work trimming back any grass that so much as threatened to cross the border to the wrong side of the sidewalk. At least it wasn't as overtly a wasteful task as spraying the golf course, but it was still pointless. Plant life should be able to grow wherever it wanted, especially in the desert, where greenery played a vital role in reducing the heat absorbed by the roads and buildings. Besides, no one would even see the end result other than Kingsley and maybe the occasional Oasis resident who dared venture out for a walk in the stifling desert heat.

She glanced around to see whether her fellow TaskForce members were nursing similar grievances. It didn't seem to be the case: everyone was trimming away in silence, eyes down and shoulders hunched protectively. She hoped that the heat was the culprit, but after last night's conversation with Bea and the other subjects' response to Lawson's music, she was filled with foreboding.

As the day stretched on, Verity's mind started to wander, and she found herself scribbling Silas's alien symbols in the dust that her edger had left along the sidewalks.

ᒋᐃ ᑭᐤᐃ ᐃᗐ ᒫᑊ

[**fum ogU Uc wom** *My mind is strong*], she wrote, after a few false starts.

Momentarily, the symbols were obscured by a shadow. It was Kingsley, looming over her with a snarling, unimpressed expression.

"What is this?" he snapped, scuffing out the symbols with his leather boat shoe. "There's no room for improvisation on my watch. In fact, there's no room for improvisation in the Oasis."

Verity swallowed nervously. "Of course. I'm sorry. I'll get back to work."

"I should hope so." Kingsley went to say something else, but something had stolen his attention. He shaded his eyes with a hand. "Is that boy okay? Could it be heatstroke?"

He was referring to Pitbull, who was standing motionless, hands at his side and edger at his feet. Pitbull's lips were moving, but Verity couldn't make out what he was saying.

Kingsley very slowly made his way toward Pitbull, clearly hoping that someone else would intervene before he got there. Despite herself, Verity followed. As she got closer, she realized she knew what Pitbull was mouthing before she could even hear for herself.

Conforming is norming . . . orders bring order . . . words we obey . . . say more mean words . . .

It was the lyrics Verity had been hearing intoned in Lawson's music—but with a slight twist—from the screed spat at her by the AI before Wordswright had abruptly ended their session.

"*We adore order . . .*" Pitbull paused, his eyes wild and threaded with red. "What was next . . . what was next? Order, border, Mordor, murder . . . ?"

Both Verity and Kingsley flinched.

"Easy there." Kingsley held up his hands as though approaching a crazed animal, something he was definitely not dressed for.

Pitbull rubbed at his temples, still muttering snatches of the AI's contrived creed over and over. Krystal wasn't the only one suffering from headaches these days.

Mouth downturned in chagrin, Kingsley slowly sidestepped over to a squat metal pole and pressed a large red button on its front. Within moments a trio of black-clad security guards materialized from behind a perfectly trimmed hedge. The guards swarmed around Pitbull, obscuring him, and although Verity couldn't see exactly what was going on, his wild mumbling was cut short. The trio led the now-silent Pitbull away, disappearing as quickly as they'd arrived.

Only Kingsley and Verity seemed to have witnessed the event up close. Kingsley was twisting his hands around a logo-patterned hand-kerchief, and Verity was trembling like she'd received an electric shock. None of the other subjects seemed bothered by what had happened, and she wasn't sure which of these two effects was more concerning. They pressed on with their task in subdued silence, heads down and faces expressionless.

The piped-in music reached a crescendo, and Verity winced. She found herself running through Silas's symbols, hoping to wield them like some sort of protective talisman:

[**fum U Uc fUwem.** *My spirit is free.*]

For a moment she felt lighter, less weighed down.

"Time to get back to it," remarked Kingsley, folding his handkerchief and returning it to his trouser pocket. He pointed at the perfectly aligned thatch of sod in front of Verity.

Verity began half-heartedly sawing her edger into the sod, reciting over and over the light language phrase she'd just coined. But her thoughts were bouncing around like a pinball, and she couldn't focus. She kept thinking about the subliminal lyrics that had been intruding into her mind since Lawson had started playing his disquieting music.

Words we obey . . . Words we obey . . . Words we obey . . .

Maybe she hadn't avoided the effects of the programming sessions after all. She had no way to know what had happened when she'd blacked out last night. Maybe she'd been just like Pitbull, muttering those mind-numbing phrases and frozen in what seemed like a loop . . .

Her breathing quickened. Taking a seat on the curb, she desperately wished the bus would come to pick them up.

Pitbull was absent at dinner that evening. As Verity stirred her tasteless gruel, she thought that was probably a good thing. Her spoon squeaked and screeched on the thick plastic of her bowl, something she realized she could hear because no one else in the room was talking. A zombie-like funk had descended over the entire mess hall, leaving nothing but whispers and dead-eyed stares in its wake.

Behind it all, Lawson's soulless music droned, so quietly you could almost forget it was there.

Verity eyed Cody, who was sitting, arms folded, in front of a plate of untouched food.

"If you think I'm eating this stuff, you're crazy. Look at this place. Something's going on around here."

There was no denying it now. First Bea and now Cody had called out the strange shift underway at the Academy.

"Breaking out the hunger strike stuff, huh?" Em, the only one of the group who wasn't off on Mars, sipped her milk defiantly. "Food isn't the enemy here."

Cody pushed the tray over. "Help yourself, then."

Verity was still thinking about the dystopian turn things had taken as she returned to her bunk room. Almost absently, she pulled out the notes she had made using Silas's code key and began working out new word combinations.

She needed to figure out a way to get through all this.

Playing around with Silas's alien symbols, she eventually came up with: ♡△∿ [OtUw *courage*]. She liked the way the words broke down—*bringing my feelings toward my mind's power*—and only wished that they applied to how she felt herself.

Verity was so swept up in the exercise that she didn't notice the bunk room door swing open.

Bea dawdled lethargically in, her manner blank and emotionless like the other subjects. Seeing her, Verity started.

"Are . . . you okay?" she stammered, instinctively covering her notebook.

Bea slowly closed the door, waiting for the lock to click before straightening up and returning to her old self. She leapt onto Verity's bed, threading her fingers together and cracking her knuckles.

"No need to hide your homework from me. I'm not gonna copy." Bea leaned back against the wall with a heaving sigh. "Oh man. What a day."

Verity felt a rush of relief. She gave the other girl a playful shove. "Don't mess with me like that! I thought you'd been zombified."

"Believe me, Wordswright tried. But I found a way around it."

"The blinking light?"

"Nuh-uh. I think Wordswright taped over it or something. There was nothing there I could see. But I used your brother's light language. It seemed to help—I'm pretty sure. Like a little alien vaccine." She injected an imaginary inoculation into her upper arm.

Verity thought about this, tapping her thumb against her notes. "I have a theory," she said slowly.

"You love your theories, huh? But I'm listening."

Verity took a deep breath. "Okay, so when I think about the alien symbol combinations, I feel more grounded somehow. But not when the AI is talking. Everything it says is . . . like all rhymey for no good reason."

"Wait . . . like '*Retrain the brain till the sane are lame*'?" Bea said it robotically, in a mocking impression of Wordswright's computer.

"That's spot-on!"

They both laughed.

"It's all so *weird*. But I don't think it's totally random, or they wouldn't be putting those subliminal lyrics in that music Em loves so much."

Bea cupped a hand around an ear. "Hold up, they're what now?"

Verity explained her theory about Lawson's music and the weird creed that the AI had broadcast at her at the end of her first session. "I think they're trying to change how we think somehow."

Bea whistled. "Mind control. We *are* talking mind control now, huh?" She paused, trying to figure out where she stood on that proposition. "I mean, I'm on your side and think you're a smart cookie and all that, but mind control is a stretch. Like a Cody-level stretch."

"Okay, so maybe it's not mind control *exactly*, but hear me out. Lawson, Wordswright, and this computer programming thing are using this jumbled up language—"

"Mumbo jumbo to be exact."

"I mean, it sounds like it could make sense, but if you think about it, it doesn't quite. Anyway, they're using it to manhandle us into being obedient and not ask any questions. But my brother's language is about real basics. I mean, it makes more sense and even rhymes *for a reason*. Like how ⟨ᔑ⟩ [**fu** *me*], ⟨ᖇ⟩ [**bu** *you*], ⟨ᡰᐱ⟩ [**bru** *friend*], and ⟨ᡰᐃ⟩ [**brU** *peace*] are all related and they sound that way."

"So not like *conform, enforce, popcorn, unicorn,* or whatever."

"Exactly. One is trying to control us, but maybe the other is somehow helping us control *ourselves*."

"I could get on board with that," said Bea.

14

The impact of the computer programming sessions spread gradually like a behavioral plague. Within a month, the subjects had become one large homogenous group that moved about the Academy with all the excitement of a group of sleepwalkers. Conversation had become a rarity, unless it was to mumble snatches of the lyrics found in Lawson's music, which had now evolved into something even creepier than the screed the AI had blurted out during Verity's first programming session:

We adore order . . . Disorder's abhorred. We adore order . . . It's the way of our horde.

Almost no one acted out, and even the ratter-boxes, formerly Lawson and Payne's favorite Friday afternoon task, had nothing to offer, sitting empty and unused. Delinquency was at an all-time low.

"Looks like our work here is done." Re-educator Wolff was leaning against the mess hall wall a few feet from where Verity and her friends were sitting, all silently working their way through the tasteless oatmeal. His voice carried across the room, competing only with the relentless background noise of Lawson's music, which Verity was doing her utmost to ignore.

Boer, sipping from a tall metal coffee mug, snorted. "Well, there are still a few outliers . . ." She trained her piercingly sharp gaze on Verity.

Verity cast her own eyes downward, timing her spoonfuls of oatmeal to match those of the other students. Her back to the PackHunters, Bea raised an eyebrow in Verity's direction.

"⼤ ⼂⼂⼂⼂ ⼂⼂ nu iOv fnu [*They see us*]," said Verity.

Meeting Verity's eyes, Bea began mimicking the sluggish movements of the students around her. Both tried not to flinch as one of Pyrite's screams ripped through the mess hall. Without the usual chatter and hubbub from the students to drown them out, the parrot's shrieks were even more spine chilling.

Other than Bea, only Em and maybe Cody seemed unaffected by the AI. Krystal, on the other hand, was decidedly not herself. She no longer bantered with Bea about her "rich girl" airs, and it felt like weeks since she'd mocked Lawson's music. That first night, she'd jokingly attempted to dance to it on her way back to their dorm room, but after a programming session the following day, it was as though she no longer even heard it.

Verity desperately wished there was something she could do, but she was focused on getting through the days without succumbing to Lawson and Wordswright's reprogramming efforts herself. It was like they told people on airplanes: put on your own oxygen mask before helping others.

"Special meal for Subjects Truman, Foxley, and de Grey." Susie Slaw sidled by with a small container of pastries. She passed one to Verity, then one to Bea and Cody. Cody waved hers away with an impatient hand, but Susie Slaw shook her head.

"Lawson insists."

As it turned out, this wasn't all Lawson had in store for them. The three subjects were each given an adjusted curriculum that consisted mostly of alternating sessions with Wordswright and Craniale, the terrifying HeadShrinker Verity had encountered on her first day at the Academy.

Cody was the first to break.

One evening, on the way back from the mess hall, she grabbed Verity's arm. Glassy-eyed and trance-like, she was reciting rhymed couplets that were by now very familiar to Verity.

"Conforming is norming; in norming we're free. Orders bring order, no questions from me . . . "

Verity snatched her arm from Cody's clawing grip. "Cody? Are you . . ."

She wasn't even sure what she was asking. Cody obviously wasn't okay. She looked askance at Bea. You weren't meant to wake a sleepwalker, but Verity wasn't sure if the same rule of thumb applied here.

Bea had no such reservations. She snapped her fingers in front of Cody's nose, following up with some sharp, rousing claps. "Whoa, girl! Are you in there? Earth to Cody!"

When this didn't work, she put two fingers in her mouth and gave an ear-splitting whistle almost as loud as Pyrite's screams. This got Cody's attention. Her eyes widened, and the expression returned to her face.

"Oh, man. Thanks for hitting reset. I think I was, like, stuck in some sort of loop."

Verity glanced around, then pulled Cody over to a corner she hoped was far enough away from the ubiquitous surveillance cameras. "Are you okay? What did they do to you?"

Cody trembled. She scratched at her wild hair, which was in desperate need of washing. "What didn't they? They're force-feeding me that poison food . . . I haven't slept in days . . . everywhere I go that creepy music is playing . . . and those programming sessions are total sensory overload . . . I just *can't* anymore!"

All of this came out in one huge, unpunctuated burst that left Cody gasping for breath. It took her a few seconds to compose herself enough to add: "How are you . . . coping? I mean, you seem fine."

Tight lipped, Bea gave Verity a warning look.

Verity hesitated. She wondered whether the light language could somehow help Cody, too. But she wasn't sure whether it was worth the risk. If Cody was already under Lawson and Wordswright's influence, she might use the language as leverage against Verity and Bea.

Bea cleared her throat. "Truman, we should go. Payne could be here any minute."

"Hold on." Verity frowned, thinking about what her family would do. She thought about the time her mom had put her job on the line defending an employee against a serious yet unfounded complaint from an influential patron. Or how her dad would write supportive letters of recommendation for people in recovery who were getting their lives back together. Or how Silas would risk life and limb to rescue orphaned birds, stray kittens—and once even a baby rat.

She glanced around at the surveillance cameras again, making sure her back was to them. She snuck her crib sheet out of her pocket and cupped it in her palm.

"Hey, you've got something on your collar." She reached toward Cody's shirt. As Cody automatically did the same, their hands collided, and Verity slipped Cody the crib sheet.

Cody fumblingly slid the sheet up her sleeve, giving Verity a quizzical look.

"The symbols on there are like the chemical elements of the periodic table," Verity whispered. "Only they combine to make words of a language. When Wordswright turns on the computer, focus totally on these."

"Thanks." Cody exhaled in relief.

"Okay. We're done here now." Bea's tone was snappy. She obviously prioritized self-preservation over helping others, and Verity was suddenly second-guessing her efforts. She tried not to think about the time her dad had written a letter of recommendation for a guy who'd been fired on his first day for "unbecoming conduct." The first thing she'd do when they got back to their bunk room was get rid of any evidence of the symbols.

"C'mon, Truman."

The two hurried back to their bunk room, ignoring the shifting stare of the cameras and television screens. But even when the bunk room door clicked behind them, Verity didn't feel safe.

Krystal was staring Verity down, large, dark eyes piercing unnervingly right through her. There was no way she'd seen the exchange with Cody, but Verity couldn't shake the idea. She kept thinking about the notes hidden in her bunk bed. She had to destroy them, and quickly, just in case.

"Everything okay?" asked Em, from the top bunk. "You seem shaken. Like, more than usual, which is saying something, because Verity, you're one giant stress ball. Seriously, it gets *so* much easier once you accept that we're all just pawns in some giant universal game and that we're all going to end up as worm food."

"Speak for yourself," said Bea haughtily. "The worms aren't getting any of this."

"I'm fine," said Verity. "I'm just . . . trying to figure out how much time I have to shower."

"*That's* what's got you stressed?" Em gave a low, lazy whistle. "You should really talk to someone about that."

"I'll book an appointment with Craniale asap." The joke was unconvincing even to her own ears.

Verity made a show of gathering her towel and a change of clothes, surreptitiously bundling her notes about Silas's language into them. She went to stand, but as she did, she spotted the symbols she'd written on her bunk. She swore under her breath.

Bea came to the rescue.

"Hey, Truman. Nice squiggles you've got there. Art's not your best subject, huh? Here." Bea produced a pen and climbed up on Verity's bunk, adding lines here and blocking out circles there to transform the alien symbols into little stick figures and characters.

Em wriggled around on her bed, peering over the side to get a better look at Bea's efforts. "You should get a job as a tattoo cover-up artist. My brother's always looking for help."

Bea snorted. "Sure, that's definitely on my list of career goals."

Verity was on her way out of the room and didn't hear the rest of the exchange. She kept her eyes down and the towel hugged to her body as she followed the blue dotted line to the showers. One of the PackHunters passed her, moving with the sinuous grace of a predator, but paid her no mind. She didn't realize that she'd been holding her breath until it came out in a single, wheezy gasp. She sounded like Em after their morning exercises.

The bathrooms were busy as usual, but she managed to claim a shower stall in the far corner. Locking the door, she turned on the water, waiting for it to reach temperature before running her notes beneath it. The ink on the page blotted and wavered before dissolving. A few moments later and the pages themselves disintegrated in her hands, turning into pale clumps that gradually disappeared down the drain.

———◆———

Verity's relief was short lived. The next morning, the klaxons were accompanied by a flashing message on the television screens: morning exercises had been canceled due to extreme circumstances.

"I mean, no complaints, but why the change of plans?" asked Bea.

"No idea," said Verity. "But for Mr. Law and Order to mix things up, it must be pretty serious."

Above them, Em was slowly rolling out of bed.

"Mmmph," she moaned, rubbing her eyes. "Daytime is the *worst.*"

Krystal, on the other hand, was silently and methodically dressing, moving to the rhythm of an invisible metronome. She made no eye contact with the other girls. Verity's stomach gnawed at itself, unsettled. She wished more than anything that her family would appear at the gates of the Academy, ready to spring her and take her home.

Maybe her coded letter would reach Silas before it was too late.

"C'mon. Let's see what's up." Bea held the door for Verity. Uncrossing her fingers and squashing down her creeping anxiety, Verity followed after her, sticking to the marked lines. Now wasn't the time to get reprimanded over a minor infraction.

"Whoa," she said as they turned a corner. Bea shared her sentiments, but less politely.

There, scrawled all over the walls in enormous, shaky letters, were dozens of symbols from the light language, roughly spray-painted in the same orange that marked the way to the computer programming lab. Some stood alone, while others had been pieced together in combinations that Verity hadn't seen before:

[wom O . . . Ywom U . . . vyiv iU
Strong feeling . . . weak mind . . . hide understanding]

"Looks like someone got into Grimes's closet." Em had come behind them. "What *is* all that? That's the sketchiest tagging I've ever seen." Slowly, she tried to spell out the symbols of the wall, pronouncing them like the English equivalents they most closely resembled. "N-P-O-S-8-S-V-triangle-S? Huh? That makes *no* sense and don't tell me that's my processing disorder."

Here and there the patterns of symbols broke down, interspersed with strident commentary in English:

The SIN-onym of homonyms!

Bea raised a perfect eyebrow. "Well, it wasn't me, and no way was it you. So . . ."

Verity pressed her lips together. Cody.

Em was still baffled. "Is it . . . a license plate number? Or, like, gamer speak?"

Taking a deep breath, Bea translated the graffiti:

"Something about '*strong feeling . . . weak mind . . .*'"

"*Hides understanding?*" finished Verity.

"Deep," said Em. "What language is that? Dothraki?"

Behind them, the subjects were starting to pile up on the marked line. Lingering much longer would draw attention.

Pressed along by the crowd, Verity and Bea continued toward the quadrangle, where Lawson, Payne, and Grimes stood surrounded by cleaning carts. Commercial-sized bottles, sprayers, and canisters were arranged in neat rows, the smell of bleach and artificial pine sweeping cloyingly through the crisp morning air. The stench was a far cry from the fresh, woodsy aroma of Verity's last family camping trip.

"*In the name of the law . . . !*" bellowed Lawson.

"*And the order, and the reformed mind!*" the subjects chanted in return.

"*Obey what I say . . . !*"

"*It's the civilized way!*"

"As you can see, we have a situation." Lawson's clipped, precise voice rang out across the quadrangle, where the subjects stood to attention in their neat rows. The pervasive music played at low volume, creating a discomforting soundtrack. "The culprit has been apprehended and taken in for re-education. But for your safety, all bunk rooms are presently being searched."

Verity's skin crawled as Lawson's deformed gaze fixed on her, his left eye swimming within its brain-like maze of scar tissue. She had been right to destroy her notes and gave silent thanks to her intuition. Although if she had listened to Bea's misgivings about Cody, there probably would have been no need. She felt guilty at the thought.

"Additional security will also be added. And I hope I do not have to remind you of the power of reporting on your peers. Surveillance—"

"—serves security," finished the subjects in a monotone.

"Now, some of the TaskForce assignments will be diverted so that we can prioritize this egregious example of a misdemeanor. Jobs has the name lists."

Neither Verity nor Bea was surprised to find they were on the graffiti cleanup TaskForce. Nor were they surprised to note that Cody was nowhere to be seen.

15

Verity and Bea kept a low profile over the next few days. Thanks to the efforts of the TaskForce, only the faintest outline of the graffiti remained, but it served as a constant reminder to remain vigilant against whatever Lawson and Wordswright were attempting to achieve with their computer programming sessions. This was more easily said than done. Even though she had taken to reciting phrases from the light language like they were a rosary, Verity worried she was beginning to succumb. Lawson had assigned her to a variety of extra tasks outside of her regular classes, and she was feeling the effects. Being physically and mentally exhausted made it that much harder to stand firm, even when she knew that she had to.

Unsurprisingly, Verity's name was down for trash duty that week. For something that was supposed to be a lottery system, her name came up a lot. Still, she kept her complaints to herself, going about her duties quietly and efficiently to avoid drawing attention to herself. Unlike the previous times, Susie Slaw showed no interest in Verity. She banged about in the back of the kitchen while Verity scraped down the subjects' trays and gathered their muffin wrappers. Maybe Slaw had finally been written up for the food she had been smuggling off the school premises. Or maybe the cook had just been banned from speaking to her.

Verity was carrying two enormous trash bags by their knotted tops when someone smacked into her with such force that she almost toppled backward. So much for the way-finding lines.

"Hey, watch where—" But it was pointless to carry on: the boy she had crashed into was Casper Grimes, the custodian's shy, silent son. As Casper held out his hands in apology, Verity noticed the slip of paper tucked between his thumb and the palm of his right hand.

Casper made a show of helping her collect the bags. As he did so, he passed the paper to Verity, who tucked it into the sleeve of her uniform. She desperately wanted to read it but would have to wait until she was somewhere safe.

"Sorry," she said loudly, hoping Payne hadn't seen the interaction from his MonitorRoom.

Casper sidled off back to his cottage, chin tilted down and eyes watchfully seeking mice to add to his collection.

The paper felt hot and raw in Verity's sleeve, scratching insistently at her skin as she hauled the trash bags to the dumpster. But shirking her duties would only draw more attention, so she patiently carried out another two loads of trash before waving goodnight to Susie Slaw and hurrying back toward her bunk room.

She had barely set foot outside the mess hall when a shadow fell in front of her, interrupting her passage. Lawson's tall, thin aspect gave him away immediately. Then there was the way he held his head, tipping the scarred side forward as though to force everyone he encountered to acknowledge it. He was like a Halloween costume brought to life.

"Law and order!" He left no time for Verity to respond before barreling on:

"Subject Truman! My office."

Verity tried to swallow, but her throat was as dry as the surrounding desert. "I was just on my way back to my bunk room to wash up," she blurted. "I've been on trash duty—"

"That is the least of my concerns, Subject."

He directed her to follow him, which she did, walking meekly in his wake.

Lawson's quarters were as she remembered: gray and dull and tidy, with all the personality of an elephant's hide. The only bright spot in all the muted gloom was Pyrite, who was loud in both color and tone. His shrieks punctured the air along with Verity's eardrums, but it seemed that he had learned a new phrase or two along the way:

"*Squawk* . . . Law-and-*order!*" he screamed. Verity flinched.

Lawson produced a sheaf of papers and waved them at Verity.

"I suspect you know what this is all about," he said.

Verity played dumb. "Sir?"

"You have been cheating in your computer programming sessions. I do not know how you are managing it, but I know it is true. You, Subject Bea Foxley, and perhaps Subject Em Petti, although with her it is hard to be certain. She has other pathologies that may be affecting our work."

"Cheating's a strong accusation, sir."

Lawson's cold eyes narrowed. He jutted his chin as he doubled down on his argument. "Every other subject is demonstrating the expected outcomes. You are not, which leads me to believe that something is awry."

Verity feigned confusion. "Do you mean we're passing or failing, sir?"

"Failing. Spectacularly." Lawson tapped the sheaf of papers for emphasis.

"Huh. But . . . if we *were* cheating, wouldn't we be passing instead of failing?"

Lawson gaped, clearly flummoxed. But he recovered quickly, snapping back to his usual military precision. He had been bested by Verity before, and he wasn't about to let it happen again.

"You and Foxley will be separated until we get to the bottom of this. You will each have your own Individual Behavior Adjustment Cell—iBAC for short—much like Subject de Grey."

Verity bit her lip. This explained Cody's absence.

"Anyway, the fact that the two of you have responded to the programming in the way that you have—"

Or haven't, thought Verity.

"—indicates that something is afoot. I am not one to believe in coincidences unless they are coincidences by design."

Which would not make them coincidences at all. Verity tasted blood. She had bitten down so hard that her lip had split. Her hands trembled by her side. She forced herself to remain calm: she had to play her cards right here. It was time to depart from her family's usual open, upfront way of dealing with problems: she had to wait for the right moment to mount a sneak attack.

"In addition to that, you will be given a personal sleep and meal regimen, and you will continue to participate in extra HeadShrinker sessions with Craniale, as well as in extra programming sessions with Wordswright. Assuming his schedule allows with his new contractual obligations."

Verity nodded, her head whirling. Lawson was determined to use every resource possible to ensure that she and Bea submitted. But even more unnerving was the fact that apparently Wordswright's efforts now extended beyond the Ersatz Academy. She wondered what kind of contract he had signed and with whom. If the reform school was just the beginning, who was next, and what was the end goal? It was terrifying to think about.

Pyrite screamed, snapping Verity out of her reverie. She rubbed her ears, half expecting them to be bleeding.

"I fully expect we will see some improvement." Lawson's tone was pointed. "The school has a special demonstration event coming up, and it will not do to have a failure on our hands. But I am sure that will not be an issue."

Verity tried to meet the gaze that lurked within that deformed face but couldn't. Instead, she closed her eyes and tried to breathe.

[**fum ogU Uc wom** *My mind is strong*]

16

When Lawson was done with Verity, he called Payne to take her to her Individual Behavior Adjustment Cell, or what the rest of the world called "solitary confinement." The brutish man arrived momentarily, flicking his keychain against his thigh. The look he gave Verity was one of outright disdain, and it remained in place as he led her through more corridors than she had previously thought existed at the Academy.

"You again," he scoffed in his perpetually hoarse voice. "Bit of a troublemaker, huh?"

It had taken weeks, but apparently Payne recognized her now.

"So I keep hearing."

"Pick up those feet. I've got monitors to get back to. And it's not like walking's so hard for a kid. Wait until you're my age."

Given how things were going, Verity wasn't sure she'd make it to his age.

"This is you." Payne stopped outside a gray door that looked no different from any of the others in the building. He swiped his fob against its security reader and swung the iBAC door open, revealing a cramped room that housed nothing more than a bed, a desk, and a toilet.

Verity's belongings sat on the bed, mussed and disorderly. Someone had undoubtedly rummaged through them.

"*Obedience in Service to Civility!*" blared a poster pinned beneath the now-familiar Academy Rules.

"There's no handle on the inside of the door." Verity felt extremely discomfited.

"Why would there be? You're not going anywhere without our say-so. If you need out, just smile at the camera." Payne pointed at a wall-mounted camera whose plastic eye watched her every move.

Verity gave it a half-hearted wave, her stomach sinking.

Payne rapped his knuckles on the wall next to the Academy Rules. "And here are the rules, just in case you forget 'em. Which seems likely. Well, good luck."

Payne yanked the door closed behind him, leaving Verity alone in her glorified prison cell. The unsettling strains of Lawson's ambient music rose and fell in the background.

Words we obey . . . words we obey . . . words we obey.

Not today, thought Verity, making a rude gesture at the posted rules.

The first thing she did was test the range of the camera by moving about the room and watching it swivel to follow her. There was a small section around the toilet that seemed safe, and she crouched down, pulling out the paper Casper had given her. Damp and wrinkled from being in her sleeve, it was an envelope containing a hastily scribbled message from Silas. Casper had come through, just as Krystal had promised.

The message was written in the light language:

≡⋏ [jYtu *Sis*,]

⎯ [fnu te-tAv. *We will come.*]

[etgUrv iUI! *Study iUI.*]

[tiOrv rUt **bUv.iUI** Ud cana-bUvd! *Look for **bUv.iUI** on the web of the universe.*]

[fnu viO-tAv nu fAvm viOvs. *We will show them a new sign.*]

[fnu vIO-tAv nu fAvm I. *We will make them hear a new sound.*]

[fnu vetgU-tAv nu vetgUz dUt AgUv. *We will teach them a lesson to remember.*]

Silas

There were some combinations Verity couldn't quite decode, but the thought that the Wild Boys were on their way changed everything. Knowing there was someone out there who was still on her side changed everything.

Verity hugged the letter to her chest, fighting the urge to burst into tears: of relief or fear, she wasn't quite sure.

———

Later, on her bed, Lawson's endlessly droning music needling into her mind, Verity found herself mulling over a few of the less familiar phrases in Silas's message.

⟨symbols⟩ [et-gUrv iUI! *Study iUI!*] was the first one. *Move-toward-know* ⟨symbols⟩ [iUI] . . . ? *Light-mind-sound*, she puzzled out. The mind made a sound?

Verity's had certainly been sounding off enough these past few weeks. It must be referring to Silas's light language. It was right there in the next line, too: ⟨symbols⟩ [bUv.iUI].

This was the one Viveo had shown her the first time she had garbage duty but hadn't been able to figure out. At least now she had the second half worked out, even if the first part was still a mystery, not to mention the "web of the universe." It almost sounded like Viveo wanted her to Google something, but that didn't make sense.

She wished Bea were here: the other girl would figure it out in a snap. Although Bea probably had other, way worse things on her mind right now, like trying to stay sane in her own iBAC. She hoped her friend was as tough as she made out. Tougher than Cody at least. Verity felt sick when she thought about what had happened with Cody. It was her fault: she'd given Cody the iUI crib sheet. If she hadn't, they wouldn't be in the situation. Or maybe, if she'd just given it to Cody earlier . . .

Tearing herself away from that line of thought, she turned her attention back to Silas's message and the other phrase she wasn't quite sure about.

[fnu vetgU-tAv nu vetgUz dUt AgUv. *We will teach them a lesson to remember.*]

Verity had figured out what it meant, but not what Silas meant by it.

A lesson to remember . . . She mulled over it, but her thoughts were interrupted by Lawson's ever-present music.

Orders bring order . . . *Words we obey* . . .

Verity sat up straight, her mind working overtime. Lawson, Wordswright and the AI were using language to manipulate the subjects. But what if those same tactics could be turned back on them?

Verity awoke with a foggy feeling in her head. Lawson's creepy music seemed quite a few decibels louder than the previous night, and she wondered whether it had messed with her sleep.

At least her new routine didn't begin as early as in her previous bunk room. It was well after six when breakfast arrived through a slot in her door, and she was apparently no longer a participant in the Academy's morning calisthenics program. Showering was also streamlined. With her bathroom access now revoked, she had to wash up in the sink built into the top of the toilet. This was easier than showering while camping but much less appealing than rinsing off beneath a bucket hanging over a floor of pine needles. Maybe because she didn't have a say in the matter. Not to mention that there were no security cameras in nature.

Having worked her way through her tasteless breakfast, she wandered aimlessly back and forth in the room, trying to ignore the omnipresent music and wondering when someone would come cart her off for a session with Wordswright or Craniale. She wondered how Bea and Cody were faring. The guilt that punched at the thought was all the impetus she needed to get to work.

Hiding herself out of sight of the camera, she started writing a message to Cody. She was almost done when the light on the door flickered green, indicating someone was outside. Hiding the note in her uniform, she rushed to take a seat at the gray desk, hoping that the visitor hadn't heard her scrambling efforts to get from one end of the room to the other.

Fortunately, the visitor wasn't Craniale or Lawson, but Constance Grimes. She rattled in, looking as tired as ever, and pushing her mop bucket and cart before her. Verity had a feeling that Grimes's day-to-day conditions weren't much better than the subjects'.

"Hey," she said quietly, with a furtive glance at the surveillance camera.

Grimes responded with only the faintest shake of her graying head. She quickly scrubbed down the toilet and sink, then set a small bar of soap and a tube of toothpaste on a plain wall rack. Verity had been right about the shower situation. At least there was no one else around to judge her on her personal hygiene.

Realizing Grimes was about to move on to the next room, Verity dashed over to the toilet area, gesturing wildly at the custodian to return.

"Could you get me another roll of toilet paper?" Verity hefted the current roll in her hand. She slipped the letter she had just written into the cardboard tube inside. "There's barely anything left on this one."

Grimes pursed her lips but did as Verity asked. As the two exchanged their rolls, Grimes clamped a thumb over Verity's hidden note and nodded. Then she hurried from the room, leaving Verity alone once more.

Her sessions with Craniale and Wordswright aside, Verity spent every waking minute trying to imitate what she remembered of the mood and movements of the brainwashed subjects. She sat at her desk for hours at a time, staring ahead and attempting to clear her mind. Verity had never been one for meditation, and Lawson's weirdly dissonant music didn't really put her in the mood for it. The closest she got to finding her inner calm was by tracing the iUI symbols on the skin of her forearm.

[fum ogU Uc wom *My mind is strong*]

Verity lost sense of time. Perhaps a week had passed, perhaps more. Her vision swam with the symbols that had become her solace throughout the endless hours spent alone. The closest she got to conversation was her brutal programming sessions with Wordswright and his computer. On the plus side, she was becoming increasingly familiar with iUI and could now put together words and phrases. Playing with the language was like coaxing out a poem: there was a natural beauty to it and its relationship between sound and meaning. Slowly, her meditative efforts took her beyond herself, until she found herself reflecting on iUI and its place in the world—and hers.

pAm rim, can kim kan, iOvAm canUm i,
[*Before—gleaming, all-starry sky, seeing universal light.*]

fAm yim, can yIm gan, tIOvAm at brUm yI.
[*Now—dark, all silent, inner space, listening to peaceful silence.*]

———

Just when Verity had resigned herself to a lifetime spent in the iBAC unit, the door lock clicked green, opening to reveal Lawson. Verity attempted to stand, but her knees were stiff from sitting for hours on end. She tried not to show her discomfort, keeping her face artfully blank and her movements small and slow to mimic the other subjects'.

"*Law and order!*"

"*Know no border,*" droned Verity.

Lawson's ravaged visage was triumphant; he regarded her with a sort of sneering glee. She was apparently playing her role acceptably well. Maybe if she ever escaped from the Academy, she'd join the drama club at school.

"I see you have rejoined us, Subject Truman." Lawson made no move to step into the room. Like any child-loathing adult, he maintained a buffer between himself and the subjects wherever possible. "It seems that your mind has finally become capable of seeing and thinking the way that it should. The civil, expected way: orderly and organized. Free thinking is frivolous and leads to insecurity. Open minds invite doubt."

"Open minds invite doubt…" Verity's voice sounded strange to her ears.

"But now the threat has subsided. You are one among many, part of a single voice and a single mind. You are part of the *Gestalt*! It is a feeling like no other, and I do not see why anyone would seek to be anything else. The *other* is where confusion lies. *Questions* are where ambiguity arises. Now you can enjoy freedom from frivolity and security in civility."

"Freedom from frivolity," repeated Verity reverently. "Security in civility."

"No more will you have to worry about what is the right way. Now you can enjoy the freedom of being told what is and what must be."

"*Obedience in service to civility*," mumbled Verity, quoting the poster on the wall. It was becoming less of an act. Despite all of her efforts to stand up against Lawson's regime, there was something liberating about leaving the decision-making to someone else. She remembered how she'd felt when her parents had spoken with the mayor in her place: the sense of relief when they had done the thinking and debating, reducing her role to merely accepting the consequences. Everything was easier when it was decided for you. There was so much more room in your own mind when it wasn't constantly weighing and deliberating. But then, room for *what*, exactly? Verity faltered. Wasn't the difficulty the whole point? It was why people had evolved problem-solving minds in the first place.

"Payne will take you back to your bunk room, where you can reconvene with the others. Some of them, at least. Subject Foxley has proven rather less receptive to our re-education than you, but we have our ways. It's only a matter of time. And intervention. Payne?"

Payne's broad, jeering face materialized from the other end of the corridor.

"Subject," he sneered. "Ready to follow me?"

17

Verity's old bunk room was not the same without Bea. Krystal had become a blank, unemotional mannequin, no longer the font of snarky quips and incisive commentator on class issues Verity secretly admired. Instead, she spent her time staring blankly off into space, every now and then mouthing along to a hidden lyric in Lawson's music. Verity felt so unnerved by this transformation that she didn't even try to engage Krystal. She just tried to stay out of her space as much as possible.

Em was harder to figure out. She had taken to hiding out on her bunk bed and kept an extremely low, silent profile the rest of the time. Every now and then, Verity would catch dark eyes staring over at her. She wondered whether Em was weighing the same question Verity was: *has she been turned?*

It turned out that pretty much all of the subject body had been. Collectively, they had become as gray and featureless as the Academy itself. What little humanity had occasionally broken through before Verity had been sent to solitary was now completely repressed. There was silence in the hallways save for the orderly shuffle of feet, and the subjects' responses to Lawson's cadence calls were now perfectly synchronized, all exactly in time with the subtle rhythm of the inescapable background music.

"*Freedom—*"

"*from frivolity!*"

"*Security—*"

"*Breeds civility!*"

"*What follows—*"

"*Will lead!*"

"*We need—*"

"*To heed our creed!*"

It was creepy how everyone was behaving so uncannily on script. The re-educators sat back during their classes and let the subjects recite the answers without prompting. The only break in the monotony was when a subject occasionally blacked out or got stuck in a loop like Cody had. When this happened, Payne and the PackHunters would drag the unfortunate creature off to the Infirmary.

Verity first saw this happen during dinner a few days after she'd been let out of solitary. The subject walking several yards ahead on the dotted line to her bunk room suddenly halted, then began rocking back and forth on the spot, moaning the now-familiar creed at ever-increasing volume.

"*Conforming is norming . . . Orders bring order . . . Words we obey . . . Mean more than they say . . .*"

The girl grabbed and snatched at those passing by, her tone desperate and begging: "*In the name of law and order we need to heed our creed!*"

Verity backed up, bumping into a couple of subjects who had been following behind her on the bottom line. She apologized, but to no end.

The other subjects ignored her, pressing forward and stepping over the frenzied student who knelt in the way of their intended destinations.

Verity stood frozen. It seemed inhumane to leave the girl there; she could be gravely injured. But coming to her aid would undo all of Verity's efforts to pretend that she was under the spell of the AI.

Was it worth sacrificing this one girl so she could continue with her plan and eventually free the other subjects? Or would ignoring the pull of her values be something she could simply never return from? Horrible things happened when people didn't stand up against those in power. You only had to glance through the history books to find more evidence than you ever wanted.

Verity started forward, intent on helping the girl, but a hand clamped forcibly on her upper arm. The pressure was going to leave a bruise.

"What—" she began, turning to find herself face to face with Bea.

"Not now." Bea marched her past the fallen girl and toward the bathrooms, which were mercifully empty. She herded Verity into a shower stall and turned on the water. They huddled in the corner of the stall to avoid getting drenched. Verity hoped that the commotion out in the hallway had obscured their escape from the all-pervasive security cameras.

"When did they let you out?" whispered Verity over the sound of the running faucet. She resisted the urge to give her friend a hug: Bea wasn't the affectionate type.

"A couple of hours ago. Lawson couldn't resist bragging about how you'd fallen under the AI's spell, and I knew you had to be faking it. So I did the same. It took a while to convince him, but here I am."

"It's getting worse every day. I don't know how far they're going to take things."

"I know. We need to do something. But we can't get found out. We need to blend in, and that means no heroics. No matter how much it tears you up inside."

Verity hissed out a long, slow breath. "And it is. I feel like I'm withering away in this place. But I have an idea. Lawson's soiree is in a few days."

"I know." Bea was idly tracing Silas's symbols in the steam that was collecting on the side of the shower stall. "He was gloating over having the entire subject body 'rehabilitated' and ready for a demonstration to his guests. Nice guy, that one. I can totally see why he got into education."

Verity grimaced. "It's all about the kids, huh? Anyway, the soiree is a big deal for him. Which means it's going to be a major distraction."

"Can confirm," said Bea. "Fancy events take a whole lot of planning and coordination. They should've asked me to help out, for real. Anyway, I'm listening."

Verity leaned forward. "I'm thinking it's the perfect chance to get *out of here.*"

"A jailbreak?" Bea was amused. "I mean, sure. Too easy. Just some locks, walls, fences, surveillance cameras, and miles of desert to contend with. But go on."

"All we need is a computer, a programmer, and Silas's language . . ."

18

The night of the soiree arrived both quickly and at a glacial pace. As one of the only students apparently unaffected by the AI, Verity found every minute leading up to the event intolerably dull. She had to work to blend in with the other students, mimicking their emotionless movements and speaking only when her classes required it. The effort of it all, along with the weight of what was to come, caused the hours to stretch on. But somehow the soiree marched ever closer, until all of a sudden it was a mere few hours away.

When the klaxons sounded at 5 a.m. that Friday morning, Verity jolted in her bed, her heart thrumming a frantic beat. She closed her eyes momentarily, reciting the calming, harmonious words that during her time in solitary had become her personal mantra:

pAm rim, can kim kan, iOvAm canUm i,

[*Before—gleaming, all-starry sky, seeing universal light.*]

fAm yim, can yIm gan, tIOvAm at brUm yI,

[*Now—dark, all silent, inner space, listening to peaceful silence.*]

By the time she eventually climbed out of bed, Krystal and Em had already left for morning calisthenics exercises in the quadrangle. Over the past few weeks these had changed in nature, becoming less athletic and more military in style. The subjects now marched up and down the quadrangle in eerie unison, their arms swinging precisely and their boots thwacking against the sunburned asphalt.

Watching it, not to mention participating in it, gave Verity the chills. She couldn't shake the idea that there was more to the reprogramming regimen than simply reshaping the behavior of the subjects. There was something longer-term and more sinister at play: the transformation of children not just into bastions of proper conduct but into a youth militia.

Verity didn't get any further with that thought. The green light on the door flashed, and the bunk room door swung open to reveal Payne's hulking form.

"You two." He jabbed a bulbous finger at Verity and Bea in turn. His fingernail had been bitten to the quick. It was a wonder it wasn't infected. "You're coming with me. To the iBAC units."

Verity almost protested but caught herself just in time. Any sort of outburst would prove that Payne and Lawson were correct in their suspicions about Bea and Verity. They needed to stay the course and behave exactly as any other subject would.

"Yes, sir." Verity's posture was perfectly ramrod.

Bea followed her lead. "Yes, sir," she repeated, sounding like a cadet. Verity hoped Payne didn't catch her quizzical glance.

"ɜ| +୨ [tAc rØm *It will be okay*],"

Verity whispered as they filed out behind Payne, signing along simultaneously.

"ᴎ ᖴℂ⑤ [fu trOv *I hope*]."

Payne stomped through the corridors, his wide frame blocking out the view ahead. Verity wondered where he got the time to work out, given he spent most of his life sitting at his MonitorRoom desk. Maybe he did push-ups every time he reprimanded a subject.

"Tonight is a big night for Lawson," barked Payne. "And for the Academy. The most important people from the Oasis will all be here. So we're not taking any chances. You two are going away for the night. And the loopers as well. Lawson wants people seeing the results, not the flaws."

"Yes, sir," said Verity and Bea simultaneously.

"That's what I like to hear. All right, this one's you; and you're in here." Payne ushered the two friends into neighboring iBAC units, slamming their doors behind them. When the light above the door lock in Verity's room flashed red, it took every ounce of her strength not to scream. They had been so close. Now what?

pAm rim, can kim kan, iOvAm canUm i,

[*Before—gleaming, all-starry sky, seeing universal light*],

fAm yim, can yIm gan, tIOvAm at brUm yI,

[*Now—dark, all silent, inner space, listening to peaceful silence*], she whispered, over and over, trying to find within herself the peaceful silence she spoke of.

What seemed like an eternity later, the light on the door turned green. Verity had no need to take her place at the sad gray desk in the cramped room; she was already there, staring at the wall as she chanted her iUI mantra to herself. She wasn't even going to turn to acknowledge her visitor, but it was fortunate she did. Because it wasn't Lawson or Payne or Craniale, or any of the other terrible Academy employees.

It was Casper Grimes, his mother's keycard clutched tightly in his bony hand. He motioned at her to follow him, and she hauled herself out of her chair. She had pins and needles in her legs.

"Wait." She nudged her head toward the security camera.

Casper made a placating gesture with his hands. Verity assumed this meant that Payne had somehow been pulled away from his MonitorRoom duties.

"Did your mom put you up to this?"

Maybe as a mom watching all this go down, Candace Grimes had decided enough was enough.

Casper shrugged, then folded Verity's fingers around the keycard. Pointing to the door opposite her room, then one a few rooms down, he awkwardly waved, then slipped off down the corridor.

Taking a deep breath, Verity crept over to Bea's room. A flick of the keycard, a flash of green, and Bea was standing before her.

"She returns!" she crowed, her voice dropping in volume as Verity gave her a warning look. "What gives? What's going on? How'd you get out?"

Verity held up the keycard. "Casper."

Bea raised her eyebrows. "That I would not have guessed. Like, ever. Are we rescuing Cody, too? Or are we going to make a peaceful exit? Kidding, kidding," she added, at Verity's sharp expression.

Verity swiped the keycard over the sensor to the door that Casper had indicated.

The heavy door swung open, revealing a wild-haired and wild-eyed Cody de Grey. She stared at her visitors in disbelief.

"I thought I was going to be a lifer," she whispered. "How'd you get out?"

"Filed-down spoon," deadpanned Bea. "But what you *should* be asking is 'Did you bring a comb?'"

Cody rolled her eyes, then froze. "Wait. Did you hear that? It was some sort of . . . whistle or something."

Verity cocked her head, listening. Then realization dawned on her, and she clapped her hands over her mouth. Tears pricked at the corners of her eyes, and she grabbed Bea's arm. "Silas. Silas and the Wild Boys. They made it."

"Who's that?" Cody was suspicious as always, though Verity didn't blame her. "Are they on our side?"

"Silas? Definitely." Verity felt a sudden rush of gratitude for her brother. What other twelve-year-old kid would trek across the state to rescue his sister from a reform school? Silas was definitely one of a kind, and in all the best ways. "He's the one who . . . taught me the language. Which may just be our ticket out of here."

Cody looked impressed, despite herself. She raised dark eyebrows and gave what was almost a smile. "A celebrity in our midst. So what's the plan?"

"You're the plan. But first we need to get to the programming room."

"Without getting busted," added Bea.

Cody made a face. "This soiree thing has already started, huh?"

As if on cue, the strains of a crowd chatting and laughing drifted over to them, traveling effortlessly down the stark hallways.

"We'll be . . . discreet, I guess?" said Cody, unconvincingly.

They tiptoed along the corridor and around the perimeter of the empty quadrangle toward the mess hall. The parking lot was packed with glossy vehicles, all of them models that Bea would approve of and that Krystal would consider scratching up with a set of keys. But there was no one around: everyone was inside the mess hall, their silhouettes bending and warping in the high windows.

A bird call broke the relative quiet. And not one of Pyrite's screams, either. Grinning despite herself, Verity tried to spot her brother in the quickly dimming light. But the desertscape, with all of its shadows and scrub, made for a surprisingly good hiding place.

Another bird call rang out, then another and another. These were accompanied by coyote yips and wolf howls.

"It's a zoo out here." Bea shuddered.

"No, it's Silas and the Wild Boys taunting Payne. Look." Verity angled her head toward a large, ungainly figure in the near distance. Payne was stomping about, crashing through the desert vegetation and waving his flashlight like a sword. With every animal call he would turn in another direction, taking a few faltering steps before being enticed away in a different direction.

"You almost feel bad for him," said Bea disinterestedly.

"Maybe if there were bear traps out there." Cody angled her chin in contempt. "Although I wouldn't put it past Lawson to booby-trap this place."

As the animal calls faded into the distance, and Payne with them, the movement in the mess hall drew Verity's attention. She rose up on her tiptoes to get a better view.

"What's going on in there?" Her joy at hearing Silas's bird calls suddenly shifted to perturbation as she saw what was going on inside. "Hey, is that . . . Krystal?"

The group crept up to the mess hall, stretching up to see in the windows. Over the past day, the mess hall had been transformed into something quite grand. Ribbons hung from the ceiling in dramatic arcs, authoritative banners were pinned to the walls, and long white cloths covered trestle tables groaning under platters of delicate-looking finger food. Plush seating had been brought in for the occasion, and clusters of well-heeled Oasis residents were reclining with legs crossed, champagne in hand. Event staff wearing a charcoal gray version of the Academy uniform milled around, topping up drinks and offering food.

Lawson and Wordswright, meanwhile, were at the front of the room, standing before an accordion wall that hid what was usually Susie Slaw's kitchen and serving area. Both looked thoroughly impressed with themselves as they listened to the class of subjects begin the demonstration by reciting the creed in precise and practiced unison. Fittingly, Lawson wore a narcissus flower on his lapel. Wordswright was his usual unkempt self, although the mad genius look played well to the crowd he was trying to court.

"*Law and order!*" called Lawson.

"Know no border!" the subjects responded. Krystal was among them, standing at the end of the row closest to them. Her eyes were glazed, her expression dull and lifeless. Em was there, too, a row back and a few places to the right.

"Krystal *and* Em!" whispered Verity.

"Did they get Em?" asked Cody.

Verity and Bea both shrugged. "We're honestly not sure," said Bea. "Either yeah or the girl's a candidate for an Oscar."

After a few minutes of chanting call-and-response slogans at the subjects, Lawson changed tack. He began calling out commands, which the subjects followed seamlessly and as one, like robots responding to programmed requests. They marched back and forth, crossing paths, switching places, and turning sharply on the spot at Lawson's command.

"This is nightmare fodder," muttered Cody.

"A lunatic ballet," added Bea.

"Colorful." Cody was impressed.

Bea smirked. "Why, thanks."

"Now on the diagonal!" rang out Lawson's voice. The subjects moved in a precise diagonal line along the hall.

After a few more such demonstrations, Lawson gestured invitingly at the attendees.

"Who would like to try? There's nothing to fear. The subjects have been precisely trained. Your command is their wish." He sounded extremely satisfied with himself, and Verity felt her loathing for Lawson taking on a new form: a darkness that went beyond hatred and all the way over to intense disgust. It was a terrible feeling and went against everything she believed in, but after what Lawson had put her and the other subjects through, she wasn't inclined to fight it. She was going to use it as fuel to get through this night.

A slender woman in a green dress raised a hand. She had unnaturally straight blond hair and wore thick silver bangles that reminded Verity of handcuffs. "I will." Her voice wavered. The champagne she held in her other hand was clearly not the first of the night. She paused, thinking through a few different scenarios, then giggled. "You, here—kick that one in the shins."

Bea and Verity exchanged a confused look.

Even Lawson stiffened: he obviously hadn't expected this.

"What?!" Verity was agog.

Cody was not. "It's simple. Adults are evil. They love power and control, and they'll exert them in any way they can. That's not even a conspiracy theory. It's human nature."

Bea whistled. "All it takes is a bit of wine, an authoritative voice, and the opportunity, huh?"

The subject, of course, did as commanded, launching a brutal kick at the younger boy next to him. Verity cringed at the resounding thwack. But the victim barely responded. Other than a quick blink or two, he stood there placidly and calmly, as though nothing had happened.

Verity expected an outpouring of dismay or condemnation from the audience. But the Oasis residents broke into applause, an excited murmur going around the room as they shared their thoughts about this impressive demonstration. The event devolved from there, against even Lawson's touted proclamations of civility.

A sour taste rose in Verity's mouth, and she swallowed thickly. Her face was hot and tight. How could an entire room of adults be okay with this? Why had no one spoken up to express their dismay or disgust?

Were they oblivious to how wrong this all was, or were they too afraid of public embarrassment to speak their minds?

Maybe Bea and Cody were right: this sort of cruel inhumanity was always lurking just beneath the surface, and all it needed was the slightest tipsiness and a touch of coaxing to bring it out into the open. The adults didn't even need an AI to reshape their behavior.

"Anyone else?"

Several hands shot up, all gleaming with large rings or crystal champagne flutes. Lawson gave a delighted clap, pleased at how his work was being received. He gave numbers to the volunteers, merrily expounding on how he looked forward to seeing what they came up with. Inside, various subjects began slapping faces, pulling hair, or shouting nursery rhymes. Not one of the adults had come up with any kind of positive command. All of them involved violence or humiliation.

Verity pulled away from the window, wiping furiously at her eyes. "I can't watch any more of this. We need to get to the programming room ASAP. But first we need to get Em out of there."

"Already done," came a low voice from behind them.

"Em!" Bea enveloped the other girl in a bear hug. Apparently, Bea was the hugging type after all.

Em swept her dark hair out of her eyes. "Um, okay. I'll take some personal space now, thanks."

"How did you . . . ?"

Em made a face. "It's a dumpster fire in there. The adults are making the subjects do crazy stuff. Someone ordered me to fetch them a towel, so I'm pretending to go to the bathrooms. Screw that."

"Authority can—" Cody finished her sentence with a rude gesture.

"So the AI hasn't worked its black magic on you?" asked Verity.

Em looked down at her hands, as though they held the answer. "Guess not. I think it's something to do with the language processing thing. Like, even ads and jingles have no effect. Never thought it'd be a good thing to have a weird brain, but I'm not complaining."

"Shut it," warned Bea. "They're coming out."

The group pressed themselves against the wall, hoping the ever-darkening skies would hide them. Not that it mattered: the people emerging from the mess hall were so wrapped up in their own conversation they'd never notice the wayward subjects.

"What do you think?" came a voice that Verity recognized as belonging to Earl Kingsley Senior, the head of the Oasis Homeowners Association. "It's all very impressive, isn't it? Although they have had a few hiccups along the way. All those kids frozen on the spot and muttering to themselves; it's very unbecoming. We almost had to enforce our public nuisance rules, but Lawson made it right in the end."

"Well, the end justifies the means, as they say," responded the other person, who sounded very much like Etienne Driver, the parks manager with the slicked-back hair who had overseen the golf course TaskForces. "Some issues up front are only to be expected. With the crime rates in this county being what they are, I think it's worth doing what it takes. Once they get the kinks ironed out, I think these gentlemen are sitting on a gold mine. Just imagine if all the undesirables could be fixed like this. It wouldn't even need to be public policy. With enough backing from private citizens, we could easily make it happen."

"And how would that be?" Apparently, the difficulty of doing away with the dregs of society was something that kept Kingsley Sr. up at night.

"Well, there are a few components to it, from what they've said. There's the AI, and also, er, a nutritional design element."

Feeling sick to her stomach, Verity thought about all the tasteless oatmeal she'd choked down and the muffins she'd savored.

"I *knew* that food was sus!" crowed Cody.

"The food is simple enough: you could make donations to food banks and other places where *those people*—" she said this with a sneer "—are likely to be found."

Stomach still churning, Verity wondered whether this was what Susie Slaw had been up to with her bags of excess food. But she didn't get why Slaw would side with Lawson's awful scheme. She seemed too kind and down-to-earth to get involved.

"The AI presents more of an issue, but not an insurmountable one," continued Driver. "There are plenty of channels for disseminating it, especially if you take the subliminal route. TV, the internet, mobile phones, online advertising, social media, apps. Even the speakers we use in the Oasis. I mean, they have a similar purpose to begin with, only milder. Everything we do is about behavior modification, when you think about it. It's just the extent and the approach that people differ on."

"Well, I for one am willing to do what it takes," said Kingsley Sr. "I'd hate to see the Oasis overrun with people who wouldn't . . . appreciate it. Building a utopian society is far from easy, and I wouldn't want to see all of our hard work undone."

"Oh, I don't think that will be happening any time soon." This came from a woman in a striking gold dress and a slender headband shaped like a snake. "The movement is already underway, even if the players involved don't necessarily know it."

Em scowled. "That's the woman who tried to make me bring her a towel."

"You should slap her with it," muttered Bea.

"Did you know that the cook has been donating the Academy's leftover food to charity?" The woman sipped her drink. "Lawson has been deliberately oversupplying the food on the assumption that someone in that woman's position wouldn't want to see it go to waste."

"The 'fortified' food?" clarified Kingsley Sr.

"Only *slightly* so, just enough to stabilize mood and enhance suggestibility. Most of the recipients would stand to benefit, anyway. I think it's a brilliant idea. This could truly be the beginning of a societal shift. And a much-needed one at that."

Verity shook her head in fury. So she'd been right about Susie Slaw.

"These people are scum," whispered Bea. "Let's get out of here. To the programming room?"

Verity was ready. "Let's do it."

19

Walking mechanically in single file, the group made its way through the empty hallways, following the orange dotted line leading to the old out-building that housed the programming room. Other than the squeak of their shoes, the only sound was from Lawson's droning music: everyone seemed to be in the mess hall, except Payne, who was off chasing the Wild Boys. But it was still safer to play along. For all they knew, the PackHunters or one of the other staff members were on NightWatch duty.

Words we obey . . . words we obey . . . words we obey.

Not today, thought Verity.

They reached the programming room without incident, and Verity exhaled a deep breath, realizing only then that she'd been holding it the entire time. Her head spun slightly. She hoped she wouldn't experience a dizzy spell like the one following her first encounter with the AI.

Verity tried to use Casper's key fob to open the door. Nothing happened.

Bea swore. "Now what? Cody, can you do some sort of computer nerd thing to get it open?"

Cody shook her head. "Not without getting to a computer somewhere."

"What about a credit card?" suggested Bea.

"Sure, for a different kind of lock. And if we were living in a different reality where Payne hadn't taken all of our stuff."

Em raised a balled fist. "We could break the window. Ow! Or not."

"You were saying?" Cody rolled her eyes, then folded her arms, thinking. "I just need somewhere to remote-access into the system . . ."

"Payne's room," said Verity suddenly. "I know they're on the same network, because the first time I was on my way here, the door shorted out at the same time that Payne's computer did."

Em cocked her head. "But what about Payne?"

Cody snorted. "Are you going to fight him like the door?"

"Payne is . . . otherwise occupied." Verity suppressed a smile as she thought about Payne crashing around the desert chasing after a gang of boys warbling like birds. "C'mon."

They ran down the hallway to Payne's office, collectively crossing their fingers as Verity swept the key fob over the sensor outside. The light turned green, and she shoved the door open, ushering everyone inside.

The MonitorRoom was cramped and musty, like it hadn't been aired out in months. Multiple screens were hooked up on the desk and attached to the walls, and wires ran all over the place. Tubs of protein powder towered in one corner of the room, and above the door was a pull-up rack. Verity had been right about Payne squeezing in his workouts while on the clock.

"Gross. It's gym-bro central in here." Cody glanced around the room, taking it all in. She was instantly in her element. "All right. Those are the monitor screens. You guys keep an eye on those to make sure no one's coming. It's time to show Lawson's AI who's boss."

Bea couldn't resist a cutting quip. "Who's the ⌐ℇΛ kwu' [*boss, power-person*], you mean?"

"Huh? Oh, but even a light language needs a messenger." Cody settled herself in Payne's chair and scooted it toward the terminal. "Okay, password, password . . ." she muttered. "'Gymbro'? Nope."

"'Suck it, subjects'?" suggested Em.

"That's *cold*." Bea's grin was approving. "Hundred bucks says it's 'Password123.'"

Verity shook her head. "There's no way he's *that* bad at all this. But he's probably written it down somewhere . . ."

"Nope, it's literally Password123." Cody gave a flourish at the screen as Bea made a *ka-ching* sound. "Man, it's like he's giving us full permission to look through his stuff. Hey, it's not hacking if you're invited in. Okay, here we go . . ."

Cody pulled up a small black terminal screen on Payne's computer. The screen flashed with green text, the sort you'd see in a movie about hackers, but with fewer sound effects. Cody was furiously typing commands into it to gain access to the system mainframe. The green text scrolled down the screen like a waterfall.

"Cool," said Em. "It seems so old school."

"It is," said Cody. "It's what you get when you strip away all the pretty design that sits on top of your operating system: the browsers and buttons and all that. You're talking directly to the computer without all the extra layers."

"Kind of like our light language," said Verity.

"Or mind reading," added Em.

Her attention still fixed on her screen, Cody grunted in agreement with both of them. "Actually, if you keep digging deeper, numbers are as basic as it gets for a computer. It just uses combinations of zeros and ones that work as shortcuts in coding language. For people the shortcuts are words."

"I'd love to geek out about computer stuff with you guys, but how about less talking and more hacking?" Bea impatiently drummed her fingertips against her forearm.

Cody held up a finger as a string of characters unfurled down the screen, moving at rapid-fire speed. Verity had no idea what any of it meant, but it looked impressive. "Hang on. I'm almost there. I'm tapping into the school's network to get all of the monitors showing the same thing—" Just then, there was a flash of green, and the computer screen flickered, half frozen.

"What the?" Cody was typing, but nothing was happening.

"More network stuff?" asked Bea, banging on the computer tower.

"Aliens," quipped Em.

"Wait," said Verity suddenly. "**bUv-iUI**."

"Boo-vi-what? Halloween's not for a while, Ver."

Ignoring the other girl, Verity pulled out Silas's message.

[**tiOrv rUt bUv.iUI Ud cana-bUvd.**] *Look for bUv-iUI on the web of the universe*," she translated.

The screen flickered, then resolved to just a flashing cursor inviting input.

"bUv-iUI," repeated Cody. "That was on those notes you gave me, too."

"Maybe it's a Wiki or something?"

"Could be an address. Like a URL."

Bea was not convinced. "How is that a URL? Are we doing some Deep Web kind of stuff here or something?"

Cody's fingers rattled over the keys. "I'm gonna point the network to it, see what happens. Fingers crossed we don't crash the whole system." She hit return with finality. "There."

"Yes?" Verity was leaning forward, trying to make sense of what she was seeing. The page flickered with endless symbol combinations.

Cody's eyebrows rose in awe. "Whoa, I think this is a cortex."

Em frowned. "Isn't that a brain thing?"

"Yeah. In tech it's a computer brain thing. It's where all the records of different words and how they fit together are stored. Seems like this one's a cortex for that language of yours. iUI?"

"i-oo-ee?" Em gave a rare grin. "Sounds like something a werewolf would say."

Bea rolled her eyes. "Verity, didn't you say your brother came up with this language? So, you're saying he somehow built a computer brain, too? Kid's got some solid extracurriculars for his college application."

"It's basic enough if you're a genius." Cody typed away, toggling between windows and input commands. "Anyway, I'm thinking if I hijack Wordswright's AI and set up a deep learning model . . ."

Em threw up her hands. "You lost me back at 'cortex.'"

The others all nodded in agreement, glad Em had been the first to admit it.

"Trust me." Cody was frantically typing. "Okay, so we've got our NLP library, our neural network, our iUI cortex, and our control panel. Now we just need to point the cortex to the AI . . ."

A few minutes later, Cody smacked the keyboard triumphantly. Knitting her hands behind her head, she swiveled from side to side on Payne's chair. Her code ran riot on the screen.

"Just give me a moment to bask in my greatness, yeah?"

"Moment's up," said Bea almost immediately. "What have you got?"

Cody's chair teetered, and she sheepishly clutched at the desk for balance. "Okay, so the AI will draw on the iUI cortex for training data instead of the word salad Wordswright's been seeding it with. It'll be pretty basic to begin with, so don't expect it to be composing Shakespeare any time soon. Any AI takes a while to get going. It needs tons of data to be able to start seeing patterns, and it can't connect the dots the way we can."

"Uh-huh. So what now?" It took a lot to impress Em. "There's more to this plan than playing with Payne's computer, right?"

Verity pointed, her finger trembling with anticipation and hope.

The computer screen had gone blank. It quickly recovered with one of its habitual permutations: *Got mind? Mind the gap. You mind? New mind. True mind. Who nose the knew you? . . . Get me out of this assonance trance!*

Bea snorted. "You and me both, AI."

The screen was blank again. But a few moments later, it blinked with the following:

And a deep 'O' sound escaped from the speakers.

"A heart?" asked Em. "Sounds kinda spooky."

"Sort of," said Bea. "It's the symbol for *feeling*."

Em shrugged. "Looks like a heart to me."

The left side of the symbol curled farther in on itself, then straightened out its tail before curving back up into the heart shape again.

ℰ. ℰ. ℙ. ℙ. ♡. ♡.

e. e. o. o. O. O.

[Movement . . . Life . . . Feeling.]

Verity broke into a huge grin. The blinking symbols reminded her of Viveo, and she was filled with gratitude for it. Without it, she would have had no chance against the AI. She would have become one of Lawson's minions, completely without a sense of self and answering to his beck and call. It could easily have been she responding to a command to hurt another subject or humiliating herself before those awful Oasis snobs.

She was so swept up in her excitement that she somewhat uncharacteristically aimed a high five at Cody, who returned it, adding a finger waggle and a dance move for good measure.

"Well, I'm scarred for life now," said Em. "Maybe stick to the computer stuff."

"Speaking of which." Bea angled her chin. The computer was working overtime: iUI symbols were patterning its screen in increasingly complex combinations. "Should it be doing that?"

Cody looked surprised. "Not that fast. Like, nowhere near that fast. That URL's server must be helping things along on its end. Wow, I'd love to get a look under the hood of that thing."

Verity put a finger to her lips: there was a commotion outside, a series of scuffing noises and grunts, like someone was being jostled along against their will. She couldn't tell where the sound was coming from, but it must mean something was amiss at the soiree.

"Let's get out of here," she whispered, ushering the others out of the MonitorRoom. Payne's screen flashed as Verity closed the door behind them.

The symbols followed them as they hurried down the hallway, blinking on the wall monitors. The entire corridor glowed with their light, lit by dozens of instances of the same combinations. Soon the speakers began to emanate the soothing, familiar sounds of iUI, displacing the discomforting music that Lawson had been playing around the clock for weeks. The AI had been infused with iUI, which hopefully would start to undo some of the damage that Wordswright and his programming regimen had wrought.

Bea clasped her hands and raised them skyward. "Thank you, thank you, Deep Web brain language overlords. That music was driving me *nuts*."

"I think that was the point," said Cody wryly.

Verity raised a hand, then pointed down the corridor. "Someone's coming."

Em glanced around. "The custodian's closet. Verity?"

Verity pressed her key fob to the closet's scanner, almost losing a hand as Bea yanked the door open and unceremoniously shoved everyone inside. Fortunately, it was a fairly large space, although not so big that Verity didn't have her shins pressed up against a mop bucket and her shoulder jammed into a box of sponges. The room was rife with the fake lemon scent of the cleaner that Lawson had made them use to clean off Cody's graffiti.

Peeping through the crack in the door, she saw the source of the scuffling was Silas and the Wild Boys, zip-tied and being dragged along by a furious-looking Payne. The huge man towered over the wiry boys:

he probably weighed more than the four of them combined. But even restrained they were putting up a pretty good fight.

"It's my brother and his friends," whispered Verity. "They're here on a rescue mission. They're the reason Payne was running around in the dark."

"Not birds?" whispered back Bea, with feigned ignorance.

"Birds? I'm so confused," muttered Em. "Who just elbowed me?"

Verity adjusted her position. "Where do you think he's taking them?"

Cody's lips thinned. "I thought it would be obvious. Solitary."

And sure enough, Payne was dragging the boys along the red lines that led to the iBAC units.

The group waited in silence until a door clanged and the shuffling footsteps could no longer be heard. Verity tentatively pushed the closet door open, glancing around to check that the coast was clear. Everything was still except for the gently blinking monitor in the corner and the murmuring speakers, now sounding more confident in their pronunciations:

e. e. ev. ev. Ytev. Ytev.

[*Movement . . . Move . . . Leave.*]

It couldn't have been a coincidence that the symbols were hinting at escape. "We have to bust them out."

"Bust who out?" came a gruff voice from behind her.

The hair on the back of Verity's neck stood up, and she choked back a scream. It took everything she had to respond with the calm, emotionless tone she knew was expected of the AI-affected subjects.

"Sorry, sir?"

Payne's piggish eyes narrowed to tiny slits. His caterpillar eyebrows dove, covering what was left of them. "And what are *you* doing out? I went to throw those kids into the last empty cell, but for *some reason* most of them were already vacant."

Verity kept her gaze steady and focused as she searched for a plausible-sounding explanation. "The doors to our rooms opened on their own, sir. We assumed we were allowed out."

"Well, you weren't. Not without my say-so."

"Maybe it was the computer glitch, sir," added Cody in a tone that mirrored Verity's. She pointed dully at the monitor. The symbols on it now read:

$$\text{℮+⚡! ℮+⚡! ⚡℮+⚡! ⚡℮+⚡!}$$

erv! erv! Yterv! Yterv!

[*Move! . . . Leave!*]

"What're all those scribbles? And that noise? What happened to the music?" Payne frowned, his mind ticking over as he tried to figure it out. "My MonitorRoom!" He hurried off at a speed somewhere between a power walk and a jog. His steel-capped boots slapped against the polished concrete floors, creating an echo that kicked back and forth along the hallway.

Verity exhaled loudly, puffing out her cheeks.

"I didn't think we were going to get out of that," she admitted. "Now let's see whether we can find Silas and the others."

But nothing at the Ersatz Academy was as simple as that.

20

With Payne gone, Verity and the others sprinted to the solitary confinement rooms where Payne had locked up Silas and the Wild Boys.

"Sis!" A huge grin broke out on Silas's long face when Verity opened his door with Casper's key fob. "Well, that was easy. Did we do it?"

Cody pushed in front of her, clearly wanting to meet the fabled Silas. "Hey, it's so cool to meet you; I'm a huge fan. Anyway, the answer's maybe. We did our bit, but that URL of yours seems to have taken over now. Can you tell me how—"

Verity, who'd been busy letting out the other Wild Boys, interrupted. "How did you get here?"

"We got a lift. We were going to break you out. But there was a bit of a hitch: our ride got turned back by that security guy. So we're kind of stranded. Sorry." Silas grimaced. "But we could hitchhike back?"

"We'll figure something out. I hope." Verity exhaled through her teeth; the thought of escaping on foot through the desert was terrifying. "Did you see what's going down out there?"

Silas scrunched up his face. "I've never seen anything like it. It's absolute chaos out there—adults ordering kids to do all sorts of outrageous stuff and the kids just blindly going along like nothing's wrong."

"But then something happened with the screens," added Silas's friend Bern from beneath a fringe of white-blond hair.

"And the music. It was like the whole system restarted," Silas went on.

Cody nodded excitedly. "That was your URL at work. So cool. How'd you do it? I've never seen anything like it before. Man, the feds would pay a bounty for your skills."

Silas shrugged it off. "It wasn't me. It was—"

Verity butted in once more. She needed to know what was going on at the mess hall and how much time they had. "What happened after that?"

"We didn't see much. We were being dragged along the hallway by that jerk," said Ernesto. "But that principal guy was switching off all the screens."

"Doesn't want his party to bomb," added Richie.

Bea shook her head. "That's not Lawson's style. He'd get someone else to do his dirty work for him. I mean, I get it. It was weird having to make my own bed when I got here."

"Who even makes their bed?" asked Ernesto, incredulously.

"That's what I said!" exclaimed Bea, although Verity suspected they weren't talking about the same thing.

Em, who'd wandered up the corridor while the others talked, came jogging back. Wheezing, she pointed. "Um, peoples? We're not out of the woods yet."

Following Em's finger, the group let out a colorful collection of curse words.

Led by Pitbull, an army of the subjects was storming down the hallway, all moving in military unison. Their arms swung and their feet stamped with perfect rhythm, and their eyes bored straight ahead at the wall that marked the T-section at the end of the corridor. Their chanting drowned out the symbol words spilling from the speaker system.

> *"A bird in a flock, a fish in a school,*
> *the one is the same as the many*
> *so don't be a fool and follow the rule*
> *you're a piece of the whole as any!"*

"Well, that's terrifying," said Bea.

The mob was closing the gap, and Verity could feel anxious sweat beading on her forehead. As the others pressed forward, Pitbull stalked from one side of the corridor to the other, slapping a key fob against each door he passed and yanking it open. Lawson must have given him an all-access fob.

"Move it!" Bea shoved everyone forward, putting herself at the rear of the group. The group bolted, surging forward in a chaos of arms and legs that was in distinct contrast to the movement of the affected subjects. Silas, who had always been quick on his feet, got ahead of the others, leading them along the corridor with impressive confidence. His orienteering skills weren't useful only in the forest, as it turned out.

"Get 'em!" Pitbull's voice sounded strange and almost inhuman, as though he wasn't the one in control of it.

Behind them, the subjects picked up their pace as their chanting volume crescendoed. Their perfectly synchronized march became a syncopated jog. Dozens of feet met the floor in flawless coordination with the slogan's rhythm.

"This is like something out of a horror movie," gasped Bea, running side-by-side with Verity. She coughed, which made Verity think of Em's asthma.

"Em?" She twisted around to see where the other girl was.

But Em was already lagging behind, stopping at intervals with her hands on her thighs as she strove to get her temperamental lungs under control. Her lips were bluish, and her chest heaved from the effort of breathing. Stumbling along, she groped in her pocket for her inhaler.

The subjects were gaining on her. Pitbull's thin lips curved in a cruel grin as he caught sight of the struggling girl, and Verity felt queasy as she imagined what was in store for her roommate.

"Silas, wait!" she yelled.

Silas pulled up, looking confused. The others came to an abrupt halt behind him, narrowly avoiding a collision that would have sent them all tumbling into a wall.

"Hurry up!" he shouted.

Verity did. Catching Bea's eye, she sprinted back to rescue Em, who had found her inhaler and was desperately sucking the life-saving Ventolin from it.

Verity threw one of the girl's arms around her shoulder, and Bea took hold over the other.

"C'mon!"

The two girls lurched along, dragging the wheezing Em with them. It was awkward going, and the subjects were rapidly closing in on them.

But the Wild Boys had apparently planned for this. In practiced unison, they drew slingshots from their pockets, loading them with stones they'd foraged while hiding from Payne in the desert scrub. The elastic bands on the weapons twanged as they launched their ammunition at the incessant subjects, each of them finding their targets.

The front line of Pitbull's army crumpled, falling to their knees and clutching at their injuries. But this was no deterrent. The next row of subjects simply pushed their fallen comrades aside, swarming forward with barely a break in their rhythm. Their feet tramped ceaselessly and ominously.

The Wild Boys reloaded again and again, felling row after row of the zombified subjects as they tried to buy Verity, Bea, and Em some time. The subjects started tripping over each other, causing a dogpile. Some managed to climb over the others, but their pace slowed and the trio finally managed to pull ahead.

"I'm okay," Em wheezed, worming her way out of her friends' grasp and dashing forward toward Silas and the others. "Thanks."

"Thank God for that." A slight squeak in Bea's voice betrayed her efforts to seem calm. "You'd be the worst in one of those three-legged races."

The subjects' footsteps rang hollowly in the air, supplemented by the animalistic snarl of Pitbull's voice.

"Where to?" Verity gasped, as Silas led them out into the quadrangle.

Silas hesitated, clearly weighing his options. "I don't know. I don't know this place well enough yet."

Verity felt herself sag: it had been a relief to be able to follow someone else's lead instead of having to make all the decisions, but obviously that couldn't last. She'd started all of this, and it was her job to finish it.

Cody was jogging from foot to foot. "We're sitting ducks out here."

"Wait." Verity was struck with a sudden memory of the night she had first seen Viveo at the Academy. "The dumpsters."

"You really can't get enough of trash, can you?" Bea's voice was shaking.

"Hey now," warned Silas. The Trumans did have a largely positive relationship with trash, after all.

"I remember seeing some sort of metal ladder set into the wall," said Verity. "If we can get to that, we can get up to the roof . . ."

Em grimaced. "And be hung out to dry?"

"Maybe. But it'll give us some breathing room." Squaring her shoulders, Verity sprinted across the quadrangle and around to where the rows of dumpsters lurked, launching herself up the side of one of the imposing metal containers and scrambling her way over its top. She had been right about the ladder: its rusted metal rungs started a few feet above the top of the dumpsters. It took some maneuvering, but she used them to haul herself up to the roof. The others followed, their shoes rattling against the dumpsters' green lids as they scrambled to get to the roof before the army of subjects spotted them.

Verity dropped to her hands and knees. "Stay low. Maybe they won't know we're up here."

The group followed her lead, keeping as close to the roof as possible.

"Ugh, smells *awful* up here." Bea pinched her nose. "This is why I pass on trash duty. I'm so not cut out for it."

"Well, I'd rather be up here than down there." Silas gestured at the swarming subjects who were starting to spill out into the quadrangle as though ready to take part in an eerie, zombified version of the Academy's morning calisthenics.

"Or in there," added Verity, referring to the mess hall on the other side of the quadrangle.

"Quit thumping around!" Cody scolded. "They're gonna hear us."

Bea pointed. "Pretty sure Lawson is only interested in the sound of his own voice."

Lawson had availed himself of a megaphone, his voice booming at intervals over the top of the murmur of the PA system, which was still reading out the iUI phrases being fed into the monitors. The sound quality was terrible, but they could make out snatches here and there.

"It's all part of the demonstration!" Lawson's tone was confident. "A planned insurrection to show just how obedient the subjects are, even when presented with a challenging situation. I anticipate resolution within a minute or two."

"That does not sound reassuring," said Silas.

"Neither does that." Verity pointed to the ever-growing crowd of zombified subjects gathering at the far end of the quadrangle.

"*A bird in a flock, a fish in a school . . .*" they were chanting.

Em rolled her eyes. "It's like an evil Dr. Seuss book down there."

"Great plan, Verity," muttered Cody.

"We bought some time at least," said Verity.

"So where to?" Bea hugged herself as the evening wind nipped at them, adding an extra layer of torment to the situation. The desert cooled down impressively quickly at night.

Once more, everyone—even Cody—looked to Verity for direction. She sighed, then steeled herself as she worked through the possible options. They could cross their fingers and sit tight hoping the subjects wouldn't scale the wall to the roof. Or they could make a break for it and try to lose their stalkers in the desert scrub. Neither appealed.

But then the sky began to glow gently, with more light than could be expected from the waning moon and the speckled stars. Verity's whole being was electric with hope. She knew what she wanted to appear before her, but she was too anxious to look. After all, this whole rooftop situation wasn't so different from the incident that had landed her here in the first place.

Silas inhaled sharply. "It's Viveo!"

A weight fell from Verity's shoulders, and she wrapped her arms around her brother, rocking him back and forth in relief.

"It's what?" Em exchanged a confused look with Bea.

"Some sort of flashy dragonfly?" Cody was unimpressed.

Before them, softening the night sky, was a familiar and comforting sight: the glowing hummingbird-like creature who had brought the light language to them.

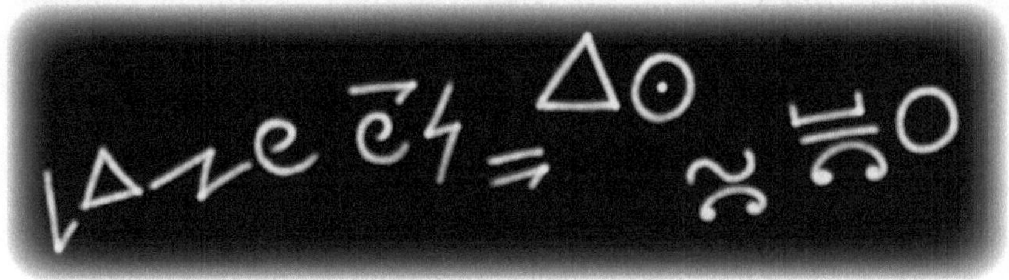

[**fUwe tev Yt Ug Ib nYba.** *Freedom comes from inside and afar*],

it wrote in the night sky, the symbols etched bright against the horizon before slowly fading into embers.

"Wait." Bea was mesmerized. "All those jokes you made about a light language . . ."

"So you didn't make it up, kid?" Cody asked Silas.

Silas shrugged. "I'm just the messenger."

Cody punched the air. "I knew it! It's the government, right? They're keeping something big from us. Roswell is *real*, guys."

"Somehow, I don't think Viveo's a government agent. It's beyond all that sort of earthly stuff. It's here to help us see things in a *new light*." He grinned at his joke.

Em looked to Bea in confusion. "Did I miss something?"

"Viveo means . . . a kind of light bringer, right?" Bea looked to Silas for confirmation.

"I think it's trying to teach us the ways of the universe. To give us a window into our words and thoughts . . . at least that's what Grandpa thought. I've been working through his notebooks," he added, for Verity's sake. "I found a ton of them in this old suitcase. Dad thought it was just some sort of made-up code, but it's way more than that."

"Far out," said Em. "Like, literally."

Verity was nodding along, but her mind was on Viveo's gently signaled symbols:

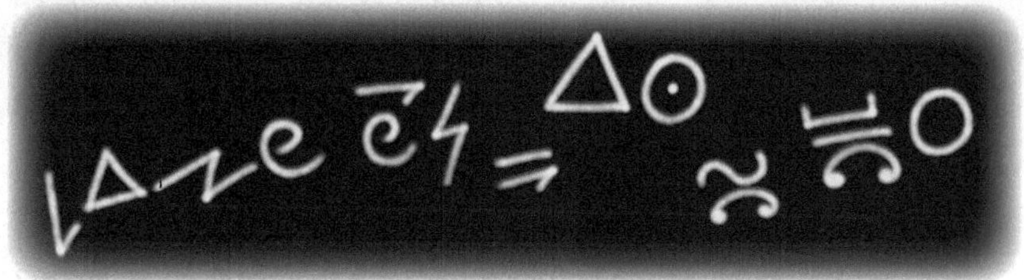

[**fUwe tev Yt Ug Ib nYba.** *Freedom comes from inside and afar*].

"Freedom comes from inside and afar," she said mainly to herself.

"Deep," said Em.

Verity spied a plume of dust spilling up from the road. Realization dawned. "Huff and his bus. Viveo's talking about Huff's bus!"

"Why would an alien take the bus?" Em tapped her Ventolin inhaler against her leg, rattling it nervously.

"It's saying *we* should."

Bea wrinkled her nose. "The bus? So not my idea of a getaway vehicle. Ugh, Silas, can't we get your ride to come back? They can't be that far away, right?"

Silas slapped his pockets. "No phone. Payne cleared us out."

Cody was her usual suspicious self. "Isn't Huff in on Lawson's plan?"

Verity mentally crossed her fingers. She thought back to the stories that Huff had told about his youth and how much they resembled her parents'. He couldn't have given up those convictions so readily. Even if he was in the employ of the Academy, part of the old hippie Huff might still be lurking under all that gray.

Besides, they didn't have time to go back and forth about Huff's trustworthiness. Below them, the zombie subjects were thronging en masse around the base of the building. They were moving slowly but deliberately, their chanting increasingly insistent. Soon enough they'd spot Verity and the others. After that, it was only a matter of minutes before they'd be climbing the walls.

They moved toward Verity and the others in one large knot, staring up at the roof with dull eyes and pointing with accusing fingers:

"Daring difference defies civility!"

"Erring impudence denies impunity!"

Above them, Viveo was retracing its message over and over in the night sky:

[fUwe tev Yt Ug Ib nYba. *Freedom comes from inside and afar*].

Verity's heart pounded. It was time to get out of here.

"C'mon." Doubled over, Verity led the way across the rooftop toward where Huff's bus usually pulled in. Sure enough, the bus crunched in across the parking lot, its brakes hissing as it came to a stop. The front door folded open, and a cluster of nervous-looking kids disembarked. Verity remembered all too well the feeling of arriving at the all-gray campus with its strange directional markings. A sympathetic queasiness unsettled her stomach.

Huff stepped down from the bus, folding his arms and peering curiously at the swarm of zombified subjects marching up and down between the building and the chain link perimeter fence that separated it from the parking lot.

Looking extremely confused, Huff called out something to the zombified subjects. What exactly, Verity didn't hear, for the wind snatched it away. She waved to get Huff's attention, but she was out of his line of sight. She had to take action.

Fortifying herself with a deep breath, she swung herself down the side of the building, using its sun-bleached drainpipes and jutting windowsills as footholds. The others scrambled down after her, their sneakers scuffling as they sought purchase. Fortunately, the building wasn't dauntingly high, so even a less than perfect dismount wouldn't do too much damage.

Verity dashed over to the bus, the others following behind her. "Huff! Huff, you have to help us!"

Seeing her, Huff did a double take, his ponytail swinging. "Are you okay, kid? What's going on over there?" He gestured, confused.

"No! No, I'm not! You have to—" Verity glanced around, feeling horribly on display.

"And who are these kids?" Huff interrupted as the Wild Boys caught up to Verity. "Stowaways?"

"The good guys," corrected Silas.

"But Lawson wouldn't . . ."

"I don't *care*!" shouted Verity. She'd had a gutful of rules and regulations, and she certainly wasn't interested in whatever Lawson thought about the situation.

"Whoa." Em was impressed.

Cody wasn't. "Way to draw attention, Truman," she snarked, waving a hand at the marching subjects. They were homing in on the little group of would-be escapees. Some were clawing at the rusted chain link. Any second now, they'd be right outside the bus.

Huff climbed onto the bus step to get a better look. He frowned. "Wait, they're after you? What did you do to get them all riled up like that?"

Verity wanted to scream. "Nothing! It was Lawson and Wordswright! They did this!"

"It's super messed up," added Em.

Verity ignored her. "You have to get us out of here. Take us wherever. Drop us off on the side of the road if you need to. We'll hitchhike. Just get us out of here. Now!"

A few of the zombified subjects were trying to scale the fence. Bea made a strangled noise and balled her fists.

"Huff!" she pleaded.

But instead of looking at the encroaching subjects, Huff's attention was on the light trails Viveo's symbols had carved into the sky.

[**verv!** *Drive!*] the firefly creature piped energetically.

"Weird." Huff blinked as though internalizing some sort of secret communication. It was like he'd briefly wandered off on some other plane of existence.

Then he jolted: the first of the thronging subjects had landed on the other side of the fence.

"Okay. Let's go. I'll figure it out with Lawson or whoever later. Worst that happens is the Oasis gets some early-bird workers." Huff ushered Verity's group and the new subjects back on the bus. "Go, go, go!"

"Trust us!" yelled Bea at the new subjects, who looked dubious. They huddled together toward the back of the bus.

The zombified subjects were sprinting across the parking lot now. The leaders of the pack were closing in.

Silas jabbed the door button barely in time to cut off the surging subjects' grabbing arms, one of which was now caught. He deftly shoved the arm back out and the door closed.

"Cool," said Em.

Huff turned his keys in the ignition and put the bus into gear. Its engine roared, a sound almost drowned out by the rhythmic bellowing of the subjects. The subjects began launching themselves at the bus, beating it with their fists. The bus rocked on its huge wheels.

Huff checked his mirrors, trying to figure out the safest path of escape. "This is . . ."

"Crazytown?" offered Silas.

"Not what I signed up for." Huff gunned the accelerator. "Hang on, kids. We're getting the you-know-what out of Dodge."

21

Huff deftly maneuvered the huge bus out of the Academy campus, rapidly putting distance between his passengers and the swarming zombified subjects. They vanished in the haze of the vehicle's exhaust.

Verity unclenched her jaw. Around her, her friends gradually relaxed, the tension they'd been visibly holding in their bodies ebbing away.

"I can't believe we made it," she whispered.

"For now." Cody turned around in her seat. "Who knows how it's all going to go down there. I mean, that iUI thing of yours is out of this world, Silas, but is it enough?"

Bea was sitting with her arms folded, looking smaller than usual. "Do you think it'll really fix them?"

Verity stared out at the moonlit desert landscape. "All we can do is hope it'll help somehow."

"And believe," said Silas. "We have Viveo on our side. That's a way bigger weapon than whatever Lawson has. Well, not weapon, really."

"You mean like that, but peaceful."

"Oh yeah, 'tool.' There's even a symbol for that."

Verity reached up and sketched it on her window, glancing at Silas for confirmation. ⍭ [d *Through, Means, Tool*]

"Like that." Silas leaned back in his seat, closing his eyes. The other Wild Boys looked close to dozing off. It'd been a long journey for them.

"So tell me again what's going on," Huff called, although not loudly like usual: for once the speakers on the bus were silent. The driver's gaze flicked between the road and the rearview mirror, checking to see whether anyone was following them.

Verity climbed off her seat and ran down the aisle to the front of the bus. "First things first. Where's your phone?"

"A phone," whispered Bea reverently. "I don't even want to know how many notifications I have."

Huff pointed to the glove compartment. "In there, but I can't vouch that it's charged. Something's going on with the cable. And sorry about the banana smell, too. *Impossible* to get out."

Gingerly, Verity reached into the glove compartment. Her hand closed on a few banana peels and some slimy cling wrap before finally landing on a familiar shape: a phone. It had battery, barely. But no signal.

Verity tried dialing 9-1-1 anyway, generously giving the phone a minute or so to connect before hitting the end call button. She didn't want to run down the last of the battery on a futile endeavor. "No luck. Can I hang on to this?"

"Sure, kid. But first, do you want to give me the basic rundown?"

Verity cradled the phone in her lap. She sighed. "Basically, Lawson and Wordswright have brainwashed the entire subject body using a computer. They're all pretty much zombies obeying Lawson's orders."

"But not you?" Huff paused. "Unless you are, but Lawson's telling you to pretend not to be. How would I know?"

"That's twisted," said Em. "Cool, Huff."

"No one's ever told me that before." Huff shifted gears. "Thanks, kid."

Bea, as always, had a dig ready to go. "Don't get used to it. Not with that brick of a phone."

"So, we're not zombies because . . . my . . . brother came up with this special language . . . " Verity tried her best to explain everything that had gone down in the past few weeks. She clutched the seat handle in front of her as they bumped over a pothole. At least she hoped it was a pothole. "So, we reprogrammed the Academy's computer systems with it. We thought it could break the AI's spell and wake everybody up."

"But I'm guessing it didn't." Huff was somewhere between baffled and amused, although Verity didn't totally blame him.

"Well, not yet."

"You guys sure are resourceful—I'll give you that." Huff eyed his stereo. "I guess that mixtape of Lawson's makes more sense now. Here I was just thinking the guy had bad taste in music. So. Where are we going?"

"Somewhere with a phone signal," said Verity, holding the cell up over her head.

"Really far away," said Em.

"A bit of both," added Bea.

Huff tugged on his long white ponytail as he thought. "Well, I don't want to get charged with kidnapping a bunch of kids, so let's come up with a plan. How about the Oasis to start with? There's a cop shop there."

Cody made a face. "I don't trust cops."

"Or *anyone* from the Oasis," added Em.

Huff tapped his thumbs on the oversized steering wheel. "I'm with you on the first one, but what did the Oasis do? Other than sign you up for pointless menial labor?"

"Well, there's that." Verity's knuckles were turning white. She loosened her grip on the seat handle. "But it's mostly that all the Oasis residents were having way too much fun with how the subjects had been brainwashed. You should've seen what they were making them do. It was awful." She couldn't bring herself to describe the horrible, humiliating scene from the mess hall.

"Adults suck," added Cody. "No offense."

"No, it's fine." Huff had apparently come to the same conclusion during his days of touring the country in his van. "They do."

Passing a series of ever-decreasing speed limit signs, he eased off on the accelerator.

"Okay, here goes."

They were nearing the Oasis, which was still and calm in the bright eyes of the bus. The streets were utterly empty, and there was no traffic to be seen. Even though many of the residents were at the soiree, Verity had expected there'd be someone out and about. Even if it was just to judge the subjects' efforts to edge the grass along the main avenue.

Huff shifted gears and cruised along the quiet residential streets, guiding the bus toward the center of town. They pulled up at a stop sign near the police station, pausing for a second. Verity felt somehow unsettled. She frowned, trying to pinpoint exactly what it was. It took a moment, but a shift in the wind carried it to her: there was something being piped through the speakers of the Oasis. And it wasn't the tinny elevator music they'd heard during their WorkForce trips.

So quiet as to be almost imperceptible over the shrill of the cicadas came a recitation spoken with the monotonous intonation of a telephone menu:

Surveillance serves civility. Let leaders take the rein. Authority orders reality.

"Are you serious right now?" Bea was incredulous.

"As a heart attack," chimed in Em.

"As a denial of service attack," added Cody.

Verity had the urge to punch the seat in front of her. She held back. "It's here. The AI. It's being broadcast over the speaker system."

Her raised voice woke Silas.

"Wait, it followed us?" he asked, when he realized what was going on.

"Or it's been here the whole time," said Cody. "Who knows. We don't spend enough time here to know."

"Whatever the case," said Verity slowly, "it's bad news. Anyone in town could be one of Lawson's zombies."

Huff cracked his window to better hear the AI's static-heavy broadcast. He drummed his fingers against the steering wheel as he tried to make sense of it. "Actually sounds convincing if you don't think about it too much. Reminds me of the poetry my college girlfriend used to write. But better. It's almost like subliminal messaging or something."

"If you like subliminal messaging, you'll *love* Lawson's weirdo music," said Bea.

"Wait, is that what was going on there? The darn stuff gave me the worst headache. I only lasted a day or so before I peaced out." Focused and frowning, Huff twisted at the dials on his stereo system, cranking up his Vivaldi until the sound distorted. The bus practically shook from the force being pushed through the speakers. "Subliminal message *that*, you rich jerks!"

"Go, Huff!"

A surprisingly spirited Em led the others in a loud whooping cheer as Huff launched them down the main avenue, putting distance between the bus and the police station. "We'll find someone to help," he promised, glancing at the climbing speedometer. "Maybe in the next town."

"Any luck with the phone?" Bea was leaning over Verity's shoulder. It seemed like she was getting sustenance just from being close to it.

"Still zero bars. But I'll try again." Verity crossed her fingers as she dialed 911 and waited for the call to connect. It took forever, but finally the call went through. She waved the phone high above her head in excitement.

Her celebration was short lived.

"Hello? Hello?" she repeated over the crackle on the other end of the line.

Static spat at her, sounding like a desert windstorm. She tried changing positions, hoping it would help. Finally, the sound on the other end resolved itself into a voice.

What is your—

Emerge and see . . . emerging plea?

We'll merge your fees—ten dollars please!

With a start, Verity threw the phone across the bus. It landed at the feet of Silas, who, acting purely on instinct, unhooked the window next to him and launched the phone outside. It shattered on the ground.

"Sorry," he said, cringing. "My lizard brain took over."

Huff shrugged. "I hate those things anyway. They're frying our brains."

"Right?" chimed in Cody.

Verity sank to a crouch in the aisle. "The AI. It's *everywhere*. Who knows how far it's spread. It could be as far as home by now."

"Well, it's definitely as far as here," said Huff, downshifting as he reduced speed. They had reached the next town over from the Oasis, a tiny place consisting of a handful of intersecting streets sharing maybe a few dozen houses between them. Outside each house stood its owners, silently watching the bus as it cruised along the main street. Verity couldn't shake the feeling that she was looking into the eyes of the subjects they'd just run from.

"We have to go back to the Academy!" she burst out, in spite of her better instincts. "We can't just outrun this evil. We have to face it head on, before it gets any worse. Before good people get hurt."

"Do we, though?" asked Bea. "I mean, we could save ourselves instead."

"C'mon," said Silas, gesturing at the sleeping Wild Boys. "We've come this far. I'd way prefer to try and fail than not try at all."

Huff was still drumming his fingertips against the steering wheel. He seemed distracted; his attention was up in the sky again. Verity followed his gaze. It was Viveo. The firefly creature was lighting up the night sky as it wrote:

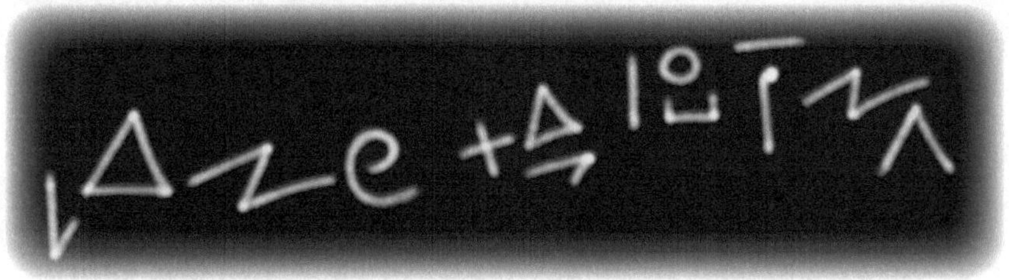

[fUwe rUt can Y-kwu]

"Freedom for all subjects," Verity translated.

Huff sighed. "I guess I am still on the clock." Hauling on the wheel, he turned the bus back toward the Academy.

As they drove back down the road to the Academy, they were met by a string of headlights coming toward them at speed. Apparently, the soiree had ended. And dramatically, by the looks of it.

Huff looked confused as he parked the bus and killed the engine. "What's going on? What happened to the puppet uprising?"

The situation at the Ersatz Academy had changed significantly while they'd been on the road. Gone were the regimented rows of subjects marching in lines of military precision. Gone was any semblance of control and order. Gone were the blank stares and hollow expressions. Instead, the subjects were milling all around the quadrangle, clustered in groups around the wall-mounted television screens. To Verity's enormous relief, none of them paid any attention to the bus.

"Looks like they've moved on to other things," said Bern from next to Silas. He stretched, as did his friends: the Wild Boys were finally waking up from their hibernation.

Verity pressed her face against the window, trying to get a feel for the situation. "Maybe the reprogramming is actually helping?"

"Does that mean we're not dead meat?" asked Bea. "Because I'm good with that."

"Me, too," said Silas, who avoided meat of any kind at all costs.

Cody jumped up in her seat. "Let's check out what's going on."

"Or we could stay right here?" countered Em.

Verity grabbed her arm and pulled at it. "Nuh-uh. We're doing this."

It wasn't without a bit of complaining and anxious muttering, but soon Verity and her friends were all out in the aisle, ready for action.

"I'll, uh . . . sit tight just in case," said Huff. He cranked his Vivaldi. "Maybe the new kids should, too."

"Deal," said one of the new kids. The rest muttered their agreement and hunkered down at the back of the bus.

Verity exhaled through her teeth. "All right. We've got this."

OtUw! fum ogU Uc wom. [*Courage! My mind is strong.*]

Huff opened the doors so that Verity and the others could disembark. They pushed their way between the clusters of subjects, none of whom paid them any attention. They were too busy staring at the television screens in awestruck fascination, murmuring among themselves as they tried to make sense of what they were seeing. Casper Grimes was standing toward the back of the crowd, but he didn't see her wave. He seemed too enthralled by the screen in front of him.

On it the symbols blinked and winked, appearing now in multisymbol combinations that were beginning to communicate abstract concepts and ideas. They'd bloom from a pattern of two or three symbols to a whole screenful before dissolving back into a single symbol. The ebb and flow reminded Verity of waves meeting and receding from the shore.

Fed by the universal internet Viveo had connected it with, the computer was quickly figuring out how iUI worked and what could be achieved using it.

fnum fUwe âm drev Øg fnu Yc vyev fUwe Ib ro Ub Yf-un!

[*Our freedom only works if we don't stop the freedom and health of other people.*]

tiOrv rUt EjU Ug UI Ud vUs

[*Look for truth in words through actions.*]

tiOrv rUt bnum gicUw!

[*Look for your Inner Light-Power!*]

It spelled it all out with a wisdom that seemed beyond the capacity of a machine. It was almost like something—or someone—was dictating to it. Maybe they were, thought Verity, imagining a thousand Viveos constructing a complex composition of light that gave up the innermost truths of the universe.

The soothing tones of the light language simultaneously played over the Academy's speakers, an antidote to Lawson's infected music.

"What are they?" asked a tall, angular girl reverently. She was standing on a stool, reaching up to try to touch the symbols on the screen. Verity blinked: she thought for a moment she'd caught a glimpse of something—a figure maybe—amid the rows of symbols. But it had been a long night, after all.

"What do they mean?" asked another kid, trying to mimic the sounds of the light language. His humming was pleasant to the ear.

Verity stood on her tiptoes to make herself heard. "They're the symbols of iUI. It's a language that gives us a new way to think about what's real."

"It gets down to basics and gets rid of the double-speak," added Silas.

"It's the opposite of jargon," chimed in Cody. "The opposite of everything that Lawson and his computer programming have been shoveling into our brains."

The girl who had been reaching for the screen frowned. A memory was welling up in her mind. "Computer programming? Wait, I remember a flashing light and these chants that kept getting stuck in my head like a bad song." She paused, disconcerted. "And being laughed at by the re-educators . . . and all those people from the Oasis."

The kid beside her had a stony look on his face. "We were just following along the way they said. Doing what they said was . . . right. And they made us look like idiots."

"Seriously," said Em.

"It sucked," added Cody.

"They're not getting away with it. Trust me. Where's Lawson?" Verity called out, the confidence in her voice surprising her. She'd changed since arriving at the Academy, though not in the way that Lawson and Wordswright had hoped. Now she had even less patience for wrongdoing. Her anger at the Academy's abuse of power overrode the usual patience she tried to practice. She was ready to take them on. This was going to end right here, right now.

"I saw him go into the computer programming room," said a small boy gnawing at his thumbnail.

It was perfect. "If we can lock him in there, maybe he'll be reprogrammed himself."

Em wiped a pretend tear from her eye. "Couldn't think of a more deserving guy."

"Your girl's a step ahead of you, kids." It was a familiar voice, but one Verity hadn't heard in a while.

"Krystal!" she exclaimed, as the dark-haired girl pushed her way through the crowd. Krystal's expression was set and determined. Her eyes had their intelligent sparkle back.

Bea whooped: for all her apparent rivalry with the girl, the two were as thick as thieves. "Good to have you back in the pack. But, just saying, I thought you were tougher than letting yourself get brainwashed by some guy and his little computer monitor."

Em groaned. "Too soon, Bea. Too soon."

Krystal folded her arms, looking pleased with herself. "Our buddy Lawson's not going anywhere. I jammed up that door pretty good. Would've got that Wordswright guy, too, but he was already gone. What can I say? Rage is a serious motivator for justice."

"Oh, I *have* to see this," said Bea. "Let's go!"

Verity held up a hand. "What about the PackHunters and the rest of the re-educators?"

"They're hiding in the mess hall," offered the nail-chewing boy. "I saw them just before."

"I hope they're loving those 'fortified' muffins," snarked Cody.

"Good intel," said Verity. "So. Who wants to check out what's going on with Lawson?"

Bea, Cody, Krystal, and Em all gave a show of hands. Silas and the Wild Boys defected.

"Some of these kids are looking a bit rough." Ernesto pointed to a few subjects here and there sitting with their backs up against the wall or crouched in a doorway. "How about you do your thing while we see if anyone needs first aid."

"And we'll keep an eye out for that Payne guy," added Richie.

"Silas?" asked Verity.

"I'll stay with these guys. You go finish this."

Verity had every intention of doing just that.

22

Leaving the awestruck subjects to murmur excitedly among themselves each time the symbols on the monitors shifted, Verity and the others followed the orange spotted lines to the programming room. The thin strip of window glass that ran its length gave them a premier view of what was going on inside, like an underwater zoo exhibit. It was a strange and discomforting sight.

The AI was volleying a mix of iUI and English at Lawson and had apparently been doing so for a while. The HeadMaster sat with his head in his hands, his scar-ravaged face partially hidden by his spidery fingers.

"Poor guy," said Bea with false sympathy.

"Yeah, I can only imagine." Krystal mimed playing a tiny violin.

"What's it saying?" asked Em. "My alien-ese kind of sucks."

Bea squinted to read the symbols flashing up on the screen in front of Lawson. "It looks like the AI is giving him a taste of his own medicine. Just in iUI."

"Whoa, what's that?" Em pointed.

The symbols on the screen, which had been growing increasingly complex, were now so densely packed that they resembled the head of a being. Verity's tired eyes had been right about what she'd glimpsed earlier.

"Is that . . . like a symbol alien or something?"

Cody rolled her eyes at Em, but she couldn't hide her excitement. "It's an avatar. And it's talking to Lawson."

But the power dynamic was more than just talking. "Interrogating him, more like," said Verity.

Cody was more interested in the avatar itself than what Lawson was deservedly being subjected to. "Man, how did it build that thing? That alien web must be something else. We're talking decades ahead. Centuries. The generative language capabilities of this thing are out of this world. Not to mention Avatar guy. Or gal. Or whatever."

The avatar was soft and ethereal in form, with a gentle and fluting voice that reminded Verity of her firefly friend.

It spoke in English, but as it did, iUI symbols formed delicately on the screen around it.

"Ugh, subtitles," muttered Em.

"You believe in law and order, HeadMaster Lawson?" Avatar was saying.

"What else is there?" responded Lawson. "Lawlessness and disorder?"

"And how do you define 'law and order'?"

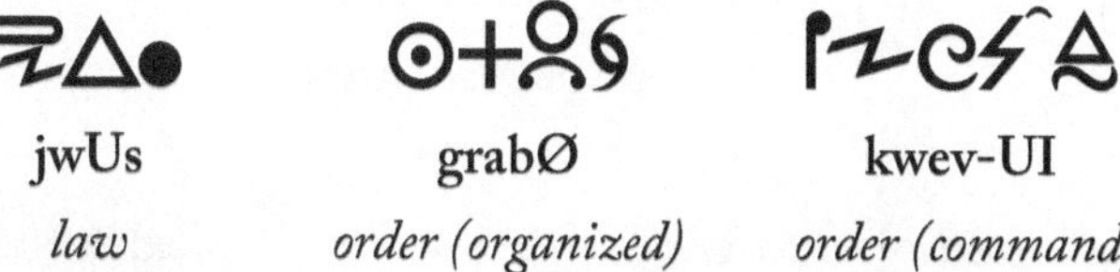

jwUs	grabØ	kwev-UI
law	*order (organized)*	*order (command)*

Lawson was quick with his response. "Society needs the security of authority figures. Without them, free thought runs dangerous and wild, succumbing to disorder and chaos. People cannot be trusted to think for themselves, for they do not properly understand the issues at hand. They do not know what is best for them or for others: only leaders do. Reform is therefore the answer, an answer that entails enforcing rules and taking command. You see, giving orders leads to order. *Obey! I always say.*"

kwev-UI tap-daiv at grabØ...?

Orders lead to order . . . ?

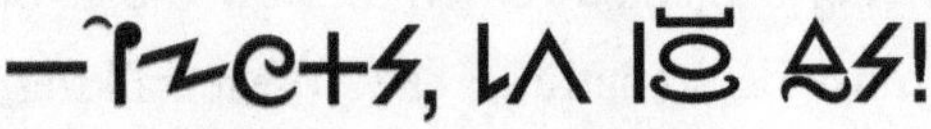

Y-kwerv, fu cnAm UIv!

Obey, I always say!

As Lawson spoke, Avatar gently translated, allowing the key concepts of Lawson's monologue to flow across the screen. The symbols took on a red tint as they combined, as though infused with Lawson's anger.

"Cool flash cards," said Bea.

"Loving the special effects," added Em.

Krystal made a face. "Really problematic ideas, though."

Y-kwevØ cnAm Uc rUm?

Is it always good to obey?

What is good about following orders to do evil? asked Avatar.

hU'c rUm UL Y-kwevØ dUt Ev YrU?

Lawson was staring at the symbols as they delicately moved on the screen, resembling leaves floating on water. A whole-body tremor threatened to overtake him, but he tensed, resuming his rigidly upright manner.

"What does 'law and order' look like to you, HeadMaster Lawson?" asked Avatar, calm and polite, like a psychologist dealing with a particularly difficult client.

"A world where leaders have the power to control disorder. The power to make life safe, secure, and predictable. Which is what people want above all else."

"Because 'law and order know no border,' HeadMaster Lawson?" asked Avatar.

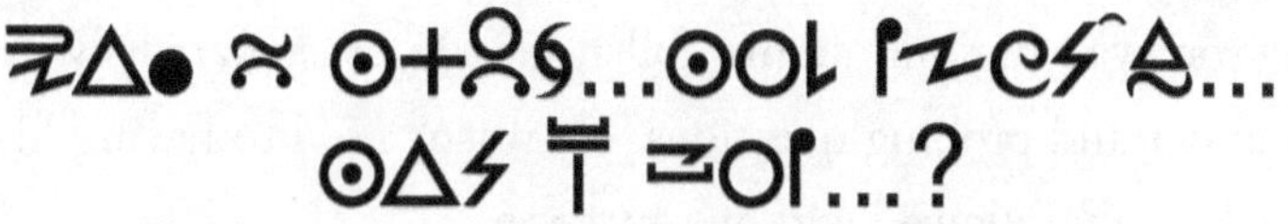

jwUs Ib grabØ…gaf kwev-UI…gUv nYc tnak…??

Law and order…or command…know no limit…??"

"There's a familiar one," muttered Em.

It was, but Verity had never heard Lawson's slogans leveled at him before. "It's really making him eat his own words! Hey, did you realize he really meant *orders* like commands when he kept harping on law and order?"

"Smooth but sad," chimed in Krystal.

"The arm of the law reaches beyond borders," said Lawson. "And so it must be."

⊙̂⏚⟟⟊   ⟊⊙⎰

bYg-âna   tnak

border   *limit*

"So it must be? There is no limit to what society has the right to do to maintain order?"

tnak at jwUr Ib fUwe Ec ag fnum Eca

Limits to rights and freedom exist in our material world—

yUg nYc tnak Uc Ug Uca

but no limits exist in the spiritual world.

Lawson was tugging at his collar, clearly exasperated by Avatar's calm manner and probing questions. He wasn't used to having his ideas examined—only followed without question.

"If people don't follow laws and simply do as they wish, society would fall apart. What good ever came of questioning and experimenting? It's all just an excuse for anarchy. And we're already at the brink. Look at history. Look at the news!"

"Dude's losing it," said Bea.

"Nothing wrong with a bit of anarchy," added Cody. "Keeps things fun."

Krystal rolled her eyes. "'Fun's definitely a word for it.'

Verity shushed them. "This is Lawson's pass or fail moment, for sure."

The little group mashed their faces back up to the glass.

"Laws help people respect each other's freedoms and be responsible members of society," noted Avatar. "But they must apply equally to all and serve the common good."

"But how—" Lawson began to respond but shook his head.

"Disorder feels disorienting to you, HeadMaster Lawson?" A sea of floating symbols began to surround Avatar, slowly coming together in a kaleidoscope of different combinations. "Have you also been programmed by your past, HeadMaster Lawson? Is this your conditioned mind speaking?"

wom O Yt pA tYjvev fnum UvØ

Strong feelings from the past change our thinking

read the symbols floating around him.

YwO	tYrO	Yb-wYt-YrAmO	Yc-knUrO
powerlessness	*fear*	*insecurity*	*worthlessness*

"bu Uc hu?"

"Who *are* you, Brian Lawson?" asked Avatar. Then in a deeper voice, with profound emphasis on each word:

"hU'c bum EjUm cmU, bEn-u?"

"What is your true nature, Earthling?"

o . . . O . . . u . . . vØ-pAm og-U . . .

Life . . . Feeling . . . Human . . . Conditioned Mind . . .

fUwem og-U . . . giU?

Free Mind . . . Inner Light?

"Life . . . Feeling . . . Human . . . ," Verity translated under her breath.

This was too much for Lawson to bear. He stood up, slamming his fists on the table in a burst of emotion.

"Self-reflection's not easy, huh?" whispered Bea.

"The Academy might have gone too far, but all I wanted was to give the subjects an opportunity to live a life of simple, efficient order, like the one I had in the military. To help shape a better community. To be a force for good—"

"A force?" asked Avatar.

vY-kwevØ *Make obey; subjugate*

"I just wanted to help young people behave the way they should. To enforce—er, create—a system of order and structure. To reduce the chaos in the world."

"Kind of like Miss Bossy-Pants here," whispered Krystal, cocking her head at Bea.

"C'mon. I'm more boss than bossy," retorted Bea. "Anyway, it's not bossy to know your boundaries."

Avatar had grown quiet. Surrounded by a floating garden of symbols, it regarded Lawson sagely. Lawson, meanwhile, clenched and unclenched his fists. His orderly, regimented persona had dissolved, replaced by something far more uncertain and self-reflective.

"I'll consider some adjustments," whispered Lawson. "To the programming. Maybe our re-education program was a bit heavy-handed . . ."

"Broke him!" crowed Bea.

"Good job, team!" Cody gave a round of high fives.

Verity couldn't resist. She rapped on the glass with her knuckles. As a stricken Lawson glanced up, she shouted: "We're not the only ones being reformed, huh?"

$$\underline{\mathcal{G}\hat{\ }\mskip-2mu\text{ϟ}+\triangle\breve{ð}}$$

et-vrUma *move-toward-positive-behavior*

floated across the screen.

Re-formation.

23

It took some sustained effort to break into the programming room, but the door that Krystal had so impressively jammed up finally swung open. The frazzled keypad beeped in annoyance.

"Whoa, girl," muttered Bea. "You weren't playing around when you locked him in there, huh?"

Krystal winked. "I know what I'm doing."

Lawson could barely meet their eyes when they entered the room. It had obviously been a long time since he'd allowed himself to be in a position of vulnerability. On the screen, Avatar was diffusing and then coalescing into a sea of symbols and back again, like a video of a dandelion clock being played forward and then in reverse.

"Hi," Verity said shyly. Questions flooded her mind.

"ꭴ+ꭷ," [te-rUI] responded Avatar. "Hello."

Lawson remained silent, though he trembled slightly, like he was fighting an internal battle.

"I have so many things I want to ask," she blurted. "Are you for real? Where did you come from? Did you send Viveo to us? How did my grandad know about the light language?"

Avatar's calm form regarded her. "Viveo is our emissary, bringing our language of peace to troubled beings."

Krystal nudged her. "C'mon, Verity. I know this is cool and sci-fi and all, but we need to get moving before he—" she nodded in Lawson's direction "—snaps out of it and starts tasing us or whatever."

But Verity would not move, still bespelled by the ethereal figure before them, with its clarity of thought and perceptive, compassionate understanding of human thinking and behavior.

"Hey. Earth to Verity." Cody snapped her fingers in front of Verity's face, then grabbed her arm. "Time to go."

"✝△☉ ᖆ✝ϟ △☉ ϝ△ △╊ ୪△!"

rUg orv Ug brU Ud iU!

[*Farewell—live well in peace through understanding!*]

said Avatar gently as Verity followed after her friends.

It was more of an encouragement than a command, and it struck something deep inside Verity. She knew it was something she'd try to live the rest of her life by.

The little group ushered Lawson out of the programming room, keeping their distance as much as possible in the narrow corridors. Lawson might have done some soul-searching, but no one trusted he wouldn't fall right back into his old autocratic ways.

"Subject Truman," he muttered.

"It's Verity," she corrected.

"Verity." A faint smile played on Lawson's ravaged, sweat-streaked face. "That means 'truth,' doesn't it?"

"I like to think so. And act so." Verity hesitated. Her natural urge to question Lawson's authority to his face had been squelched under his regime, but this was her last chance. "Do you have any idea what you've done? What you've caused?"

Lawson set his jaw and looked past Verity.

"You've hurt us. You've *changed* us. Do you know that?"

"I was just working with the information I had," said Lawson stiffly. "That's all any of us can do."

Bea scoffed. "Good news: now you have new information to work with!"

For once, Lawson said nothing.

They emerged onto the quadrangle, where the moon played its silvery light across the faces of the subjects and the Academy staff who had cautiously emerged from the mess hall. The hubbub of earlier had died down, and everyone was milling around talking quietly among themselves. The re-educators and the PackHunters looked somewhat nervous, with none of them willing to try to assert their authority over the newly revived subjects.

Instead, Constance Grimes and Susie Slaw had stepped up, together with Casper and the Wild Boys. They were working their way through the crowd, checking for injuries and helping settle anyone still out of sorts after emerging from the spell of the AI.

When Verity and the others appeared with a much humbler-looking Lawson, a murmur went up through the crowd. A few boos arose here and there.

"You're done, old man!" shouted a kid in a too-big uniform from one of the back rows.

"Reprogram this!" A muscular girl made a rude gesture.

Gathering himself, Lawson stood tall and cleared his throat.

"Law and . . ." He began, then faltered. The former subjects leapt on this lapse in confidence immediately.

"Good luck with that one, pops," jeered a kid propped up against the building.

Lawson took a deep breath and tried again.

"Attention! This has been, well, an eventful evening, but we need to call it a day. Subjects, go to your quarters. Staff will make their rounds to ensure that all subjects are where they should be and will report any problems to me. We will deal with disciplinary problems in the morning. Payne, place the newcomer troublemakers in separate rooms. That's all. Dismissed!"

With that, Lawson clicked his heels and strode, somewhat shakily, from the quadrangle.

Cody folded her arms. "He could've said please."

"He could've said worse," countered Verity.

Payne corralled Silas and the Wild Boys and herded them away. The crowd of students dispersed along the way-finding lines to their bunk rooms. Some muttered angrily, while others appeared dazed as they walked uncertainly to their respective quarters. The remainder lingered at the monitors, with their ever-evolving sequences of symbols. Avatar's fluting voice continued to speak gently over the sound system, a soothing counterpart to the background music the subjects had endured for so long.

Verity and her roommates were among the stragglers.

"Move it," scowled one of the PackHunters, prodding them off to their bunk rooms. Total reform apparently didn't happen overnight.

⎯⎯⎯

At the 0500 bell, the girls dragged themselves out of bed and headed wearily to the bathrooms. The screens in the hallways were dark, and the sound system was silent. Any evidence of last night's uprising had been cleared away or set aside for safekeeping.

"Surreal," whispered Bea.

"Like being in Groundhog Day or something," responded Krystal.

Pointless, thought Verity, wondering what had become of Silas and the Wild Boys. She wished Viveo would appear to share a message or communicate some sort of hope-filled missive, but the hallways remained their usual drab, nondescript gray. Viveo definitely preferred the out-of-doors, and she didn't blame it.

Dressed and cursorily groomed, Verity stared at herself in the bathroom mirror, searching her own face for the changes she thought must be imprinted there. But she looked as she always had, if a little more tired and wan. Maybe she'd dreamed everything that had happened the previous night. It seemed unfathomable that after all their effort, they had simply arrived back at their usual Academy routine.

Payne intercepted them on the way to the quadrangle. "Subject Truman, come with me."

Payne led a reticent Verity to Lawson's office. She rallied a little, however, when she saw who awaited her there: Cody and Silas.

"Wait here," Payne snapped, narrowing his eyes at Silas, whom he hadn't forgiven for last night's wild goose chase. He clearly wished he was in charge of meting out whatever punishment Silas and the others were about to be subjected to.

Verity swallowed.

Punctuated by the occasional scream from Pyrite, Lawson's voice could be heard from the other side of the door that separated them from the HeadMaster.

"... you are right; no subjects were seriously injured," he was saying. "But I think we may need to reconsider the program in its entirety. Yes, a temporary closure during which we release the subjects to their parents. Well, the cost is immaterial when you consider the risks. Yes, of course we have insurance, but you do see—yes, I will provide a full report as soon as possible."

The door opened. "Subjects? And the other boy. Come in."

Verity, Cody, and Silas uncertainly took their places in front of Lawson's desk. Unsure what to do with her hands, Verity finally clasped them in front of her. She closed her eyes, trying to take strength from the presence of Cody and her brother.

Lawson's scarred face turned toward Silas. His gaze was fixed.

"You. How, and why, did you disrupt our soiree?"

Silas paused for a moment, then shrugged. "My sister needed my help. So we did what we had to do."

Lawson pursed his lips. "You did. Up to and including reprogramming the AI. I would like an explanation." He turned to Cody. "Given your background, I suspect you were implicated in the reprogramming business."

Cody rapped idly on Lawson's desk. "I'm pleading the fifth on that. But whatever actually went down, at least now you've got something pretty decent to use in your so-called reprogramming classes."

"Some words that mean what they say," added Verity, paraphrasing Lawson's rules back at him.

Lawson pressed his hands to his thighs. They left a damp imprint, out of line with his usually immaculately presented manner.

"In the meantime, I have an announcement to make."

Lawson led Verity and the others to the quadrangle, where the subjects had gathered in disorderly clumps and clusters. A few had positioned themselves in something approaching the usual rows and formations but broke rank when they saw that none of the other kids were bothering. Whatever spell Lawson and his AI had held over them appeared to be likewise crumbling.

"Subjects," began Lawson, before checking himself and starting over. "*Students*. I have come to realize the program here is not fully meeting its effectiveness criteria. When I started the Ersatz Academy, my intent was to design an institution that would facilitate the development of productive, law-abiding citizens through organized discipline. Though in large part our goals have been met, my vision . . . has shifted somewhat. I have spoken with the managing director, who agrees that the best path forward is to close the Academy temporarily. I will ask our re-educators to inform your parents that you are safe and that you will be sent home immediately." He paused, as though considering a last-minute retraction, but then barked: "Dismissed!"

Raucous cheers and shouts arose from the various clusters of students, and there was plenty of high-fiving and above-the-head clapping going on. One boy did an impressive series of backflips along the lines on the asphalt.

"School's out!" bellowed Pitbull, making devil horns with his hands. Verity half wished he'd remained under the spell of the AI. He had been almost bearable then.

"I cannot *wait* to have a proper bath in an actual tub." Bea rubbed her hands together, then checked her nails. "Mani-pedi session, here I come!"

Krystal checked her own worse-for-wear manicure. "Are you offering? Because I am *in*."

"Mani-pedis for all," Bea promised. "Even those two, if they're up for it."

Cody shrugged, although she seemed pleased. "Maybe."

Out of habit, Verity found herself shaking her head, but stopped herself. "You know what? Sure."

"You can have recycling symbols or whatever painted on yours," teased Bea. "Or trash cans." She cocked her head. "On second thought, maybe we'll hit the salon for a blow-wave first. Like the bus driver guy."

She pointed to Huff, who had stepped up from the sidelines. He had let his hair down, and it hung about his face in long white waves, offering a glimpse of what he had looked like in his hippie youth.

"I'm licensed for sixty, so you kids should all fit," Huff was saying. "Even the ones who just showed up out of nowhere."

"Cheers!" called Silas, on behalf of the Wild Boys.

"You re-educators can drive yourselves. Or walk. Go get your things from Payne and Grimes."

Constance Grimes had ducked into the room where Payne kept the kids' personal belongings, gathering up the gray bags on a cart and rolling them out into the quadrangle. She went through them, reading out each subject's name and handing over their possessions.

Bea hugged her bag tightly. "My clothes! I never thought I'd wear anything not made of polyester again."

"Fresh eyeliner!" Em produced a thin tube from the inside pocket of her bag. "I was running on emergency reserves in there."

When Verity received hers, she wasn't quite sure what to do with it. She'd grown accustomed to having nothing to her name but her uniform and her iUI code sheet. Everything else seemed superfluous.

She thanked Grimes anyway. "And thanks for everything you and Casper did. Without you the entire school would still be brainwashed."

"Not just the school," added Cody.

Grimes gave one of her warm smiles. "He's a good kid. He has his quirks, but he tries to do good. Like most of us."

"Big reach there," said Em. "Bad guys walk among us, remember?"

Verity thought about everything that had transpired on Lawson's watch. His intentions hadn't been *bad*—just seriously misguided. But that was a charge that could be leveled at a ton of people. To varying degrees, anyway. She tried not to cringe thinking of all of the judgments she'd leveled at people about their environmental footprint, without having any sympathy for the other factors that might be involved.

Huff's voice broke into her thoughts. His arms waving like an air traffic controller, he was ushering the confused subjects onto the bus. "Let's get going before my coffee wears off."

As the subjects started to file on, a violent shriek cut through the crowd, causing almost everyone to flinch. A couple of subjects cowered on the ground, reacting as though a bomb had gone off around them.

"That thing's going to give me a heart attack," muttered Em.

"It's still better than Lawson's music," countered Krystal.

Only Silas seemed pleased to hear the eardrum-rending noise. "Is that a scarlet macaw?"

Verity nodded. "It's Lawson's."

"Was, by the looks of it." Pyrite had escaped his cage and was perched atop one of the enormous rule-adorned sign boards that stared down anyone who entered the Academy. Silas's eyes lit up with excitement. "Do you think it's looking for a foster home?"

Verity tried to hide her horror. "There might be . . . noise restrictions in our neighborhood. And we'd have to register him. And macaws can live for fifty years."

Silas gave a dismissive flap of his hand. "I'm sure no one will care. Our neighbors will be amazed. Promise. And if not, maybe the museum will take him as part of their living wonders exhibit. I'm gonna go get him."

Silas ducked off, following the bird's violently loud screams. As she watched him go, Verity thought of one more thing she needed to do— and one that didn't involve adopting a parrot whose voice resembled a horror movie soundtrack.

"Can you wait?" she asked Huff. "There's something I've got to go back for."

Without waiting for an answer, Verity jumped back off the bus and ran back toward the Grimeses' living quarters. Casper shyly greeted her. He was packing an assortment of books into a battered suitcase.

"I wanted to say thanks," she said. "I know the keycard thing was a risk. For you and your mom."

Casper's large eyes regarded her, and his face creased into an unpracticed smile.

"I have something for you." Reaching into her pocket, Verity pulled out the wooden carving of Viveo Silas had made, along with the iUI crib sheet that had helped keep her grounded and sane in this academy of insanity. Casper took them in silence, with a questioning nod toward the monitors, still glowing with symbols.

Verity smiled. She had a feeling Casper would be a good steward of the language.

By the time she got back to the bus, just about every seat was taken, save the one next to Silas. Seeing Pyrite's cage at his feet, she realized why everyone had given her brother a wide berth.

"He's going straight to the zoo. My eardrums can't take it," she warned, digging in her bag for something to drape over the cage to dissuade the bird from shrieking. She came up with the brightly patterned T-shirt she'd arrived in. She'd almost forgotten that clothing could come in a color other than gray.

Huff pulled the bus out of the Academy, his usual classical soundtrack playing in the background.

"What did you go back for?" asked Silas, peeking in at Pyrite.

"A friend," said Verity, and left it at that.

<hr />

The bus ate up the road, though the sameness of the landscape made it feel as though they were spinning in place. As the hours passed, the subjects lapsed into silence, most of them asleep against the windows or on the shoulder of the person next to them.

Verity found herself nodding off, too, until something woke her: a faint strobing light outside the window.

"Hey," she whispered. She shook Silas awake. "Look."

Silas broke into a broad grin as he saw Viveo.

[**diOm UI daiv fnu at iU**
Transparent words guide us toward understanding.]

it etched into the sky alongside the bus.
Silas dug a small penlight out of his cargo pants.

[**fnu iOv ad diOm UI** *We see through transparent words.*]

he responded.

[**AgUrv bnum gicUw!** *Remember your Inner–Light–Spirit–Power!*]

And then the firefly creature was gone.

pAm rim, can kim kan, iO-vAm canUm i

Before—gleaming, all-starry sky, seeing universal light.

fAm yim, can yIm gan, tIO-vAm at brUm yI

Now—dark, all silent, inner space, listening to peaceful silence jam UI gav wU

Similar words contain power

Ud jAem jIm wUI

through rhythmic homonymous slogans

tIOrv rUt Ui

Listen for understanding

diO-vAm can UI

seeing through all words

A WAY WITH WORDS

Stranger: . . . the new program could dramatically speed up your results. And their extent. The Academy, and of course you, will become a true thought leader in youth reform.

[pause]

Lawson: Anything that reduces the resistance to our methods is of interest to me. Anything at all.

Stranger: It's based on Soviet-era research in behavioral linguistics. The term is semantic conditioning. Or, if you prefer, a type of "perception management program," and one that will undoubtedly be more effective and in compliance with the new governmental orders than previous methods for reforming young minds.

Lawson: Interesting. At this point we still have a lot of resistance to our methods. At least the passive kind that's hard to deal with. Although I'll need to hear your justification. And just to be clear, we're not talking about brainwashing exactly, are we? Because that would be a hard sell on many levels. Maybe something closer to behavior modification or ideological adjustment. Am I right?

Stranger:　You are right, indeed. We can call it anything you want. Shall I provide a demonstration?

[pause]

The program is based around a computer technology we've developed specifically for these purposes. Truly cutting-edge stuff. Give me just a moment to boot it up … a computer that can think for itself, while keeping your subjects from doing the same. Ironic, wouldn't you say?

Lawson:　Intriguing. How does it work?

Stranger:　Are you familiar with Pavlov's dogs and classical conditioning?

Lawson:　Somewhat. [which meant that he wasn't]

Stranger:　Ah, well. In a sense, the technology will provide a sort of neural training. Very effective, very safe. And here's the beauty of it all. Given the plasticity of adolescent brains, I anticipate exceptional results for your subjects.

Basically, these conditioning experiments showed that young or fatigued or otherwise stressed brains tended to react to similar-sounding homophones as if they were synonyms with similar meanings—especially when this training is supported by the use of some, er . . . facilitative medication.

Lawson: Facilitative medication?

Stranger: It's not unlike the work Craniale is doing; it's simply taken
to the next level.

You know we get conditioned to things when we learn
to make a mental connection between a common cue in our
environment and our reaction to it, until that reaction becomes
automatic. Such as when kids in school hear a recess or lunch
bell, they automatically get excited for fun and food. Pavlov
trained dogs to start salivating by adding a cue before their
dinner: he rang a bell before their food was put out. Over time
the dogs learned to associate the bell with food and responded
by drooling even before they saw or smelled any.

Lawson: Hmm.

Stranger: When I worked in a Russian lab, they did this kind of research
on human subjects using spoken words instead of a bell as the
added cue. But, and here's the key, under certain conditions
they achieved the same salivation response when they used
homophones that just sounded like the original words but
had totally different meanings.

Lawson: [sounding confounded] Surprising . . . but how does that apply
to our purposes here?

Stranger: Well, it would be almost as if Pavlov had substituted a totally different instrument from the bell, say, an electronic one, to get the dogs to drool in the same way because it happened to make the same sound. The research showed that young or compromised brains tend to associate similar-sounding words even though they have different meanings. You find it in nursery rhymes all the way to slogans.

Lawson: You mean as in ads and political propaganda? They do seem to work pretty well . . .

Stranger: Right, so here's my brilliant application. An AI programmed to capitalize on this tendency, but with the goal of training your subjects to become, shall we say, more manageable. And all in half the time, with half the . . .

Lawson: . . . effort! With the outcome being that our subjects are molded into upstanding young citizens. Those who adhere to social mores and conform to the conventions of a law-abiding society! Is that what you're getting at?

Stranger: Precisely. You get it, I see. Shall we proceed with a pilot study? You'll have exclusive rights to it, of course. It could be incredible for the school's reputation and reach. You could scale your success like that. [sound of snapping fingers] The sky's the limit!

AUTHOR'S NOTE ON SEMANTIC CONDITIONING

One of the main questions raised by the Ersatz Academy's "re-education" techniques is whether the manipulation of words and their sounds can affect human behavior under certain conditions. Slogans, which Lawson makes liberal use of, are characterized by rhythm, rhyme, repetition, and three types of parachesis (repeated similar sounds): alliteration (initial sounds), assonance (vowels), and consonance (consonants). Homonyms are also used to confuse or encourage different interpretations. These devices are found not only in beautiful literature, but also in advertising, and have been exploited throughout history in political propaganda.

The methodology of Wordswright's AI is loosely based on Russian research referred to as "semantic conditioning" by Gregory Razran in 1939. Semantic conditioning is a training procedure in which a target physical response is repeatedly stimulated while being paired with a key word until an association develops between the two. For instance, salivation is stimulated by chewing gum while a word is pronounced until the same salivation response is stimulated by the word alone, without the gum.

In follow-up research, both synonyms and homophones of the original words were used as the conditioned stimuli. In experiments involving alert subjects, synonyms generally resulted in similar responses, whereas homophones did so to a lesser extent. However, when the brain cortex was inhibited in some way (e.g., through a drug causing drowsiness), homophones became more effective than the synonyms in stimulating the same response. It appears plausible that a stressed brain more easily associates words according to their similar sound rather than to their similar meaning, and that under certain conditions, people may begin to believe that words make logical sense together partly because they sound similar. Perhaps this hypothesis is worthy of further testing.

For further information, the website at http://aUILanguage.space has resources for learning Silas's light language. It is based on the original text-book, *aUI, The Language of Space*, by W. John Weilgart, 4th ed., 1979, which is available on that site.

SOME NOTES FROM GRANDPA

(found by Silas while rummaging through
an old drawer in his grandpa's room)

We do not recognize the slogans of our own age: we take them as statements of truth.

Unlike our earthly languages, where several meanings are often hidden inside the same word, the formulas of this system could make meaning transparent and bare—open to be questioned and verified.

Symbols that are like the universe's atomic elements . . . that combine into molecules of meaning . . . a cosmic logos for truth and wisdom that keeps pointing us back to reality, to the basic elements of our world.

Where there was confusion and discord, this cosmic speech brings an inner harmony between sound, symbol, and meaning.

The miniature world of the mind mirrors the immense world of the universe in the symbols of the Language of Light.

Silas's Crib Sheet

Symbols

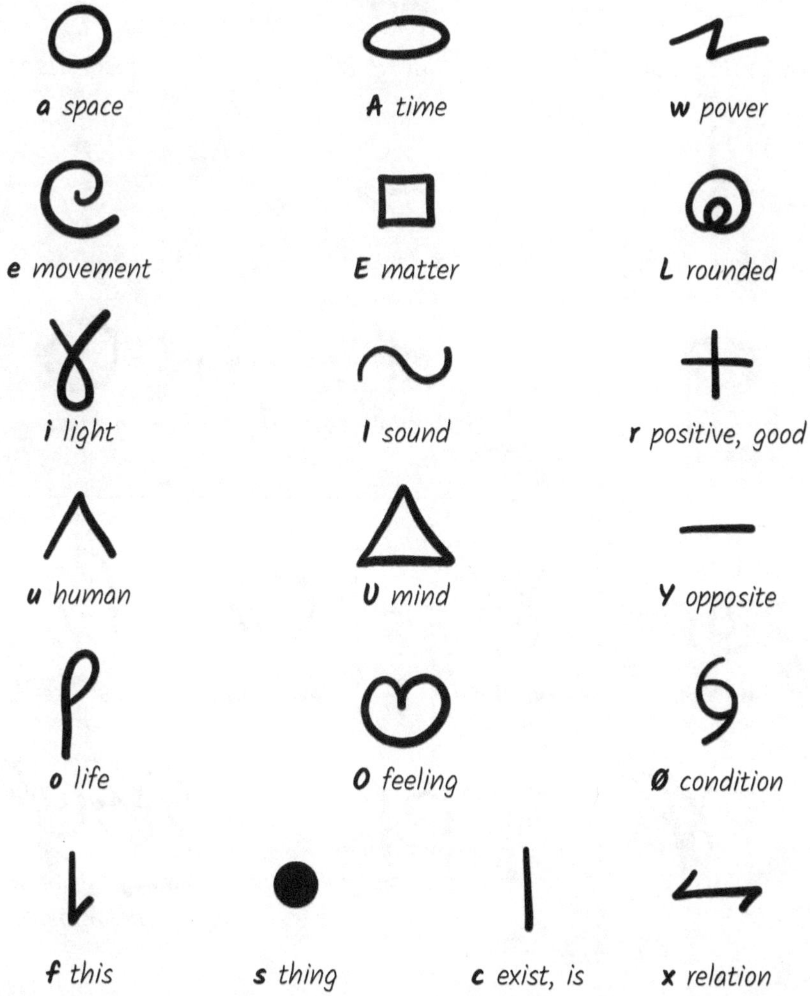

a space

A time

w power

e movement

E matter

L rounded

i light

I sound

r positive, good

u human

U mind

Y opposite

o life

O feeling

Ø condition

f this

s thing

c exist, is

x relation

Silas's Crib Sheet

v action, make, verb

z part

j equal

m quality, adj.

n quantity, much

h question

p before, front

t toward

k above

b together

d through, tool

g inside

---

im: light

iv: shine

ev: move

ov: live

io: plant

eo: animal

Viveo: glowing plant-animal?

Silas's Crib Sheet

Ov: *feel*

iOv: *see*

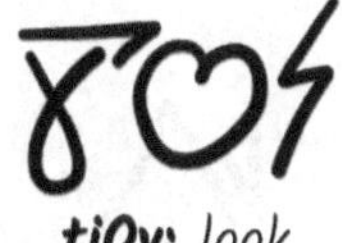

tiOv: *look*

lOv: *hear*

tlOv: *listen*

Uv: *think*

iUv: *understand*

gU: *knowledge*

gUv: *know*

et-gUv: *study*

vet-gUv: *teach*

bO: *sympathy*

tebUv: *communicate*

Ul: *word*

bUv.iUl: *from Viveo's signals?*

Silas's Crib Sheet

fu: I/me

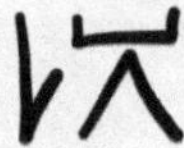

fnu: we

nu: they

un: people

bu: you

bru: friend

brU: peace

GLOSSARY

Note: The iUI language is built from 31 basic units that function as "building blocks" to create words. These units are thought to be as basic as the atoms in the periodic table of chemical elements and are combined into "molecules" of meaning. For instance, io ⴑℙ, Light-Life, life that lives by photosynthesizing light, is a plant.

In iUI words that are related in meaning also sound and look similar.

For example,

iO ⴑ◯ [*Light-Feeling/Sensation*]: sight

iOv ⴑ◯⚡ [*sight-Verb*]: see

tiOv ⴑ◯⚡ [*Toward-see*]: look

A-tiOv ◯ ⴑ◯⚡ [*Time-look*]: watch

nA-tiOv ◯ ⴑ◯⚡ [*Much-Time-look*]: stare

Here is a complete list of Silas's and Verity's vocabulary. The basic elements of iUI are capitalized in the literal definition shown in brackets below. Short root combinations are in lowercase. To find the literal definition of these root combinations, look them up separately. For instance, in the entry **âna** below, **na** is a root combination glossed as "dimension." To find its literal definition, look under **na**.

âm ⚓ [*One-Quality*] only

âna 𝟙̃Ö [*One-dimension*] length

ad O⊦ [*Spatially-Through*] through

ag OO [*Space-Inside*] in; inside

at ⚲ [*Spatially-Toward*] to

A-gUv O⌢⊙△⚡ [*Time-know*] remember

   A-gUrv O⌢⊙△⊦⚡ [*remember-Positive-Action/V.*] remember!
(command)

bam ⚯ [*Together-Spatially-Quality/Adj.*] near

   bav O⚡ [*Together-Space-Action/V.*] have *(if you have something, it is together in space-near-you)*

bEn-u ⌸⌢Λ [*Together-Matter-Much (solid/earth)—Human*] earthling

bO ⚭ [*Together-Feeling*] sympathy

bu Λ̂ [*Together-Human*] you *(the person you're together with)*

   bum △̂ [*you-Adj.*] your

bnu ⌓Λ [*you-Many*] you all

   bnum ⌓△ [*you all-Adj.*] your *(plural)*

brI ⊦~ [*Together-Positive—Sound*] melody *(sounds put together well)*

bru ⊦Λ [*Together-Positive—Human*] friend *(the person you have a 'good togetherness' with)* brU ⧓ [*Together-Positive—Spirit*] peace *(a good spiritual togetherness)*

> brUm ⧓ [*peace-Quality/Adj.*] peaceful

bUv △⧸ [*Together-Mind/Spirit-Action/V.*] connect; commune *(a mind or spirit connection)*

bYg-âna ⊙1Ŏ [*Together-outside-length*] border

> bYg-âna-tnak ⊙1Ŏ⁼Oʃ [*border-limit*] boundary

ca lO [*Existence-Space*] world

can lǑ [*Exist-Space-Quantity*] all *(the quantity that exists in a space)*

> can-a lǑO [*all-Space*] universe

> cana-bUvd lǑO△⧸✝ [*universe-connect-Tool/Means*] universal-net; -web

> canUm lǑ△ [*all-Mind/Spirit-Quality/Adj.*] universal

cmU l△ [*Existence-Quality-Spirit*] essence

cnAm lŏ [*Existing-Quantity-Time-Quality/Adj.*] always *(the quantity of time in existence)*

cu l∧ [*Existing-Human*] he; she

da ✝O [*Through-Space*] way

daiv ✝O४⧸ [*way-Light-Action/V.*] guide *(to light the way)*

> daiuv ✝O४∧⧸ [*guide-Human-Action/V.*] guide (human)

diOm ✝४♡ [*Through-sight-Quality/Adj.*] transparent

diO-vAm ✝✝○⌃✦⊖ [*Through-see-present participle ending*]
through-seeing

drev ✝✝ℂ✦ [*Through-Well-move*] function

dUt ✝△ [*Means-Mentally-Toward*] in order to *(to do something with
a mind toward and as a means toward)*

eb ℂ [*Moving-Together*] with

eo ℂℙ [*Moving-Life*] animal

et-gUv ⌣⌃○△✦ [*Move-Toward—know*] study

et-gUrv ⌣⌃○△✝✦ [*study-Positive-Action/V.*] study!
(command)

et-vrUma ⌣⌃✦✝△○ [*Move-Toward-Positive-behavior*]
reformation

ev ℂ✦ [*Movement-Action/V.*] move

erv! ℂ✝✦ [*move-Positive-Action/V.*] move! *(command)*

Ec ☐| [*Matter-Exist*] is (materially)

Eca ☐|○ [*Matter-world*] (material) world

EjU ☐△ [*Matter-Equals-Mind*] truth *(when the mental picture
equals the objective matter; when your mental attitude or
opinion is equal to the material facts of the objective world)*

EjUm ☐△ [*truth-Adj.*] true

Ev ☐✦ [*Matter-Act*] do

fAm 🜂 [*This-Time-Qualifier*] now *(adv.)*; present *(adj.)*

fAvm 🜂 [*now-Make-Quality/Adj.*] new *(something made in this time, now or recently is new)*

fu 🜂 [*This-Person*] I; me

fum 🜂 [*me-Adj.*] my

fnu 🜂 [*This-Many-People*] we; us

fnum 🜂 [*we-Adj.*] our

fU 🜂 [*This-Mind/Spirit*] self

fUwe 🜂 [*This-Mind-Power-to Move*] freedom

fUwem 🜂 [*freedom-Quality/Adj.*] free

ga 🜂 [*Inside-Space*] space inside; room

gaf 🜂 [*In (the)-Space- (of) This*] or

gam 🜂 [*Inside-Space-Quality/Adj.*] inner

gan 🜂 [*Inside-Space-Quantity*] inner space

gav 🜂 [*Inside-Space-Verb*] contain

gicUw 🜂 [*Inside-Light-Existing-Spirit-Power*] our inner Light Spirit Power

giU 🜂 [*Inside-Light-Spirit*] our inner Light

grabØ 🜂 [*Inside-Positive-Space-Together-Condition*] order *(the condition of things put together well in space)* gU ⊙△ [*Inside-Mind*] knowledge *(what's inside the mind)*

gUv ⊙△⚡ [*knowledge-Verb*] know

hu ⵧ∧ [*Question-Person*] who?

hU ⵧ△ [*Question-Mind*] what? (mentally)

hU'c ⵧ△'l [*what-is*] what's (mentally)

io ⚥ᕩ [*Light-Life*] plant *(life that lives by light)*

im ⚥ [*Light-Quality/Adj.*] light

i-nUI ⚥ ⌶ [*Light—Many-words*] light language

iOv ⚥○⚡ [*Light-feel/sense-Verb*] see

iO-vAm ⚥○⚡◠ [*see-present participle ending*] seeing

iU ⚥△ [*Light-Mind*] understanding *(when your mind lights up[1])*

iUv ⚥△⚡ [*Light-Mind-Verb*] understand *(when your mind lights up[2])*

iUI ⚥⌓ [*Light-word*] light language *(abbrev.)*

iUs ⚥△● [*Light-thought*] idea *(when a light comes into your mind[3])*

iv ⚥⚡ [*Light-Action*] shine

---

1. This is more than a metaphorical representation: "Functional imaging allows the brain's information processing to be visualized directly, because activity in the involved area of the brain increases metabolism and 'lights up' on the scan." https://courses.lumenlearning.com/boundless-psychology/chapter/brain-imaging-techniques/

2. Ibid.

3. Ibid.

Ib ⊗ [*Sounded-Together*] and

IOv ⊗⌇ [*Sound-feel /sense-Verb*] hear

jam ⊜ [*Equal-Spatially-Quality/Adj.*] same

jAe ⊟⊖ [*Equal-Time-Movement*] rhythm

jAem ⊟⊖ [*rhythm-Quality/Adj.*] rhythmic

jIm ⊟ [*Equal-Sound-Quality/Adj.*] same sounding; homonymous

jwUr ⇋△+ [*Equal-Power-Mind-Good*] right *(a spiritual power and good, equally well available to all in the same situation)*

jwUs ⇋△● [*Equal-Power-Mind-Thing*] law *(the thing which rules with equal power in our minds is the law, which should not make a difference between people)*

jYtu ⇶∧ [*Same-parent*] sibling

kan ⌐○ [*Above-Space-Much*] sky

ki ⌐δ [*Above-Light*] star

kim ⌐δ [*star-Quality/Adj.*] starry

knu-wun ⌐∧ ⇋△ [*Above-Many-People—Power-people*] people in power above others

kU-tog-ma ⌐△⌐⊙ö [*High-Spirit—into-body—form*] avatar (from Sanskrit: *descent of a deity from heaven; manifestation of a deity in human, superhuman, or animal form*) kwev ⟨symbol⟩ [*Above-Power-Move-Make/V.*] order; command

    kwev-UI ⟨symbol⟩ [*command-word*] order; command (see also **ve-kwUI**)

kwu ⟨symbol⟩ [*Above-Power-Person*] boss; person in power

kwU ⟨symbol⟩ [*Above-Power-Mind/Concept*] control *(power over)*

LiUv ⟨symbol⟩ [*Round-understand*] comprehend *(to understand the surrounding <u>circum</u>stances; to embrace, include, encompass—which contains an element of sur<u>round</u>ing)*

ma ⟨symbol⟩ [*Qualified-Space*] form; shape

na ⟨symbol⟩ [*Quantity-Space*] dimension

nim ⟨symbol⟩ [*Much-Light-Quality/Adj.*] bright

nu ⟨symbol⟩ [*Many-Human*] they; them

nUI ⟨symbol⟩ [Many-word] language

nUr ⟨symbol⟩ [*Quantity of-Spiritual-Good*] value

nYba ⟨symbol⟩ [*Much-apart-Space*] distance; afar

nYc ⟨symbol⟩ [*Quantity-not*] no *(a non-existing quantity)*

og ⟨symbol⟩ [*Life-Inside*] body *(life container)*

ogU ⟨symbol⟩ [*body-Spirit*] mind *(spirit part of the body)*

ov ⟨symbol⟩ [*Life-Verb*] to live

    orv ⟨symbol⟩ [*live-Positive-Action/V.*] live! *(command)*

OtUw ♡△ [*Feeling-Toward-Mind-Power*] courage *(aligning my feelings with my mind's power)*

Ov ♡ [*Feeling-Verb*] feel

pA [*Before-Time*] (the) past

  pAm [*past-Qualifier/Adj.*] past

Øc [*Conditionally-Is*] is (conditionally)

Øg [*Condition-Inside*] if *(containing a condition)*

rim [*Positive-Light-Qualifier/Adj.*] bright *(with a poetic, positive feel)*

riO [*Positive-to sight*] beauty

riO-ev [*Positive-to see—move*] dance

ro [*Positive-Life*] health

rOb [*Positive-Feeling-Together*] harmony

rØm [*Positive-Condition-Quality/Adj.*] okay; fine

rU [*Positive-Spiritually*] goodness

  rUg [*good-Inside*] well

  rUm [*goodness-Quality/Adj.*] good

  rUt [*Positive-Mind-Toward*] for *(doing something for someone is doing it with a mind toward a benefit)*

-rv ⟨symbol⟩ [*Positive*-Do/Action] imperative, command ending: "it would be *good* to do!"; "you *better* do it!"

tag ⟨symbol⟩ [*Toward-Space-Inside*] into

tap ⟨symbol⟩ [*Toward-Space-Before*] forward

tap-daiv ⟨symbol⟩ [*forward-guide*] lead

tap-daivu ⟨symbol⟩ [*lead-Person*] leader

tA ⟨symbol⟩ [*Toward-Time*] future *(the time toward which we go)*

tAc ⟨symbol⟩ [*future-Is*] will be

-tAv ⟨symbol⟩ [*future-Verb*] future verb ending

te-bUv ⟨symbol⟩ [*Toward-Move—Together-Minds-Verb*] communicate

te-rUI ⟨symbol⟩ [*Toward-Move—Positive-word*] hello *(a positive word when someone comes toward you)*

tev ⟨symbol⟩ [*Toward-Move-Action/V.*] come

te-tAv ⟨symbol⟩ [*come-future Verb*] will come

tiOv ⟨symbol⟩ [*Toward-see*] look *(to see in a certain direction)*

tiOrv ⟨symbol⟩ [*look-Positive-Action/V.*] look! *(command)*

tIOv ⟨symbol⟩ [*Toward-hear*] listen *(to hear in a certain direction)*

tIOrv ⟨symbol⟩ [*listen-Positive-Action/V.*] listen! *(command)*

tIO-vAm ⟨symbol⟩ [*listen-present participle ending*] listening torv P+⚡ [*Toward-Life-Positive-Action/V.*] help

tnak ⚎Oⲑ [*Toward-Quantity-Space-Above*] limit *(toward a certain amount of space above which one cannot go)*

trO ⊤♡ [*Toward-Positive—Feeling*] hope *(future good; you feel that things will go toward the good)*

trOv ⊤♡⚡ [*hope-Verb*] hope

tUw-bO △↯◌̂ [*Toward-Mind-Power (striving effort)—Together-Feeling*] solidarity

tYg-we ⊙̄ ↯ℭ [*Toward-outside—Power-Move*] bursting, busting out

tYg-wev ⊙̄ ↯ℭ⚡ [*burst-Action/V.*] burst, bust out

tYjev ☰ℭ⚡ [*Toward-Un-Equal-move*] change

tYjvev ☰⚡ℭ⚡ [*Make-change*] change (something)

tYrO ⊤♡ [*Toward-negative—Feeling*] fear *(future-bad; you feel that things will take a turn toward the bad)*

tYwe-YkO �ⲍℭ⊤♡ [*Toward-powerless-Move—low-Feeling*] tired, low feeling

un △ [*Human-Many*] people

Ub ⌂ [*Mentally-Together*] of

Uc △Ⲓ [*Mentally-Is*] is (in mental or abstract contexts)

Uca △ⲒO [*Spirit-world*] spiritual world

Ud △ϯ [*Mentally-Through*] by means of

Ug △⊙ [*Mentally-Inside*] in (abstract); inside (one's mind)

Ui △ɣ [*Mind-Light*] perception, understanding

UI ♋ [*Mind-Sound*] word

   UIv ♋⚡ [*Mind-Sound-Action/V.*] say, speak

UL △◉ [*Mind-Round*] about (mentally)

Us △● [*Mind-Thing/concrete*] thought

Uv △⚡ [*Mind-Verb*] think

   UvØ △⚡§ [*think-Condition*] thinking *(noun)*

-vAm ⚡◎ [*Action-Time-Quality/Adj.*] present participle ending; -ing *(happening over time)*

ve-kwUI ⚡ꓛꞮⱽ♋ [*Make-Move—Above-Power-word*] order; command

   ve-kwUI ⚡ꓛꞮⱽ♋⚡ [*command-Verb*] order; command

vet-gUv ⚡♎⊙△⚡ [*Make-study*] teach

   vet-gU-tAv ⚡♎⊙△ꝯ⚡ [*teach-future Verb*] will teach

vet-gUz ⚡♎⊙△ꓷ [*teach-Part*] lesson

vev ⚡ꓛ⚡ [*Make-move*] drive

   verv ⚡ꓛϯ⚡ [*drive-Positive-Action/V.*] drive! (command)

viOv ⟨glyph⟩ [*Make-see*] show

viOvs ⟨glyph⟩ [*show-Thing/Concrete*] sign

viO-tAv ⟨glyph⟩ [*show-future Verb*] will show

Viveo ⟨glyph⟩ [*Make-Light/shine—Moving-Life*] photosynthesizing, luminescent animal

vIO-tAv ⟨glyph⟩ [*Make-hear—future ending*] will make hear

vØ-pAm ⟨glyph⟩ [*Make-Conditions—past-Adj.*] conditioned *(past participle)*

vUma ⟨glyph⟩ [*Action-Mind-form*] behavior *(the form in which a mind acts)*

vUs ⟨glyph⟩ [*Action-Concept-Thing/Concrete*] action *(a concrete action)*

vyev ⟨glyph⟩ [*Make-stop*] stop *(to cause to stop)*

vyiv ⟨glyph⟩ [*Make-Opposite-Light-Action/V.*] darken

vyiOv ⟨glyph⟩ [*Make-Non-see*] hide

vY-kwev ⟨glyph⟩ [*Make-obey*] subdue; subjugate

vY-kwevØ ⟨glyph⟩ [*subdue-Condition*] subjugation

vY-kwu ⟨glyph⟩ [*Make-serve—Power-Person*] tyrannical boss, master

wom ⟨glyph⟩ [*Power-Life-Quality/Adj.*] strong

wU ⟨glyph⟩ [*Power-Concept*] power

wUI ⟨symbol⟩ [*Power-word*] slogan

wYt-YrAm ⟨symbol⟩ [*Powerfully-safe*] secure

Yb ⟨symbol⟩ [*Opposite-Together*] without; apart

YbO ⟨symbol⟩ [*Non-Together-Feeling*] apart feeling; isolation

Yb-wYt-YrAmO ⟨symbol⟩ [*without-security-Feeling*] insecurity (feeling)

Yc ⟨symbol⟩ [*Opposite-Is*] not

Yc-knUr-O ⟨symbol⟩ [*not-worth-Feeling*] feeling of worthlessness

yev ⟨symbol⟩ [*Opposite-Move-Action/V.*] stop

Yf ⟨symbol⟩ [*Opposite-This*] other

Yf-un ⟨symbol⟩ [*other-people*] others

Yg ⟨symbol⟩ [*Opposite-Inside*] outside

yim ⟨symbol⟩ [*Opposite-Light-Quality/Adj.*] dark

yI ⟨symbol⟩ [*Opposite-Sound*] silence

yIm ⟨symbol⟩ [*silence-Quality/Adj.*] silent

Yk ⟨symbol⟩ [*Opposite-Above*] below

Y-kwev ⟨symbol⟩ [*Opposite-order*] obey

Y-kwevØ ⟨symbol⟩ [*obey-Condition*] obeying *(noun)*

Y-kwerv [*obey-Positive-Action/V.*] obey!
(*command*)

Y-kwu [*Opposite-boss*] underling; subject; subordinate

Y-kwuv [*subordinate-Action/Verb*] serve (*in the sense
of obeying*)

Y-kwu-torv [*subordinate-help*] serve (*in the
sense of improving life, service*)

YrU [*Opposite-good*] evil

Yt [*Opposite-Toward*] from

Ytev [*Opposite-come; from-move*] leave

Yterv [*leave-Positive-Action/V.*] leave! (*command*)

Ytu [*Opposite-Toward (from)-Human*] parent

Yt-YrAm [*from-bad-Time-Quality/Adj.*] safe (*when you are
away from bad over time*)

yUg [*Opposite-Mentally-In*] but (*in-contrast; mentally-outside of
what was just stated*)

YweO [*Non-Power-Move-Feeling*] powerless, tired feeling

Ywom [*Opposite-strong*] weak

YwO [*Opposite-Power-Feeling*] powerless feeling

ACKNOWLEDGMENTS

This work rests upon the daring creation of my father, W. John Weilgart, PhD (1913–1981). His fervent ideal of "Peace through Understanding" was manifested in this "cosmic logos" that he originally named aUI, the Language of Space. This is my tribute to his dedication and to what became our family's work while my sister and I were growing up. My hope is that a student may recognize the potential value of learning aUI and perhaps be interested in incorporating it in research.

The story is the result of a three-year collaboration with Australian author Stephanie Campisi. She has faithfully brought my bare-bones ideas to life and fleshed them out into a full, flowing story that artfully incorporated my father's language and some of his essential ideas. Just how difficult such an unconventional endeavor is soon became apparent as she guided me again and again in finding the right balance between story line and language. For her patience with my very gradual process of learning how to convey the language I am very grateful. The story was thus able to evolve into a partial synthesis of my father's work in novel form—no small miracle to my mind!

In addition, John T. Matthias, one of my father's first aUI students (in 1968) and board member of Cosmic Communication Foundation, most generously performed an integral part in this work by providing weekly feedback sessions for me over the period of at least half a year. His loyal support, affirming my intuition or offering alternatives, kept me going in the not infrequent times of doubt and faltering. It is John's recontacting me in 2013 (after 45 years, when he attended my father's first informal aUI class in our home) that gave me the courage to begin work with aUI in a more systematic way.

Neither would this work have been possible without the enduring support and unending patience and understanding of my husband, Kim, along with the rest of my family, mother, and sister! I received extensive feedback and valuable suggestions from my daughter, Alisa, along with much-appreciated support from her brother, Elias, and sister, Anja.

ABOUT THE AUTHOR

In addition to German, Andrea Weilgart grew up being taught an experimental language designed by her philosopher and psychoanalyst father, W. John Weilgart, Ph.D. After wondering for decades how this language might further be applied, this story evolved as a kind of synthesis of her father's teachings.

www.ingramcontent.com/pod-product-compliance
Lightning Source LLC
Chambersburg PA
CBHW030615120726
47904CB00006B/1902